BLACK AND WHITE DEVILS

LAURENCE BEERMAN

BLACK AND WHITE DEVILS

iUniverse books may be ordered through booksellers or by contacting:

iUniverse
1663 Liberty Drive
Bloomington, IN 47403
www.iuniverse.com
844-349-9409

ISBN: 978-1-6632-0435-6 (sc)
ISBN: 978-1-6632-0436-3 (e)

Print information available on the last page.

iUniverse rev. date: 08/03/2020

CONTENTS

FOREWORD

THIS BOOK WAS BORN OF blood, the blood of thousands of slaughtered animals, whose only crime was to have their habitat in a war zone. The blood of thousands of young men in Angola, who butchered each other, doing the bidding of their leaders, each believing their politics were the correct path to follow. The blood of all the women and children who were raped, tortured and killed by the warring factions and lastly the blood of the South African soldiers and my people, who died protecting their border from those who wanted to take over their country. The fact that the country was finally handed over to the black majority with no additional blood shed, stands forever as a monument to the black and white leaders of the day.

CHAPTER ONE

I HAD SPENT A YEAR in the bush up on the Caprivi Strip, then a further two years in the police college, courtesy of the Minister of Defense. It had a sense of unreality about it all and if it hadn't actually happened to me, I certainly would have been most skeptical. Now I was a police captain with a degree in criminology, assigned to state security. At odd moments, my mind wandered back to the Caprivi Strip and the bush I had grown to dislike so much. The bush war had a really bad effect on me. It could do that to a man deeply involved in the killing of his countries' enemies. Many of my days, merely a prelude for the dreams that followed at night, the faces of the dead flashing by in silent condemnation, but there was nothing I could have changed, they were classified as terrorists and I had my orders. This book stands as a small memorial to all those now forgotten, but not by me. I remember what a sad and vicious son of a bitch I became, haunted by the past, fearful of the future. It seemed almost a dream, if I could just allow myself to believe it. Now, I found that bush covered, overgrown areas smelled sickly and offensively sweet. My body was covered with many scars and I always insisted on always sitting with my back to a wall, so I could not be crept up on. Now and then, I would thrash about in my sleep fighting demons and I found the company of a big, trained dog, comforting and calming. When does reality become a dream? I stopped on my walk along Kloof Road, which high up on the side of the mountain, looked out across the Atlantic Ocean. As I rested and gazed out at the beautiful view, dog at my side, I could hear the waves breaking onto the rocky shore far below. It sounded familiar, like the distant sound of artillery fire, shells exploding on impact and it all came rushing back to me, the black and white devils were never far away. So what were the "Black Devils?" If you were a so called freedom fighter, we called them terrorists and you were prepared to and in fact did kill some of your own people, men, women and children to further your cause and ensure the co-operation of the rest of the community. If you stole or kidnapped boys as young as ten years old from their villages, marched them a couple of hundred miles into the bush to a training camp, gave them AK47 assault rifles and turned them into your soldiers, who would kill anyone they were instructed to. If you were happy to kill farmers, their families, their staff, farm animals and burn their buildings to the ground, raping the women as you did so and if you were prepared to die for the cause without question, then you certainly were a "black devil." We had finished our first trip to the east, along the Caprivi Strip, past Katimo Mullilo towards the Victoria Falls. It was our reintroduction to thousands of square miles of bush. The following day we left Rundu at sunup and headed in the opposite direction, west. The dirt road went in a north westerly direction, parallel to the Okavango River for about a hundred miles, then the river changed direction, coming from the north, while the SWA border swung due west. I noticed that the bush was much taller and thicker in the area, probably due to the river overrunning its banks in the rainy season. I felt a little claustrophobic, thick tall bush on both sides of the lousy road, zero visibility, narrow, pot holed, rutted and that sweetish smell of the bush, all pervasive. At around twelve miles an hour, it would take all day to get to where the border swung west and so we rumbled along slowly. It was around three thirty in the afternoon when the radio crackled into life. "R1 to K1, R1 to K1, do you copy, over?" I reached across and picked up the mike. "K1 to R1, we copy loud and clear, over." The voice on the other end sounded agitated. "K1, state your position, over." I looked down at the large compass, mounted on the dashboard and gave Rundu our position. "K1, there is a group of enemy soldiers headed towards your position, they managed to break through the line last night and should be very near you. They counted twenty five men in the group. Deploy and stop them. They are sending troops up behind them, but it will be a few hours before they get there, copy?" I jerked into action, "turn the truck around now," I shouted at Piet, then I pressed the send button. "We are taking action now, K1 out." "K1, K1, do not attempt to capture, do not attempt capture, shoot on sight, do you copy?" "I copy R1, out." Piet had meanwhile managed to turn the truck around. "Piet, go back a few yards then hide us." Piet reversed the truck down a narrow side path and we disappeared into the bushes. He turned off. I turned to the guys. "We are going to do this by the book. Mick, myself, Joe and Henry will go across the road and hide there. The rest of you will stay on this side, follow Jack's lead and in the meantime stay hidden. We will all get as close to the road as possible, lying down out of sight. If control is right, they will come onto the road somewhere near us. If they are fifty yards or closer, I will fire one shot and you all join in, make every shot count. As you lie, first man takes the left, next takes the middle and last man takes the right, same for us on the other side of the road. Do not let them cross the road. If they are too far away, we will have to crawl closer to them. When I fire the single shot, you all join in. When it is all quiet, we will come back to this side, get into the truck and get the hell out of here down the road. We will call in the chopper to bring twelve dogs, the tracker and the kennel hands. The chopper should get here by five thirty to that clearing we passed down there," I pointed down the road. "If any of them are alive they will have retreated back the way they came and the tracker will tell us how many there are left. Then we use the dogs. By the book guys, I don't want anyone getting shot, but if it happens, you all keep going, even if it's me, no heroics, it may be our only chance, so get the dogs, understand?" I glared at them. They all nodded. "Ok, we are going now" and I dashed across the dirt road, followed by Mick,

Joe and Henry. We dived into cover and lying flat, peered cautiously down the road. I hoped they would appear on our right, so the setting sun would be in their eyes. I looked across the road, but could not see my men. They were well hidden. I hoped control's information was good or we could be here for hours. Fifteen long minutes slipped by and suddenly there they were, a rather ragged group of men in mostly torn khaki uniforms coming silently out of the bush on to the road. They were only about thirty yards away on our right, with the sun in their eyes. I found myself holding my breath, while my heart pounded away. A big man stopped in the middle of the track and faced his men as they gathered in front of him. We couldn't hear what he was saying. I looked at the man next to him and felt sick, he could not have been more then fifteen years old, one of the so called "toy soldiers." As they started to cross the track, I shot the man at the front through his head and it exploded. The next man I shot was the toy soldier, the kid. As his head disintegrated, at that very second, I became a "white devil," killer of children. The guys had instantly joined in with me and three seconds later there was just a pile of bodies on the road. The hours and hours spent on the rifle range had paid off big time. I removed the empty magazine from my rifle and smacked in a full clip, then released the slide and the next round clacked into place. The guys were doing likewise, then we all lay quietly and waited. I couldn't help doing the math. Eight rifles, each with a thirty round magazine. That meant we had fired two hundred and forty rounds in three seconds. Amazing. I had sort of disassociated myself from the bodies on the road, after the fact I felt nothing. We were far enough away from them to remain isolated within ourselves, later on, who could tell? I felt certain there were some of the enemy troops still alive and hiding in the bush. It was just too much to believe we had got them all, also, nightfall was coming closer, we were running out of time. I slid over to Henry on my left, Piet and Joe were further down. I whispered to him. "Tell the guys, when I start firing, you will all jump up and run like hell back to the other side, while I keep their heads down. When you are ready, you will all fire at the bush area near the bodies and I will run over and join you. We all get on the truck then complete the plan with the dogs. Get ready." I settled myself and then began firing at the area behind the bodies. Henry, Piet and Joe jumped up, sprinted across the road and vanished into the bush, there was no answering fire. Five seconds later, a hail of gunfire came from across the dirt road, I jumped up started to run across the road and found myself flying through the air, I had been shot through the upper part of my left leg. It felt like a red hot needle had gone through my leg, I couldn't move. I heard the truck start up and drive away, they were following my orders, I was on my own. My leg was settling down to a steady throbbing ache, marginally better than the first hot needle feeling. I tried to lift myself and crawl away, but suddenly there was a pair of filthy boots in front of me and one of them lifted up and kicked me in the face. I was knocked out. When I came round again, I was lying on the ground and I couldn't move. I was tied up, hands and feet and was lying on my side in a small clearing. Through narrowed eyes I counted five black men, sitting close together talking very quietly. My leg throbbed on and the right side of my face hurt like hell where the bastard had kicked me. I hadn't been given any first aid, which probably meant they were going to kill me pretty soon after questioning me. I had no insignia or badges of rank on me, so I could play ignorant, just following orders. As far as I could tell, it was still very much day light, but the thick, tall bushes blocked out a lot of the light. I wondered where the guys were and if the dogs were on the way. One of the men stood up and came over to me. He squatted down in front of me and I looked back at him with one eye. "So, African whitey, you are awake?" "Yes." "My men want to hurt you a lot and then kill you slowly. You killed all our friends." He pointed a finger at me as he spoke. "It is war," I said. "You are trying to take our land, so we have to fight back." "You are wrong" he said, "it is our land and we want it back." "It's not yours, we developed and improved the land, we employed people to help build the cities and roads. Where were your people while it was all going on?" "We will see who wins, whitey, but you will not be around. It is nearly dark. We will stay here tonight and in the morning we will have some fun with you before we leave. My men will chop off your toes, just one foot, then ten minutes later we will do the other foot, then ten minutes later, chop off the foot and ten minutes later the other foot. We will work our way up your legs a piece at a time. We want to see how long you take to die, white pig. We use belts, tightly around your legs, so you will not bleed to death before we are finished with you. One man in Angola only died after we chopped off his knee caps, do you think you can beat that?" He gave an evil chuckle. I stayed silent, what was there to say, my stomach twisted into a knot as fear took over. The leader of the group turned and went back to his men. He said something to them and they all laughed. I trembled all over. They were eating cold rations and drinking from water flasks. I wasn't offered any. It had got darker, sunset was on the way. I thought I had heard helicopters in the distance a little earlier. I said a little prayer to myself that my guys and dogs were on the way, it was my only chance. My bullet holed leg throbbed painfully and there was a burning sensation from the lower part of my other leg, I must have been bitten by something. The men had spread blankets on the ground and were ready to sleep. There was nothing else they could do. They could not light a fire or show any light at all that would give away their position. Suddenly it was dark, the sun had gone down. I started counting to myself. When I reached fifteen I heard a faint snorting noise in the distance, the dogs were coming. Five seconds later the snorting could be clearly heard and seemed to come from all directions at the same time. The sudden loss of light was disorienting and the men in the clearing were muttering to each other. I closed my eyes and waited. If the dogs were going to kill me too, I would be dead in a few seconds. They arrived like an avalanche, crashing through the bushes and fell onto the men in the clearing with snarls of fury. It was so terrifying, I thought I would die from shock there and then. I couldn't breathe properly. There were choking, grunting, ripping, tearing and snarling noises, the men were screaming and I got trodden on by big paws and I groaned out loud. It didn't matter if the men heard me, they were too busy dying. As suddenly as it started, it was all over and there was silence. All I could hear was the panting of the dogs lying around the clearing. I opened my eyes and as they got accustomed to the gloom, I could make out the dim outline of two of the dogs sitting next to me. The one moved its head towards my face and I froze, but it didn't bite me, it licked my cheek and whined softly. It was Jet and Zee, sitting with me, the guys had sent them to protect me. "Hi chaps," I whispered softly. They both poked me with their noses, licked my face and gave excited whines. I couldn't help it, a couple of tears trickled down the side of my face. I told them to down and stay and then we waited for the guys to arrive. The other dogs were all lying quietly as we had trained them to do after an attack was completed. I wasn't on the menu that night. I shuddered. The men's bodies were just shadows on the ground and I was not unhappy I couldn't see the savaged and neck ripped corpses, there would be plenty more in the weeks to come. Never was I so pleased to see anyone, as I was to see my men that night. They had brought a doctor with them from the Rundu medical unit. They quickly untied me and stretchered me out of there to one of the waiting helicopters. After a quick examination, basic cleaning of my wounds and a couple of injections, I was ready to be flown out. I couldn't thank my guys enough, they all looked pleased and embarrassed at the same time. They had stuck with the plan and we were all alive. We couldn't have got a better outcome. The dogs, kennel hands, Abe the tracker and Petrus our interpreter were all choppered out of there and back to base with me. My guys had to retrieve our transporter and drive it back, but everyone was elated, we had killed twenty five, very dangerous men. They would not be hurting anyone else. Back at Rundu, the doctor told me I was very lucky, the bullet had not hit a bone or artery. I would be okay, but would be limping for a while. In the meantime, I had to stay in the hospital for a couple of days, so I could be treated. On that note I fell asleep. Early the following morning, a private brought in a radio telephone. "Good morning Lieutenant, General Myburgh wants to speak to you." I picked up the handset. "Good morning Sir, it's DeBeer." "Are you all rightDeBeer?" "Yes sir." "Can you continue with our plan, yes or no and do not lie to me?" "Really Sir I am fine, I will be out of here in two days and the plan goes ahead." "Good, I will be in touch and I am proud of you my boy." The line went dead and I put down the handset. Who would have thought, old "Pigiron" had a softer side and I wondered what the nasty side was like. I had a steady stream of visitors, in and out the whole day. The camp Commander, Colonel Villiers came to see me. After enquiring about my welfare he said, "You know the whole camp is talking about you DeBeer. They seem to think you single handedly killed off a group of terrorists." "Sir that's not true, it was my men who did most of the work." He looked at me with a smile. "That's the story and you need to acknowledge it, otherwise there will be awkward questions about everything, including the dogs, who they think are just border patrol dogs. So, that is why you need to accept the fame and remain anonymous, it will all be forgotten in a couple of days." So I became known as a security police killer, along with my men, but our mission remained secret. My men came to see me later that morning, all grinning and relaxed, it had taken them half the night to get back to camp.

I told them what had happened after they drove away the previous day, but I left out the torture details. There was no need to burden them with it. "Whose idea was it to send Jet and Zee along with the other dogs." "It was Jack," one of them said. Jack was a little red faced. "My, man, it was a stroke of genius, thank you." Jack mumbled it was nothing, he was just doing what was needed, but I knew he had probably saved me from a far more serious injury. It turned out, that the group of men we had stopped and killed, was part of a SWAPO force, fighting alongside the MPLA, the communist force supported by Russia at that time. They really were an evil bunch of bastards, using intimidation and torture of the local population in southern Angola, to achieve their own ends. No one would miss them, but our mission in Caprivi was just beginning.

Years before, as a youngster, I had watched a simple idea put into practice by a farmer to save his sheep. Never in my wildest dreams could I have seen it resulting, years later, in the army program I had implemented and was in control of. My plans for a successful business future cast aside as I got caught up in the struggle to defend the border. This is how it happened.

CHAPTER TWO

THE TWO BIG LAND ROVERS rumbled quietly along the dirt road in the early pre-dawn light, heading north-west towards the desert. The sun peeked over the horizon about fifteen minutes later, just as they neared the area bordering the Namib desert, scrub bushes and sand as far as the eye could see. I was sitting in the front passenger seat as the guest, next to Pieter Lombard, who was driving. Henry and Dirk sat in the back, commenting on our chances of seeing Jackal. The Jeep behind us carried two of the farm staff and the dogs. Pieter said, "Ok, get your binoculars ready, I'm heading for the nearest koppie, the sun will be behind us and we should have a good view from the top of the next rise." Holding onto the powerful pair of binoculars, as we stopped at the crest of the hill, I jumped up with the others, the roof was open. We began scanning the hill for signs of life. The koppie was about half a mile away, crystal clear in the early morning sunlight, a rocky and boulder strewn slope and there at the top, looking down towards us, was a Jackal. "There he is," we shouted together. "Shut up," snapped Pieter, "you'll scare him away." We fell silent. I stared at the animal through the glasses, magnified so he looked to be only a few feet away. A big specimen can weigh up to about 40 pounds and looks a little like a small, skinny, German Shepherd, with a narrower, pointy muzzle. As a scavenger, he will eat anything he finds lying around. He will also kill and eat any animals or birds smaller or weaker than himself, if the opportunity presents itself, so a sheep is a really easy target, a sort of jackal fast food to go.

That having been said, they serve a really useful purpose, together with vultures and hyena, they keep the land clean of dead and rotting carcasses, helping to prevent disease and unhealthy conditions on the vast African plains. However, when they over multiply, as when conditions are ideal and they start killing farming stock, a conflict situation arises and the farmer will then cull the renegade Jackals, to save his sheep. Pieter Lombard had trained a team of dogs to do the culling, two Greyhounds and two Bull Mastiffs. I did some dog research when I got back home and found out that a Greyhound was an amazing breed of hunting dog and in more recent times used for dog racing. The breed dates back hundreds of years. There are drawings of dogs that look like Greyhounds on the walls of tombs and pyramids in Egypt, although there is disagreement on the origin of the dogs' name and they come in several colors. A Greyhound can weigh up to eighty pounds and be about twenty eight inches tall at the shoulder. He can reach speeds up to forty five miles an hour for around 350 yards effectively, although he could go further, up to about 500 yards before he runs out of steam. He will cover the 350 yards in eighteen seconds, which is about sixty six feet per second, around sixteen feet per bound. Going flat out, their paws hit the ground, four to five times a second. Man, can they run. The Greyhound was bred to hunt small game, like hares, rabbits and small antelope, so, a Jackal that fought back when cornered, was not an easy kill for them. They could keep it at bay until the other part of the team arrived, being two Bull Mastiffs, they were the executioners and a different proposition altogether. They can also be up to twenty eight inches at the shoulder, but are heavily built and can weigh up to 120 pounds. In spite of this they can be quite speedy over shorter distances, not anywhere near the Greyhound league, but not at all bad, considering their size. The breed dates back about two hundred years and was bred as a guardian for grounds men and gamekeepers on English estates, to keep poachers away and protect their masters. They have a big broad head and very large jaws, easily capable of killing a jackal in one or two bites, so that was the team, the Greyhounds to get there fast and keep the Jackal at bay, the Bull mastiffs to carry out the killing. The Landrover moved slowly forwards as we continued to watch the Jackal, who, in turn, was watching us. The other Landrover behind us kept pace, waiting for the signal to release the dogs. Pieter said, "Let me know if the Jackal turns to leave?" "Yes dad," the guys answered. The Jackal, being a very curious animal, stayed where it was, watching us. "We are about a quarter mile from the hill, I'm going to keep moving and get as close as I can," Pieter said. We kept going for a few more seconds. "He's getting nervous," Henry said, "he's like jiggling about, moving back and forth." The Rover stopped and Pieter waved his hand out the window. The Rover behind us skidded to a stop sideways on, the door facing the hill crashed open and the four dog hurricane bounded out and headed for the hill. The Jackal stayed a second longer, then turned and ran. The four legged rockets covered the distance to the hill in seconds, leaving the mastiffs behind. I had never seen dogs run like that, it was spellbinding. As the dogs were released, Pieter accelerated the jeep towards the hill and around its base, bouncing us around over the rough surface, but getting there in time to see the dogs slide into the Jackal in a shower of sand and snapping teeth. The Jackal fought back, which rabbits do not do, but five seconds later the mastiffs arrived and just fell on the Jackal with snarls of fury. A couple of huge bites and the Jackal was dead. It screamed as it died, abruptly the sound was cut off and I felt a bit queasy, as the dogs tore the Jackal to pieces. I slumped back down in my seat, the preparation and anticipation of the hunt had completely overshadowed the actual kill and I felt a bit sick, some hunter I was. Henry and Dirk were elated and discussed the hunt excitedly, I remained quiet. "Not quite what you expected?"

Pieter said to me. "Well, not really. Do you have to kill them with the dogs, isn't there some other way?" "Well, I tried with a rifle, but if you only wound the animal, you have to go into the dunes and bush to track it down. No self respecting farmer will let a wounded animal die in pain out in the bush or desert, but one trip on foot into the dunes in the heat of day and you won't try with a rifle again. Poison is out of the question, god knows how many animals would die, which leaves my dog method. The cost of fencing everything in on the border of the desert with shifting sands would be prohibitive, not to mention, that as a game farm, the wild game comes to the water holes we made for them and I could never deny them access, no, my way is the least expensive and most practical. I only cull the excess jackal population, which ensures the survival of the rest, they get enough food away from the farm and leave the sheep alone." I realized that was it, "least expensive method," after all it was a farm, they had to make a profit. My mind snapped back to my child hood, my first dog and how I became a knowledgeable dog trainer. I started nagging my parents for a puppy when I was seven years old. When I turned nine, my parents finally gave in and bought me a puppy Fox Terrier we named Bobby. I had been fascinated by dogs since I was a toddler. Every dog I came in contact with, I had to pat, stroke and scratch behind its ears, while telling the dog, "good puppy." It was amazing that I never got bitten or even growled at by any of the dogs I patted, perhaps I gave off some sort of doggy vibe that granted me instant acceptance as a sort of kindred spirit, who could say? When I turned ten years old, my puppy was one year and I wanted to train him, to be able to communicate with him, but how? He would play with me all day, but would not listen to a word I said, or so it seemed. Then one week end, wandering through a local flea market, I found a small book entitled "The Bob Martins Dog Book" I handed over my ten cents pocket money and hurried home to try out the training your dog lessons. Later, I sat on the sidewalk crying, having been painfully nipped several times on my legs and reduced to tears. It left me wondering how I could carry on. I decided to put the book away and try again the next weekend, but during the week I had a breakthrough. Every day around six in the afternoon, I would take Bobby for a walk. He pulled at the lead all the time and refused to walk at heel. If I jerked him back he would spin around and nip me on the legs, so I let him pull. On the Tuesday, I walked past the rear entrance of a hotel, a few blocks from our house. There were a lot of large trash bins at one side of the driveway and as we neared them, Bobby barked loudly. I saw several rats vanish into the nearby bushes, they had been eating from the trash bins. Bobby seemed upset there were no rats left there and sniffed around aimlessly. I was depressed that he had barked and scared the rats off so soon. The next afternoon, as we left the house to go for our walk and headed towards the hotel, without thinking, I hissed "shooooosh" at Bobby and waved my hand at him in a push back motion. To my amazement, he stopped pulling on the lead and fell back next to me, while going into a half crouch hunting posture. We crept along towards the trash bins, but once again, as we got closer, his excitement got the better of him and he let out a volley of excited barks and so the rats all vanished by the time we got there. I was very upset and I shouted at him, "bad dog," several times. He looked very miserable, his tail and ears were down and he was very quiet as we walked home with no pulling on the lead. The following afternoon, as we left to go on our walk, I turned in the opposite direction from the trash bins. Bobby tried to pull me in that direction, but I was having none of it and pulled him in the direction I was going. He hung back, he tried to stop me but I kept going, he whined loudly and I actually had to drag him a few feet, before he finally gave up and walked along next to me. His ears and tail were down and he looked really miserable, I had won at last. A couple of blocks further along I turned around and headed for home and he continued to walk next to me. As we got to our garden gate, instead of turning in, I carried on down the road towards the hotel. As Bobby realized we were going hunting again, his tail and ears lifted up and he went into the half crouch position as we walked quietly along, but he remained at my side. I picked up a stick that was lying on the sidewalk and carried it along with us. I once again said "shooosh" to Bobby and waved my hand in a push back motion at his face. When we got near the bins, creeping along in silence, everything was very quiet, it being the back entrance of the building and at that time of the afternoon the driveway was deserted. I reached down and held the clip on the leash with my left hand while I smashed the stick against the nearest bin, yelled, "hah, hah, hah" and unclipped Bobby. The rats shot out of the bins and Bobby went into action. I never knew a dog could move that fast. It was a series of lightening fast pounces, combined with a vicious snap to the back of the neck, a simultaneous shake of his head to break the rats neck and discard the body at the same time while already pouncing on the next one. After about thirty seconds, the rats had vanished back into the nearby bushes, leaving six of their number dead on the driveway.

My dog was happy and pleased with himself. I was also happy, but for an entirely different reason, I had realized that the key to training a dog, any dog, was motivation and incentive. His motivation would be the enjoyment he would get out of doing any task, his incentive to listen could be almost anything. The expectation of a treat if he listened for example, or not having to wait for his dinner because he was a good boy. I found many other forms of incentive over the years, including some unpleasant ones, but they all led to the same thing, obedience, doing whatever their master wanted without question. So there I was, at ten years old I knew that in the years to come, I would be able to train dogs to do anything I wanted, I had grasped the basic essentials to getting it done, something many dog trainers never understood and so remained mediocre. By the time I was eighteen, I was training dogs privately all over the neighborhood and had amassed a library of highly technical books by some of the best dog trainers in the world at that time. I had read and studied the books again and again, until I was sure I understood what the authors were saying. Then I opened my weekend dog training center at a nearby field and put all my acquired knowledge to good use, including teaching dogs protection and guard work. It was generally acknowledged in the Cape Town area, that I had produced some of the best trained security dogs ever seen there.

My mind clicked back to the present and I climbed out of the truck with the others and had hot coffee from the flasks and cookies that Pat had sent along, the dogs got water and after a short rest we were off again, heading North towards a distant hill, at least three or four miles away. The temperature was rising as the sun rose higher and I made a silent wish that we find nothing at the hill except rocks. It would soon be too hot to make a third attempt. My small prayer went unanswered because when we were about a mile away, there it was, half way up the hill, a smaller Jackal, probably female, moving up towards the crest.

The boys, very quietly, this time, notified Pieter that we had another one in our sights. He slowed the Rover right down and we rumbled very quietly onwards. At the top of the hill, the jackal turned and looked around, the sun now well up, must have been shining into its eyes from the right, because it looked away to the left, but I am sure it heard the engines, because it became jittery.

Henry was muttering to himself, "stay there, don't run yet, don't run." I was staring at it through the glasses and suddenly it occurred to me that her pups were probably in a den under the rocks I was looking at, which was why she wasn't running yet, first identify the danger before you make a decision. This time, well in range, when we stopped, the Rovers' side door opened quietly and the two greyhounds were pointed in the right direction and released. The mastiffs followed in a hurry. The little Jackal died in silence, it was over in seconds. They picked up the dogs and the jackal remains and we were on our way back to the farm. I was right, it had been a small female. "What if she had pups hidden under the rocks." I asked. Pieter answered, "Well, they will not survive for very long, that is part of the process of keeping the jackal population at normal levels." Henry and Dirk were silent, no one had really thought about pups. Back at the farm, the twisted fascination of my first Jackal hunt behind me, I hoped I wouldn't soon be seeing anything like it again. I had been mesmerized by the thrill of the hunt, only to feel ill and guilty afterwards, it was almost as though,

I, a self confessed animal lover had condoned the gratuitous killing of wild animals. All across the continent wild animals were being slaughtered, Elephants for their tusks, Rhinos for their horns, Lions, Leopard and Cheetah for their heads and skins, Buffalo and all the antelope species just for sport. Different of course if a wild animal kills to feed itself, but it was not a happening I wanted to be part of, but we are not masters of our own destiny as I would find out one day. No matter ones personal aspirations, life tends to get in the way. We spent the afternoon relaxing at the swimming pool and had a great barbecue that night, when I got my first taste of venison, wild buck meat, what a flavor, but even then I felt guilty eating a wild animal. I rationalized that food was different to killing for sport, after all I had been eating meat in various cooked forms since I was a small child. The following day we were up early again for a tour of the farm and out into the surrounding bush. The farm itself was covered by scrub bushes, about the height of a sheep, growing in an uneven patchwork, in clumps, as far as the eye could see. The sand was whitish in color, probably related in some way to the desert sand dunes. There were patches of open ground where nothing grew, creating natural pathways in between the bushes, which twisted and turned in every direction. It would have been easy to get lost there without a compass to show the way. The area looked a lot like the Karroo in South Africa, thousands of square miles of we stopped about fifty yards from the watering hole and waited to see what game would stop by for a drink. We did get to see some Kudu, I counted six of them, the biggest of the antelope species, with big spiral horns, wandered by and stopped for a quick drink, before vanishing into the bush again. A couple of Jackals trotted out of the bush for a drink before also disappearing. An hour later, some Gemsbok appeared, had a quick drink and also vanished back into the bush. We called it a day and headed back towards the farmhouse. The guys told me there were no Lions in the area any more, hunting had driven them away from the farming areas over the years and they had moved towards the north east, on the border of the desert, but there were still Cheetahs around. We didn't get to see any that day and I was a little disappointed, I felt I deserved to see at least one, but it was not to be.

CHAPTER THREE

FOR ME, IT HAD ALL begun in 1967, mid November it was, the start of summer in South Africa. I had just been accepted for a position with a large clothing factory. I was due to start end of the month, which left me with a forced two weeks vacation.

was close to Sunday lunch time when I remembered the Lombard brothers had invited me to visit them on the family farm in South West Africa, any time they were there. We had met on the beach at Clifton the previous year and hit it off immediately. We spent the next three weeks together chasing pretty girls on the beach and I showed them the night life in Cape Town, introduced them to everyone I knew that we met as we partied our way around. We had a mostly drunken good time. I prided myself on being something of an expert on the cities' night clubs and also got us invited to some really great parties. Their holiday went past in a flash and I took them to the airport that last day, to catch their flight to Windhoek. We parted sadly, vowing to get together soon. They went back to university, I went back to work. Henry and Dirk were both studying at Wits University in Johannesburg, Henry was in medical school, Dirk was studying political science and law. "What could he do with such a combination?" I had thought, probably become a politician or a professional military man. I dragged myself back to the present. They would have to be on summer vacation from university already, so I put a call through to them, no easy feat in the days of manual telephone exchanges and no cell phones.

First I called the main exchange and gave them the name, phone number and city I wanted. They put me through to the nearest exchange to the farm, which was Otjiwarongo, (there's a name to remember) and finally they called the farm, then called me back and connected the lines. It always took a long time, so patience was essential. Eventually my call went through and I had Henry on the line. " Hey, it's me, Rolf, how the hell are you?" " Ja man, we are all great, when you coming to visit?" "Well, I have two weeks vacation now, when can I come?" "Man that is great, we are going to do a Jackal cull on Tuesday, you have to see it, come now!" he shouted at me. "What's a Jackal cull" I asked, is there something wrong with them?" "No man, just over population, they are killing the sheep, so we need to lower their numbers a little. We are going to use the new dogs. Dad has been training them for weeks and this will be their first hunting trip, I will explain it all when we see you. Get going and let me know what flight you are on, man this will be great, the folks can't wait to meet you and Dirk will be mad he was not here now, but we will see you soon," and he shouted again, "get moving now!! "I jumped up and ran out to my car, leaving my bewildered parents calling out to ask what was wrong, "Nothing" I shouted to them, "I'll be back later" and I got into my car and drove off. I went down to the main SAA airways office, open on Sundays and booked a ticket to Windhoek, on the 7am flight the following morning, which would land me there about three hours later. I went back home and booked a telegraphic message to Henry, they would call him and read it out, then send a copy in the next day or two, as long as he got the message, who cared when the copy went out? The previous year there had been political uprisings in SWA and demands made by African leaders to take over SWA. The United Nations tried to assume direct responsibility for SWA and officially changed the country's name to Namibia, recognizing the South West Africa People's Organization (SWAPO) as the official representatives of the Namibian people. The South African government largely ignored the UN's efforts and continued to administer SWA, so at the time I went to SWA, politically, on the surface at least, all was calm, but sub Saharan Africa was really just like a full cauldron, simmering away, just waiting to boil over. South Africa itself, waited unknowingly, for the ANC, (African National Congress, a banned and outlawed political party) to rear up. SWA was already busy with SWAPO. Angola, on SWA's northern border was about to be engulfed in a vicious civil war, as the MPLA, Russian communist backed, UNITA, backed by the west, being the USA and Great Britain and the FNLA backed by China, would begin to butcher each other, as each group sought to gain control of Angola. Meanwhile, Cuba, at the behest of its Russian masters, would send many thousands of troops to Angola, to fight on the side of the MPLA. As I saw it, years later, Castro 32 had his own agenda as well. Break through the South African lines and take SWA, then on into South Africa and he would control all the diamonds, gold and raw materials of Southern Africa, making himself and Cuba a force to be reckoned with on the world stage, if he succeeded. Was he in for a shock when he tried and grossly underestimated the power and sophistication of the South African army as it was drawn into the bloody conflict, to protect its interests in SWA as well as their own Northern border. South Africa had at that time, developed new artillery pieces, known as the G4 canon. The beauty of these, were, that for a big cannon, they were highly portable. They could be assembled or pulled to pieces in around fifteen minutes, then attached to the rear of a troop transport and on its big wheels, could be towed at around forty miles an hour. This canon could fire a shell that weighed as much as a mini motor car about fifty miles. They had three or four of those canons and moved them all, back and forth along the border with Angola, firing those huge shells into the massed ranks of Castro's soldiers, decimating them. Because they were so mobile, the enemy never knew where they were going to fire from and they were always set up miles behind their own lines in relative safety, then hurled the huge shells into the massed Cuban ranks. When one of those shells landed, it would clear a couple of hundred square yards, literally vaporizing anything that was there. It was said that Castro went wild with rage when he saw his plans coming to nothing and he decided, that what he needed was his aircraft, Mig jet fighters that could bomb the enemy, flying into South Africa and bombing Johannesburg. He would bomb South Africa into submission. To that end, they loaded the Migs onto a couple of freighters in Cuba and then the ships left port, heading for Angola. The word got out almost immediately and it was said that the USA President, Jimmy Carter, then sent an urgent message to Castro, basically telling him, that the day one of those jets took off and flew against South Africa, would be the day Cuba would vanish from the face of the earth. This must have scared the hell out of Castro, because the freighters turned around and went back to Cuba and Castro took what was left of his men and they all went back to Cuba as well. Within a few months, the warring factions got together and worked out a power sharing agreement. The Angolan civil war was over. Botswana, along SWA's eastern flank, took little part in the goings on, relying heavily on South Africa for most of its needs, but thousands of animals fled to the south, into the safety of Botswana's Okavango Delta, driven there by the war and the slaughter of thousands of animals on the border and in the Caprivi Strip. On Angola's eastern side sat Zambia and Kenneth Kauanda its president, who gave bases to the SWAPO terrorists, and rapidly increasing poverty, until his people voted him out some years later and got rid of him. In the meantime, SWAPO members, mostly black political activists from South Africa who had run away to their bases in Angola and Zambia, continued to try and infiltrate South West Africa, with a view to killing farmers, their families and their staff. Also, they would burn and destroy farm houses and buildings if they got the opportunity. The plan was simple, if you could destabilize the country, it would be much easier to take it over. In addition, they had friends within South West Africa who would not hesitate to help them if the opportunity presented itself. SWAPO was an outlawed political organization and the men that tried to cross the border into SWA on their behalf were declared terrorists. On getting home I had told my parents I was off to SWA for a few days holiday at the Lombard's farm, leaving the following morning. My mother leapt into action and rushed around the house gathering up clean clothes for me and even tried to pack my suitcase. I guess it's a mother thing. She produced a large box of chocolates from a kitchen cupboard for Mrs. Lombard, as she admonished me, "Don't you and the boys go eating them, you make sure she gets them." " Yes ma" I sighed. Packed and ready, I tried to read the Sunday papers, but couldn't concentrate. The day dragged by and I went to bed early. I was up at four am and at the bus stop fifty feet down the road from our house at five. The first bus of the day stopped there a little after five and I was in town fifteen minutes later. The airways office was just across the street and at 5.45am I was on the shuttle to the airport with my single suitcase and a small carry on bag. In 1967 they were still using twin engine, turbo prop Viscounts for the flight to Windhoek, fairly noisy, but reliable and in due course we landed at the Windhoek airport, which was surprisingly small, I thought. The only other airport I had seen was Cape Town, enormous by comparison. Years later, after seeing London and Los Angeles, I laughed, thinking about how big I had thought the Cape Town airport was, all those years before. Windhoek Airport was off to the east of the city, the drive to the farm was west and then turn off to the north up the highway, bypassing the city for the seventy mile drive to the farm on the edge of the Namib desert. Henry and Dirk were waiting for me and with lots of backslapping and shouting, grabbed my case, threw it into the back of the old Land Rover. It was like a small bus, with a canvas top and could seat about ten people. The spring weather was perfect, a mildly warm day, with no wind. Henry drove off and we were on our way. It was much like driving through the Karroo, semi desert, scrubby bushes and sand as far as the eye could see. Rocky, stony hills punctuated the landscape, in colors of brown and red, fading away into the distance. There were very few cars on the road and we hummed along smoothly. Henry said, "Okay, so tomorrow we will be going out at daybreak, we will wake you at four am and we will leave around five thirty. The sun comes up at about six and then the hunt begins. We had a very mild winter this year, so the Jackal have done well and when there are too many of them, they start killing sheep, so we cull them a little to keep them off the farm. They have killed four sheep in the last month and dad is very worried. Each sheep is worth a few hundred rand, so we have to stop them. If we kill a few of them and stop them breeding, it will normalize the population in our area and save our sheep. Sad in a way, but dad says we have no alternative." So that was how I ended up on the Jackal hunt. I arrived back home around lunchtime and thereafter followed a week of anticipation, waiting to start my new job in the clothes factory. Three years later, I completed training and was given the entire city area as my sales division. I needed a driver, assistant combination, who could help with the day to day running of the office and showroom, as well as driving me around to appointments. Parking was an impossible task, so a driver was essential. I placed an advert in the local newspaper and waited for applicants. To my surprise, there were only seven replies and I made appointments with each man to interview them. What a disappointment that turned out to be, three of them were very dirty and stunk of stale booze, two were illiterate and the sixth one was so high he could hardly speak, his pupils were dilated and his eyes bloodshot. I turned him around and pushed him out of the door. He staggered off down the corridor. One applicant had not arrived. It was late afternoon and I was getting ready to leave when there was a hesitant knock at the door. I opened the door and there stood my last applicant. "I'm sorry I'm a little late," he said, "the bus was not on time today, I'm Tony James. A big man, over six feet tall, neatly dressed, dark pants, highly polished black shoes, checked jacket, white shirt and tie. I invited him in and we sat down in the lounge area of the showroom. He looked African, but had lots of dark curly hair. He was a good looking young guy, with a big smile, full of very white teeth. I looked across at him and asked for his unemployment card. All ordinary, employed people in South Africa had a card opened for them when they first started working, All work history was listed on the card, together with starting and finish dates of each job. In addition, there was a comments column where the reason for leaving was filled in. The card, when folded open was almost as big as an A4 page and was made with a strong fabric backing, made to last, I thought. I folded the card open and was absolutely amazed to see the card was full, every line filled in, twenty five positions in three years. I remained expressionless however and looked at the comments line. All I saw was resigned or laid off, all the way down the page, there were no other comments. I looked over at Tony and said "I see you've had quite a lot of jobs." "Yes," he answered, "that's been a big problem for me." "Okay," I said, "I wasn't that much of an angel growing up, that I can sit in judgment of anyone else, so tell me, what happened at this place?" and I pointed at a business name listed on his card. "Oh yes," he said, "I remember that place well. I was there for about a month, during which time, the manager I reported to, referred to me as "that black bastard." "When he was talking to me directly, every day, he called me "you black bastard or kaffir, it depended on his mood at the time, so I had to choose between killing him or leaving the company." I left and for three years I have gone from position to position after having been faced with racial insults, racial slurs, sworn at, denigrated and humiliated, because I am a black man. There were a few positions that I left after a little while, just not for me, but mainly, the hatred I have experienced for being black, just overwhelmed me. I don't know why I am telling you this, you just seem different." His voice trailed off. I was speechless with horror. Was he telling me the truth? Surely, no one in his position would lie about something so personal? He sat across from me, gazing at me with big brown eyes. I kept my face expressionless, but I knew I had gone bright red with embarrassment. I could feel my face burning, while inside myself, for the first time in my life, I was ashamed to be a white man in South Africa, a part of the system dedicated to marginalizing and keeping the black people of the country as irrelevant and almost subhuman. No! I thought to myself, you are not going to be part of the perpetuation of the system, starting now. "Where do you live?" I asked. "I live with my granny in a little house in Maitland." "What does it cost you?" "seventy Rand a week. The man we rent from said if we stop paying, he will send his people to throw us out on the street and he was not joking, With granny's pension and my little wages now and then, we scrape by. Granny keeps telling me how proud she is of me, I just get embarrassed." "I thought about my own one bed roomed apartment in Sea Point, thirty five Rand a month was what I paid, my G-d, talk about extortion. I looked across at him, cleared my throat and spoke very carefully. "I don't care if you are black, white or green with yellow stripes, if you come and work with me, you are either with me all the way or you are gone. Have we got a deal?" His face broke into a huge smile as he said, "I'm with you." I reached over the table and we shook hands. We celebrated with coffee and cookies, negotiated his starting wage and that was how we met and then worked together for years, becoming more than close friends in the process. Little did I know how intertwined our lives would become years later. Tony quickly settled in to the routine of taking me to my appointments. I would jump out of the car, taking my briefcase and samples with me. Tony would find parking and then bring in the rest of the samples and help me with the presentation. A few months later, I came down with a cold and woke the following morning, to find I could not speak, only whisper. I had an important meeting scheduled with a major customer of mine at nine that morning and in due course presented myself at their offices to show the latest ranges. Tony came with me and we were ushered into the conference room. I found my voice had almost completely gone, so I turned to Tony and whispered that he would have to show the range. He did very well indeed, I merely handed him the correct samples, he did everything else. From then on, he regularly showed ranges as we swapped over and in all the months and years that followed, there was not one instance of racial animosity, although we did business with a large cross section of the population, white, colored, Asian, Moslem and Indian business owners and buyers. Driving to a customer out of the city one morning, we had time to chat. Tony said, "You know, I've never thanked you for helping me get a new life, it's been amazing, people of all races just being people, no one cares about my color, who would have thought it could be like this in South Africa? Why do think it has been like this for me?" I considered his question. I had never thought about it, just accepted it, after all, he was a really nice, good looking young guy, very helpful and informative. I thought my customers and business associates just appreciated him for who he was, as I did, but Tony was right, there had to be more to it than met the eye, finally I thought I had the answer, I turned to him. "I think, in the type of business we are in, at first all our customers accepted you because you were with me, so you were not a perceived threat. You know how they think, that every black guy wants to rob them or worse. They knew you were not there to harm them in any way, so they relaxed, this allowed them to get to know you as the nice guy you are. Now, because we supplied them with goods they wanted and they made money out of the deals, you came to represent profits to them and that transcends everything else, congratulations, you became colorless, they don't care about your color any more, business is more important. Isn't that crazy? The sociologists could have a field day with this one." We both burst out laughing. "You know, the reverse must also be true," Tony said. "What reverse?" "Well, there are big businesses in the black townships that could place large orders with us, so if we go in, I will lead and you can be my backup, exactly the same as we are doing, but reversed, are you game to try?" "Sure I'm game, as long as you feel it's safe?" "Of course it's safe, I would never take you any place where you, or I for that matter, would be at risk." "Okay, deal, set it up and we'll go. "So, we started a new sales area, it was very successful and sure enough, I became colorless, the business of making money was more important. A couple of weeks later, Tony was waiting for me in the office early morning as usual, but as I walked through the door he jumped to his feet and said, "We need to talk urgently please." " Of course we can, what's wrong." He took a deep breath. "A couple of years back, I was a gang member. I decided to leave the gangs and start a new life, so I took my granny and we ran away. I found us the little house in Maitland, where we live now, but the gang has found me. I must have been recognized out in the townships and followed. You are not allowed to leave your gang, if you do and they find you, they will try to kill you. There were a few of them across from my house last night pointing at it. That means they are coming to get me tonight. They always attack after two in the morning, so I will be waiting." "What are you going to do?" I asked. "Wait for them and fight. If I beat them, I win the right to leave, there is no other way." "What about the police?" "You're joking. You think the police will help a black man. They will come and pick up the pieces, nothing else." "Okay, that settles it, I'm coming with you, we'll take them on together." Tony gave a horrified bellow of outrage. "What, are you crazy? You can't go with me and put yourself at risk because I was a gang member. These guys would slit your throat for fun, no, you stay away, it's my fight. If I win the fight they will let me go, it's my only way out." He glared at me. "Okay, okay, if that's what you want, but this is not right, you could get badly hurt, even killed." He shrugged his shoulders. "I have no choice, it's win or die, so if I'm not here early tomorrow, send the cops" and so saying, he turned and left. My day was ruined, I couldn't work worrying about Tony, so I quickly called the few businesses we had appointments with and changed them, then headed for my parents' house. There was no one home, so I left a note on the hall table and went back outside. Around the side of the house was a parking space I kept my old car in, a little Renault I just couldn't bear to get rid of, so I kept it there with a little trickle battery charger attached, so it could be used when needed. I disconnected the charger and moved the car out into the street, then moved my regular car into the parking space.

CHAPTER FOUR

I HAD DECIDED WHAT I was going to do, I was going to park down the street from Tony's house at around one in the morning and wait for the gang to arrive. My old car would fit in well in that neighborhood, not attracting any attention. I drove back to my apartment, had a small lunch and tried to nap. The day dragged by. Around six, I went across the street to Ricks, a little steak house and ordered dinner. An hour, small sirloin, fries and grilled mushrooms later, followed by a couple of coffees, I felt much better and headed back across the street. The evening dragged by, the radio just irritated me. Finally, midnight rolled around and I got dressed in black. I found the knitted black cap I had got for a present some months before in a cupboard and put it on. It hid most of my face. Lastly, I took my nunchakus out of their bag, they were going with me. I had never hit anyone with them, only practiced with them for many pleasant hours, as I had been taught to. I took some snacks and a soda with me, sitting for a few hours in my car would be hungry work. Tony's house was three blocks from the main road, close to the suburban rail line and Observatory Station. The little house was in the middle of the block on Wylie, on the left side of the street, off Station Road. I drove past Station Road on the Main Road and turned left two blocks further on, then turned left onto Tony's street. The streets were empty, no traffic at all, it was very quiet. Just before the corner, I found the perfect parking spot, where a tree hung over the road creating a dark shadowed area. My car was almost invisible. I parked, turned off and settled down to wait. It was just after one in the morning. At one thirty I saw Tony come out onto the street, he looked around, then crossed over and disappeared into the alley between the two houses on the other side. He did not come out again and I wondered what he was up to. There was no way I could check, I just had to wait and see.

Just after two thirty, there was movement a couple of blocks down the street, a group of people was heading my way. I quickly turned off the radio and got ready. As they got closer, I counted twelve men. How could Tony fight them all and win, also, where the hell had he disappeared to? The group stopped outside his house and started picking up things on the sidewalk, of course, stones. Ready, they turned towards the house and started throwing the stones. So far, it was all done in silence, a prearranged plan of course. I heard the sound of breaking glass, then everything went crazy. I saw Tony hurtle out of the alley behind the gang, carrying a trashcan in his right hand and the lid in his left. He took them completely by surprise, they never expected an attack from the rear and he went through their line like a charging bull, using the trashcan as a battering ram. Four of them went down, unconscious from his first effort, smashed over their heads with the trashcan, then he spun around like a whirling dervish, arms extended with the trash can and lid held out and took out another three, five to go. At that moment, two men came around the corner from Station Road and stopped dead in their tracks as they stared at the fight taking place down the road. "Jesus," the one said, "he's killed half the guys." "Let's get him," said the other and as they started towards the fight, I sort of erupted from the shadows and was on them before they realized I was there. I hit the first one across the top of his head with my nunchaka, flipped the end back to my other hand and smashed it sideways across the side of the other guy's head as he turned around. I doubt if either of them actually saw me, both were very much out cold, probably with concussions, in any event, neither would be taking any further part in the evenings proceedings. I glanced down the street, there were two left, in the distance I could hear sirens, someone had called the police. The two leftovers turned and ran towards where I was standing in the shadows. They paused as they saw their two friends lying in the "Shit, what the hell happened to them?" shouted the one, "I don't know man," shouted the other. "It's me," I shouted and as they both jumped around in fright, I did the one two with my nunchaka. A very fast strike to the left side of the head of the one closest to me, flicked it back over my right shoulder and then a down strike to the top of the head of the last one and they were all bye, bye. It was all over in seconds. Tony stared down the street at me. I shrugged my shoulders, jumped into my car, started it and turned on the bright lights. He would not even be able to say what car it was. I reversed hurriedly away from him down the street and at the end of the block, reversed around the corner and kept going. At a safe distance, I turned the car around and headed for home. Interesting weapon, the Nunchaka. It started life as an agricultural implement, being used to knock the rice husks off rice plants in the paddy fields in Japan, around five hundred years ago, by rapidly twirling it so that the one spinning end would hit the rice husks as the peasants walked along the rows of plants. It was made of very hard wood, two pieces, around eighteen inches long, each piece two inches in diameter, tapering to an inch at the other end. Holes were drilled at the tapered ends, to allow the two pieces to be joined together with cord. The farmers owned the land, but were not allowed to have weapons. The emperor's soldiers had the weapons, but were not allowed to own land. If the soldiers thought the farmers were not producing enough food, rice being their staple diet, they would attack the farmers and kill them in the fields, so the farmers learnt to use the nunchaka as a weapon of self defense, very effective it was too. Meanwhile, I reached the Main Road, turned left and then right, heading up the hill to the De Vaal drive freeway. I had avoided the police and ambulances and was back at my apartment a half hour later. I cleaned my nunchakas, packed it away and had a shower, then I went to bed, it was three thirty in the morning.

I rose early and was at my office around seven, Tony was already there. "How are you?" I asked, "what happened?" I was greeted with a big grin. "You know exactly what happened, you were there." "Not exactly, you told me to stay away, so I did. I was at least fifty yards away and I never interfered in your fight." "What about the four guys lying in the street where you were?" "Well, two of them were running away from you and were no longer in your fight, so I just stopped them from leaving and the other two tripped over me coming up behind you and I was forced to deal with them because you were quite busy at the time. I don't think any of them knew what happened to them and they wouldn't recognize me even if they walked into me. Just big headaches when they woke up, so what happened when the cops arrived?" "I was the only man standing when they got there. I had put the trash can back down the alley and I told them there was a street fight and these guys were attacked by a gang of others while just walking along. The other guys ran away and left these guys just lying there. I told them I came out of my house to see what all the yelling and screaming was about and saw some men run around the corner and they were gone. They accepted my story because I lived there. It took three ambulances to take them away and my story saved them because I had turned them into victims, clever yes? Anyway, that final good deed was witnessed by my old gang leader, I think his arm was broken but he was conscious and as they carried him past me to the ambulance he said very quietly that I was a good guy, I was free, no more problems. So here I am, a new man, I can get back to work." So we did.

CHAPTER FIVE

YEARS BEFORE, I HAD MISSED being called up for army service, due to not being balloted, then they changed the rules and with the advent of the Angolan civil war, instituted a new ballot. I got caught in the net, so at the age of thirty two, I was off to the army for two years. I was annoyed and really pissed off, but there was nothing I could do about it, so I accepted it. It was fortunate that I had no idea what a bastard of a trick fate had played on me. "Ok, this is it, I'm off to the army next week, I told Tony and explained what had happened. I had received my call up papers some months before and had been trying to get out of going. My final appeal had failed and so I was leaving the next week. Tony looked troubled. "Are you nervous?" "More irritated than nervous, I would really prefer to be someplace else." Tony said, "Listen here, you have to come with me tomorrow to see Auntie." "What! what auntie? You said your only living relative was your granny." "Well I have "Auntie" as well, I just don't talk about her." "Why, what's wrong with her?" "Nothing, well not really nothing, it's just she's a bit strange, sometimes very strange, oh what the hell, she's a "Sangoma." It was my turn to stare at Tony. "You're joking right, you haven't really got a witch doctor for an aunt, have you?" "Yes I have. Granny had four kids, all girls. The first two were still born, the third was my mother and then came "Auntie. She was born blind and has lived on the farm in Malmesbury all her life. You'd think after two still born kids, she would have stopped trying, but it was the late eighteen hundreds and what the hell did they know about anything, let alone birth control. Any way, Auntie survived. She must be around eighty four years old, which puts her birth date around 1894. Granny was an African type of herbalist, taught by her mother and her mother before her. She taught Auntie what she could, but when Auntie was still a young girl, granny said she started acting funny. She started having visions about the people in the area, she would tell them about good or bad things that were going to happen and then she started seeing things about people from further away. There is no doubt she is an amazingly clever woman, she learnt to read braille at the local church with the help of the minister, then proceeded to educate herself, far beyond the norms of a simple black farm girl. Almost unbelievable. As you know there were no schools in South Africa for black kids way back then and black Africans were not allowed in the "white mans" libraries. The minister got all the books for her and was instrumental in finding a braille teacher for her, he must have been quite a guy, a black man in South Africa in those far off days of inequality, moving mountains for one of his flock. Granny told me, auntie would send messages to strangers that she thought she could help, but they thought she was a nut case. She kept sending messages to arbitrary people and one day a man from a nearby farm fell out of a tree and died, after she had warned him to stop tree climbing. Coincidence you say, but after that it kept happening. Bad things happened to those who ignored her and those who listened stayed safe. Who can say if anything would have happened to the others, if they too had, just gone their own way, but how did she know the names of all those people, where they came from and what they were doing? Anyway, the local communities declared her a "Sangoma," witch doctor, to be ignored at their own risk and after that people started visiting her and requesting councelling. She never asked for payment, these were very poor people, but somehow a little money made its way to her, offerings from grateful folk, also food would be left at her door. This has been going on for many years. The farmer would have liked to get rid of her, but was too scared to do anything. I don't blame the poor bastard, he showed good sense. I'm her great nephew, I'm terrified of her and I don't know why. When granny left the farm, auntie got the little cottage and still lives there today. She sends me a message when she wants to see me, with a little list of herbs she needs. This time the message said to bring the white man, she wishes to see him. You are the only white man I know, please, you must come with me?" Looking at Tony, my stomach lurched and I got an uneasy feeling. If big Tony was that nervous, how would I hold up? I gave myself a mental shake, I was being ridiculous, witch doctor indeed. "Okay, okay I'll go with you, but you are driving, you can pick me up at eight tomorrow morning." "Good," his face cracked a small smile. "By the way, what's her name, what do I call her?" "I only know her as Auntie, but you will not need to call her anything, she talks, we listen and then go away, okay?" "Okay. Listen here," I said, "should we take her something, a little present maybe?" "That's up to you, I have already bought the herbs she wanted." "Then I will get her some food." Tony stood up. "I have some people to see, you have to finish packing. I will pick you up at eight tomorrow and thanks man, you're a good guy." I left the office and headed for the supermarket to prepare for my meeting with Auntie. I grinned as I wondered what would appeal to an elderly witchdoctor. I decided on some chocolates, hand soaps and sodas to play safe, then headed for home. The army had supplied me with a list of items I could take with me if I wanted to, things they would not be supplying free of charge. The list included a clothes iron, shoe polish, playing cards, writing paper, envelopes, stamps, a good flashlight, cookies, snacks, extra underwear if you preferred your own and not army issue. The list went on and when I first read it, I had laughed, a list for a boy scout camp, but I stopped abruptly, the reality was, where I was going was no holiday camp, the guns and bullets were real and there would be men waiting, happy to kill me if they could. The bush war and I were on a collision course. The following morning Tony was his usual punctual self and we were on our way, the big, pale blue Ford Granada purring smoothly along the highway. We headed up the west coast road through the residential areas of Milnerton and Tableview, then branched off heading north west towards Malmsbury, a large farming area. The farm was about seventy miles away and beyond the city limits. We drove alongside mile after mile of vast, empty, brown colored maize fields. It all looked ominous and lonely and matched my feelings exactly. I had a bad feeling about my coming meeting with auntie. The growing season was from spring through mid summer, then came the harvest. I could see enormous grain silos dotting the landscape, silhouetted against the sky as we passed by, I wondered if there was anything left inside them or had they been cleaned out, waiting for the new seasons crops. We drove mostly in silence, branched off west at the town center and turned off onto a gravel road about twenty minutes later. On our left, built against a small hillside were about thirty cottages and just after them were what looked like a few long bungalows. Tony pointed, "see, the cottages are for the permanent staff, the long bungalows are for seasonal temporary staff, about thirty guys to a bungalow. The toilets and wash houses are at the end and the permanent staff, have their own bathrooms down here, near the cottages. The actual farmhouse is about a mile down the road." It all looked quite pretty, the buildings white washed and gleaming in the early morning sunlight. There were lots of flowers and trees scattered about. There were no people to be seen and no children. I assumed the kids were at school and the adults at work on the farm somewhere. There was a small empty parking area on our left, for about six cars, they certainly were not encouraging visitors.

We parked there, gathered up our parcels and got out. I could hear a baby crying, a sign of life. It was a pleasantly warm day, the air smelled sweet and fresh, I could hear birds tweeting and warbling in the trees, otherwise all was quiet. "Follow me,"

Tony said, so I did. We followed a gravel path that climbed upwards and around to the left. Auntie's cottage turned out to be the one at the end of the first row. There was an empty flower bed at the front, waiting for spring to arrive no doubt. The plain brown front door was set in the middle with a small shuttered window on each side of it. The door stood open, held in place by a quilt covered, brick door stop. The quilt had a little head like a dog, small paws and a tail, much better than a plain brick. Tony rapped on the door with an extended knuckle. "Come in," chirped a high pitched voice, it was an instruction not an invitation. I followed a little hesitatingly behind Tony. The inside of the cottage was unlit except for a small fireplace on my left, in which some logs were burning, the flames looked quite cheerful, lighting the dim interior. The floor was covered with linoleum, shades of brown in a square block pattern. There was a curtain drawn across at the back, no doubt the bedroom area. On my right was a wooden table with only one chair, the other three chairs were in front of the fireplace, one chair facing the other two. Auntie sat on the single chair, a tiny woman wearing a bright floral housecoat, her head was covered with a matching scarf, wound around her head and pinned down. "Put the parcels on the table and come and sit with me." "Yes Auntie." We piled the stuff we had bought onto the table and went and sat down. Now that my eyes were accustomed to the dim light, I could see the cottage was spotlessly clean. There was a fresh clean smell in the air and also something else I did not recognize, probably an odor from the strange herbs Auntie used, but it was not an unpleasant smell. I was looking down, not quite ready to look into the sightless eyes of Auntie. She was wearing brown felt slippers and wooly socks. "You, white man, pull your chair up close to me so I can feel your face." I jerked upright in fright, recovered, then moved my chair forward until my knees almost touched hers. "Okay," I said. I leaned forward, so did she, extending her arms until she found my face. Her touch was soft as she examined the shape of my face, my eyes, my chin and even my ears. Her fingers felt warm. I took the opportunity to examine her face at the same time. She could not have been more than five feet tall, her face was small and oval in shape, her eyes were milky white, like eyeballs with no iris at all, just round white balls, almost no eyelashes or eyebrows. Her nose was small but quite flattened, not protruding in the conventional sense. Her ears were covered by the scarf, but I could see wisps of white hair, sticking out at the edges. Her skin was a medium brown color and remarkably unlined, her face looked strangely peaceful and scary at the same time. I suddenly felt quite sad for her, what a struggle life must have been for her. The high pitched shout gave me such a fright, I nearly fell off my chair. "Don't you dare pity me white man, you do not have the right," she shrieked. "Reserve your pity for those poor souls who have yet to come to terms with the consequences of their own actions, by which time it will be too late." Her shriek of fury faded to silence, my heart was beating like a trip hammer, I was frozen to my chair. With her face still inches from mine, her voice dropped to a harsh whisper as she pointed a forefinger at me, she seemed to be in a trance like state.

"The Devils are coming, black and white, what you cannot see you cannot fight. Look to the left, look to the right, it's in the center out of sight, off you go there will be another, thank your luck that there is a brother." Her voice rose to a shriek again.

"Many will die and you will suffer too, before you see the light and what is true. You are not an inherently bad man, but you need to know, if you walk with the devil, you can always choose to walk along a different path, but if the devil walks with you, the only way out is death. I do know, you will carry it all with you to your grave, for you there is no escape. A weaker man might be driven insane, you to your credit, will accept the blame.

Remember, the devil is never your friend, never." She sat back and all was silent, several moments passed, then she spoke again.

"You must go now, I am tired, thank you for the gifts." I struggled shakily to my feet as she spoke again, "Tony?" "Yes Auntie." "Look after this white man, you need each other." "Yes Auntie, I will" and then we were outside hurrying down the path. Tony's hands were shaking so badly, it took a couple of attempts before he could get the key in the lock and open the car door. I was feeling strangely weak and my legs felt like lead. I pulled my door open and collapsed into the car. Both of us were badly shaken by the encounter, it was an experience way beyond anything I could have dreamed of. Tony started the car, turned it around and we drove slowly away, heading for the freeway, both of us busy with private thoughts. My mind was in a turmoil, so many unanswered questions. Once we were on the freeway, I started feeling a little better. "You okay man?" I asked Tony."

No I am not bloody well okay. I am still shaking and what the hell was that left and right devil crap Auntie was screaming about?" "I was going to ask you the same thing, because I have no idea. I have never been involved with devil worship, the stuff you buy for her, do you think she uses it on the fire to create some sort of hallucinogenic daze if you're sitting there breathing it in?" "Sure it's possible," Tony answered, "but then why does she stay unaffected and the things she says always come true, so how does she know and what does it all mean?" "Perhaps she is using the word devil just to mean bad or evil things, the old folks do that you know. Perhaps it's just a warning to watch out for something bad that may come along in the future?" I didn't believe that any more than Tony did, but we left it at that and did the rest of the drive home in silence. My final thought was about carrying it all to my grave, "all what?" I wondered, my God, she had really unnerved me, it was as though she could look into my soul and rational thought brought no relief or explanation either.

I was on the train at Cape Town station at one pm, my folks came to say goodbye, I was hugged and kissed together with a thousand or so other young guys, by their parents, girl friends and assorted relatives. Tony had badly wanted to come and see me off, but had decided against it, it was a sad goodbye the day before, but I was happy Tony would run the office in my absence and the factory was okay with the arrangement. My steel trunk, known as a trommel, was packed in the goods container section of the train with all my belongings in it, except for my kit bag, which I had with me. There was a strong lock on my trunk to minimize theft. The next time I would see the trunk, would be when we got to the army camp outside Bloemfontein. The train had about twenty carriages all full of young men plus the goods section with all the trunks and luggage, around a thousand men on their way to the army. The train trip was not pleasant. There were six of us cramped in the compartment, me the thirty two year old, the others were eighteen, nineteen and twenty. I felt like a grandfather. They wanted to know how I had ended up in army, I told them it was just bad luck, I had been balloted and that was that. They laughed. I spent my time reading and dozing. They asked if I preferred a particular bunk, I said they could all pick, I would take whatever was left over, which turned out to be a bottom bunk, which was fine with me. Dinner was a pack of chicken sandwiches, a mug of coffee and an apple. An officer poked his head in the door, looked us over, checked our names off on his list and suggested we go to sleep early, we were going to need the rest. He left. Pajamas for me, were shorts and a tee shirt. At about eight, I paid a visit to the toilet at the end of the carriage, then back to the compartment and brushed my teeth. I was ready for bed. Outside the compartment it was noisy, men shouting, laughing and hurrying up and down the corridor, inside the compartment it was much quieter, I was surprised the insulation was so good. I estimated we would get to Bloemfontein around seven in the morning, so I planned to wake at four thirty, be dressed and ready by five thirty, which would leave time for breakfast. I mentioned it to the guys in the compartment, they groaned but agreed, if they wanted breakfast, they had better be up and ready at the early hour. One of them, a big, dark haired kid by the name of Badenhorst, I forgot his first name, had been overly loud and aggressive since we got on the train. The other guys were obviously irritated by him, but had said nothing. He turned on me and demanded to know who had died and made me king. "Don't be ridiculous, it's just a suggestion to try and help out. You don't have to do it. If you want to sleep later, you go right ahead." He muttered something under his breath and turned away. He was going to get a rude shock if he continued to behave like an idiot. I hoped I wouldn't end up in the same barracks with him, I would find out soon enough. We moved the seat backrests up into the bunk position and pretty soon were all asleep. I woke up at four thirty, picked up my shaving gear and clothes from the end of my bunk and headed off to the bathroom. To my great joy, it was open and the corridor was deserted. I hurried inside and around twenty minutes or so later, relieved, washed and shaved, came out to find a line for the bathroom was forming. "Jeez, what the hell time did you get up?" one of the guys asked. I just smiled at him and kept going. Back at the compartment, the guys were getting ready and treading on each other as they all tried to use the basin to shave and brush their teeth at the same time. The door slid open and a sergeant stood there. "You men go and have breakfast now, fourth carriage down, you've got thirty minutes starting now." He pointed in the direction of the dining saloon. I was ready, so I took off in a hurry, followed by my compartment companions. The saloon was filling quickly, we grabbed a table, six of us where there were normally four. Badenhorst the bully was sullen and quiet, I ignored him. Breakfast was cereal, followed by fried eggs, one sausage, toast and coffee, no choices allowed. I wolfed down my food, drank the luke warm coffee, then back to the compartment to wait, it was just after five thirty in the morning. We tidied up the compartment, put the seats back together and sat down, three to a side. Badenhorst sat opposite me and glared around him, but mostly at me. I could see pent up rage on his face and I knew he would have loved to take a swing at me. I knew, if I hit him, I could easily end up in army prison for assault, he knew it applied to him too and that was all that was holding him back. The uneasy silence was broken when one of the guys thanked me for getting them up in time for a decent breakfast. I answered I was happy to have helped. Badenhorst sneered and said it was a clever Jew move. I said it had nothing to do with Jews, it was just commonsense and experience, something he was sadly lacking. He knew I had insulted him, but wasn't quite sure how to respond. I wondered how I could needle him into trying to hit me. He looked up and said, "so you're a Jew lover as well, hey?" I replied, "I know what I am, but you, you have no idea that you're an unpleasant, ignorant young man, you lack manners, you're uncouth, your breath smells disgusting, your clothes are dirty and as for my Jewish friends, any one of them is worth a dozen of you, you revolting little prick." I delivered my little speech in a quiet even tone and as I finished, I smiled at him. I could see he was boiling with rage, he clenched and unclenched his fists, going red in the face, but he just would not take the bait.

It crossed my mind that when it came time to be issued with our assault rifles, I had better watch my back. I smiled inwardly, I had really asked for it, no going back. I sighed and settled back in my seat. Not long afterwards, we arrived in Bloemfontein and were lined up outside the train, checked off against a list, put our kit bags in a trailer behind a troop carrier, climbed on board and were driven to Tempe, the army camp. The army base was enormous, I estimated at least ten thousand men were there at any given time, it could well have been more. The truck stopped at the main entrance and the drivers' documents were examined. The rear flap opened and the duty guard looked us over and counted us. He compared this with drivers' list, closed the flap again and we drove off after the trucks in front of us. A few moments later we stopped again and were ordered out of the truck. We found ourselves outside the barracks. There were row upon row of them, we were D3. I could see the steel trunks stacked up near the entrance. A corporal appeared, lined us up again, then he led us inside. Forty men to a barracks in double bunks. "I'm Corporal Moser," he announced, "I'll give you ten minutes to pick your bunks, after that I'll just allocate." He turned and left. I said I would take a bottom bunk, so did several other men. I grabbed one down the end, near the bathroom, there were six guys left over, they spun coins and that settled everyone in bunks. The guys from my train compartment were all there except Badenhorst. I asked what had happened to him. They told me he was not supposed to be in our compartment, he had made a mistake and the Sergeant at the station had shouted at him for being an ignorant idiot and had sent him down to the other end of the platform. I was sorry I had missed seeing that, but relieved he was gone. The guys started swapping names and of course, my name got the usual, "where are the diamonds?" question, the guys laughed as I answered I was out of stock. The Corporal appeared again. "Okay, everyone outside to the trunks." At the trunks he said. "Two men to a trunk that belongs to one of you, carry it to your bunk, then come back for the next one. The trunk for the upper bunk goes at the foot of the bunk and for the lower bunk against the wall. Get going." It took about fifteen minutes and the trunks were all in place. The next six weeks went by in a blur. We were woken up at any time of the night, even five minutes after lights out. We had to put on full battle gear and go running around the parade ground, then back to the showers, soaked with sweat, then back to bed and repeat a few hours later.

During the day we had lectures on armaments, army procedures and battlefield drill. We were issued with R4 rifles and learnt how to strip and clean them. We spent hours on the range learning to fire them and of course we also spent time learning hand to hand combat and it was during one of the early sessions that the sergeant major called me out to the front and said I should try and hit him. I asked where and he said anywhere, face or chest and to go ahead. I was about a yard away from him and with my years of martial arts training I knew I could hit him. I leapt forwards but at the last split second punched next to his face to avoid hitting him. I could see the shock on his face as he grabbed my arm and dumped me unceremoniously onto the ground. We had to practice each self defensive maneuver on each other again and again until we were performing at a high level. It was a few days later, just as I leaving the lunch hall to go back to the barracks, the Sergeant Major beckoned to me. I went over to him. "Yes Sir." "Come with me DeBeer, I want to talk to you." He turned and walked away, I followed him to a quiet spot around the corner of the building. "Okay, DeBeer, I want to know why you didn't hit me the other day when you had the chance to?" "Sir, I know there is a good chance we will end up on the border quite soon. Our survival could very well depend on what we learn from you and to humiliate you in front of the men you have to instruct, could serve no useful purpose. The men need to respect you at all times and I could never be a party to losing you that respect." It was the first and last time I ever saw him smile. "Right then, off you go." "Yes Sir." I turned and headed once more for the barracks. It was my intention, once at the bungalow, to have a quick nap before the afternoon started. It was going to be a full program of gunfire at the range. I went down the few steps, the mess hall was raised off the ground, as were all the bungalows. I wondered why, as I walked around the corner of a bungalow, but before I had a chance to speculate further and almost as though he had been waiting for me, the Sergeant Major appeared again. "DeBeer." "Yes sir." "Pack your bags, you are going to Pretoria this afternoon, you leave in an hour. They are sending a helicopter to pick you up, pack for three days." I stared at him blankly. "Well, get moving man, do you not understand English any more?" "Yes sir, but why, what is going on?" "General Myburgh wants to see you urgently and when he calls, you go. He will explain when he sees you and I have no idea what is so urgent. You will say nothing to anyone about the General, tell your bunk mates you have to go home for a few days on personal business, you got it?" "Yes sir." "Good, now get moving and be at the helipad in forty five minutes."

"Yes sir." I hurried away, my mind racing. Why did the General want to see me, as far as I knew I had done nothing to bring myself to his attention or for that matter to anyone else's either. For a moment I went cold, perhaps something had happened to my family back home. I instantly brushed that aside, any bad news would have been given to me at the camp, as I had seen done with a couple of soldiers who had lost a family member. I became even more apprehensive, I was totally mystified. I packed my kit bag and of course the guys coming back from lunch were curious as hell. I told them what I had been instructed to say, emphasizing the personal aspect and they dropped the subject. As I hurried away I shouted,

"I'll see you guys in a couple of days, make notes for me, hah, hah."
I hefted my kit bag over my shoulder and headed for the helipad
on the far side of the parade ground. It was a circular concrete slab,
about fifty feet across, with a large white stripe around the perimeter
and a big white cross in the center. The Sergeant major was waiting
for me. "They will be here soon sonny boy, good luck to you" and
he stuck out his hand. I grasped it and got a vigorous hand shake, he
turned and walked away. My stomach churned nervously, what the
hell was going on? My thoughts were interrupted by the alarm for
incoming aircraft, I looked around but couldn't see anything, then
I heard the faint characteristic chop, chop noise of an approaching
helicopter. The noise got louder and a couple of minutes later a large
army green, twin prop transport dropped out of the sky and settled
neatly in the center of the pad. The props had hardly slowed down
when a small tractor, pulling a flat bed trailer, arrived from a nearby
storage building. The hatch in the side of the chopper slid open and
two men in flying suits jumped out. The warehouse crew climbed in
and started unloading crates of goods, marked only with numbers.
The one airman started supervising the unloading, the other came
towards me, standing on my own to one side. "Hi there, are you
DeBeer?" "Yes I am."

"Good, I'm Lieutenant Sharp, call me Dave, what's your name?"
"Rolf, nice to meet you." His hand shot out and we shook. What a
very strange, informal day this had turned into, no formalities, no
saluting. "You are getting priority treatment, my instructions are to
get you to Pretoria immediately. Soon as we have unloaded, we'll
put in some fuel and be off." A tanker had driven up to the other
side of the chopper and was preparing to fuel it up. Thirty minutes
later we were on our way. I was put in a fold out seat at the back of
the pilots' cabin, I strapped myself in and we chopped our way up
into the sky. Dave said the trip would take around two and a half
hours, so I could sleep if I wanted to, big joke, I was wound up like
a piano wire, there would be no sleeping, so we chatted instead.

There was a big flask with coffee and a box of assorted cookies, but I wasn't in the mood.

Dave was from Bloemfontein, his co-pilot Mark someone or other, I forgot his last name, was from Durban. The seat I was in was comfortable enough, but the lack of insulation in a transporter made for plenty of noise. The loud droning of the engines for one and there was lots of netting and straps hanging from the walls all clicking, clacking and rattling, together with the vibration, which made conversation a real task, as one had to shout questions and answers. I gave up and tried to doze off. I actually did fall asleep because the next thing I knew, I was being shaken by the shoulder. "Wake up, Rolf, we are landing."

CHAPTER SIX

WE LANDED ON A HELIPAD in a large courtyard, somewhere near the
government buildings in the center of Pretoria. It was around 6pm
and getting dark. I was ushered to a waiting, unmarked, dark blue
Ford, the driver was in plain clothes, not an army uniform in sight,
more secrecy. The driver introduced himself as "Guy," tossed my
kit bag into the trunk and we were off. About ten minutes later, we
stopped outside a plain white, four storey building and he let me
out. "You are staying at the Holiday Inn, I'll take your bag there
and get you set up and I'll pick you up here later, okay?" "Sure,
thanks very much." "Go on in, security will take care of you." As
I climbed the stairs to the double glass doors, the gold lettering on
the wall read, "ARMY HEADQUARTERS." Underneath was the
coat of arms, in the form of a shield, prancing unicorns and the
words, "Eendrag Maak Mag," unity creates strength, at the base. I
went up to the door and peered in through the glass. It was a large
reception office, with a counter running across it, left to right and a
thick glass wall from the counter top to the ceiling, with small slots
in the glass at each cubicle, just like a bank. The office was deserted
at that time, except for a uniformed guard at a desk on my left, next
to the doors. He examined me through the glass, then pressed a
button on the phone console in front of him. "Yes, can I help you?"
His voice came through a speaker set into the wall." "I'm DeBeer, I
have an appointment." "ID in the box please." I pushed my id and
letter through the steel slot, set into the wall. He collected them on

the other side, looked at them and picked up his phone, spoke briefly into it and replaced it on its cradle. A few seconds later, the door next to his desk opened and a large, heavily armed soldier appeared. The glass door clicked open and I went in. "Come with me sir," I followed him into the building to the elevators. We got into the first one and he pressed four. He handed me back my id and letter and by the time I had them back in my wallet the bell rang and the door slid open. Waiting there was a middle aged woman, conservatively dressed in a black skirt, white blouse with a frilly thing in the front, black, graying hair, pulled back into a bun on the top of her head, small gold ear rings, set with small pearls, black low heeled shoes and dark stockings. I put her age at around fifty. "Welcome," she said, "I'm Hettie, follow me," so I did. The soldier watched us walk away. I decided Hettie must have been a knockout twenty five years ago, she was still very attractive. She hurried through an open door on the left, at the end of the corridor and moved to one side as I followed. There I was, in the lion's den. It was a large office with a desk to match it and rising from behind the desk was a man unlike any of my prior visualizations, of which there certainly had been a few. "Here he is General, Rolf DeBeer" "Welcome DeBeer." "Thank you Sir," I responded. I had been expecting an army general in uniform, with lots of gold braid and badges, instead, standing before me was a man in a dark gray suit, white shirt and red tie. He was a lot taller than me, which made him way over six foot, very thin, with snow white hair and a small pointy Van Dyk style beard.

He had those very pale blue eyes, the ones that look like they are looking through you, not at you, only the pupils stand out. I had never liked eyes like that and this only reinforced my dislike. He had small wrinkles in his facial skin, but no smile lines at the corners of his mouth and eyes. I decided he was in his mid sixties. He had a quiet voice that had a sharp edge to it, he was obviously used to being listened to, so had no need to raise his voice. I wondered again why he was known as "pig iron," man, was I only going to find out. " There was no hand shake. He pointed at an easy chair in front of a coffee table on the other side of the office. I sat down and he sat on the other side, gazing at me, studying me. Before I could say anything his secretary came in with coffee and some small cakes. While she bustled about serving us, I looked around the office. Big windows on the one side, with closed, beige venetian blinds I had no idea what they overlooked. There was a big painting of P.W. Botha on the wall behind the desk, which was a dark wood, probably mahogany. On the desk were two phones, black and red. A large, closed diary lay on top of a desk calendar and a gold colored desk lamp stood on the desk corner. The floor was covered with a large persian carpet, in colors of black, burgandy and beige and in the corner on my right was a gold stand with the South African flag. The coffee table matched the desk and we were seated on two of the four armchairs, very comfortable dark leather. I thanked the secretary for the coffee, I had already forgotten her name, not a good start, I had to wake up if I was going to get through this meeting and as yet, I had no idea what it was about.

The General was born 1912 in Pretoria, South Africa. His parents enrolled him in the local preparatory school when he turned five and there he stayed until he finished his schooling at the age of sixteen. He went from there into Pretoria Military College and four years later graduated with a B.Mil degree. It was 1931 and he was just nineteen years old. He enlisted in the army as a permanent force member and was given the rank of Corporal. He was very tall, a six foot four young man of imposing stature with a shrewd mind. Whatever tasks he undertook were completed quickly and efficiently, earning him the respect of the enlisted men and his superiors as well, so by the time the second world war started, he had earned his Sergeants stripes. He found himself fighting along side the British forces as they finally drove the Germans out of Africa. He returned to Pretoria as a Captain, the result of distinguished service during the war. Around that time he was introduced to the daughter of one of the older officers and after a whirlwind courtship he married Leonie and they had a daughter about two years later. When

South Africa became a Republic in the early 1960's our captain was advanced to Colonel and given the job of planning a new modern army for the future, together with his fellow officers. This they did with amazing results, South Africa becoming known to have one of the best smaller armies in the world. In 1975 with the Angolan civil war in full swing, Cuba interfering in the war and South Africa as well, a new problem of terrorism on the border of South West Africa became evident. One or two men at a time were being sent across the border into South West Africa from Zambia or Angola, with the aim of killing farmers and their families. The Colonel, now a General, came up with a plan to stop the terrorism and carry the fight to the enemy, all he needed was the right personnel to carry out his plan. If the General had a character weakness, it was not readily apparent. In actual fact, his biggest weakness was his greatest strength. He had an almost pathological fear of losing any of his men in battle, so in consequence, all operations were planned in great detail to try and avoid any loss of his men's lives. It did not always work that way and the General suffered severe emotional stress when ever he lost soldiers in battle. Now at last, he could see a way to stop the border incursions once and for all, but what he could not see was the detrimental effect the stress would have on his health in the months to follow.

"DeBeer, I had you investigated by our special branch before inviting you to come and see me." I was shocked, no small talk, no minor pleasantries, just a punch to the face in a manner of speaking. In reaction, I couldn't prevent the anger in my voice showing through. "I don't understand sir, why would you do that, it's an invasion of privacy, what have I done to deserve this?" "DeBeer, I had to find out if you are a man of your country, a man willing to die for his country?" "I cannot answer a question like that, it would depend on the circumstances. I certainly would not want to just die uselessly for a cause I didn't believe in and even if I did believe, I would do my damn best not to die without a great deal of consideration and fighting back." "Fair enough," he paused. "I selected you because you are known to be an expert on security dog training, you show leadership qualities, your country needs you and I believe you will not let your people down."

I sat there in silence and waited for the General to continue. "I'm going to explain to you what I want done and then you will carry out my instructions." His voice dropped to a softer level. "A few weeks ago, I was invited to spend a weekend on a farm in Northern SWA. I and a couple of other officers accepted and we had an interesting time there. They were having trouble with the jackals coming out of the bush and killing sheep, so we got to see a culling of the excess jackal population." "The Lombards sheep farm," I blurted out, unable to keep my mouth shut. The General's eyebrows rose. "You know them?" He sounded surprised. "Yes sir, I was friendly with their sons years ago, but we just drifted apart, the sons live in Johannesburg, one is a doctor, the other is a lawyer. I know all about the way they cull jackal with dogs. I didn't approve and I guess it broke up our friendship." "DeBeer, your approval or otherwise is immaterial to the situation, what I really want to know is, what do you really know about dogs?" "Quite a lot actually." My mind churned away. What the hell was all the dog stuff about, I really did not want to be a dog handler.

"So DeBeer, I am told you are using psychology to train dogs?" "Yes Sir, I am. It's still pretty new in terms of specialized training, but I actually started using it all those years ago as a small kid. The so called experts used to say a dog was a loner, related to the Jackal, it didn't need a pack. Today they agree it is a pack animal, it adopts its human family or owner as its pack and obeys the laws of the pack which are in its genetic memories, until it gets trained or educated differently, then it obeys its training." "Okay, DeBeer, now tell me something about dogs in a more general sense." "Yes Sir, let me tell you about the first army to use dogs in warfare, seeing as I am here at army headquarters." The General nodded and I started talking again. "Well, the Rottweiler is the oldest living breed of dog known to man. We can trace its history back to pre-Roman times. It was used as a cattle herding dog and of course would protect the stock from wolves, bears and thieves, protecting its master as well. When the Romans were marching across Europe, laying waste to everything in their path, these dogs lost their homes and masters and were found around the village dumps, scavenging for food. The soldiers had wooden handcarts in which they kept their possessions, armor and weapons and wheeled these handcarts along as the army moved from place to place. Thievery among the soldiers was a big problem, until one day on a break, a soldier tossed a scrap of food to a starving, half grown pup that was nearby. The dog promptly attached itself to the soldier as a food source and he kept the pup as a pet. Shortly afterwards, when another soldier tried to take something from the dog owner's cart, the dog chased him away and so a bond was formed. The soldier decided the dog looked strong enough to pull his little cart, so he made a harness out of some old strips of leather and the dog happily pulled his cart for him. Soon there was a scramble to find dogs as more and more soldiers saw what was happening and also wanted the advantages of dog ownership. The big change came when a soldier running into battle, found his dog had got free and was running with him. The first enemy soldier who came to attack him, was in turn attacked by the dog and killed. When the officers found out about this, they decided to turn those dogs into the official Roman war dogs, with their own armor. Imagine how terrifying it must have been to face a thousand Roman soldiers, each one with a Rottweiler war dog. The male Rottweiler has a very large mouth and is known to be able to take a mans' leg off in two bites, the first down to the bone and the second straight through. Their average bite pressure has been measured at around ninety pounds per square inch, multiplied by the inside surface area of their jaws, top and bottom. The average is around fifteen square inches, but some big dogs have as much as eighteen square inches, so they can exert between thirteen and sixteen hundred pounds of pressure." I paused, the General looked quite interested, so I continued. " Since those days, the Rottweiler has become the main component in many different breeds of dog all over the world. Bulldogs, Bull Mastiffs, St.Bernards, Boxers, Bull Terriers, Old English Sheep dogs, Dobermans, Weimaraners, Pyranneans, Bouviers, Briards, Boerbulls and there are probably more, all first cousins to the Rottweiler." I stopped and looked at the General. "Sir, may I ask why you are so interested in hearing about dogs?" "Not just yet DeBeer. Tell me, if I wanted to create a special breed of dog, how would I go about it?" "That is not an easy undertaking. First you have to decide what characteristics you want your special dog to have. Then you have a look at the dog world and see what breeds each have some of what you are looking for. If you put their characteristics together, would they match what you had in mind and that is where your problems will start. I use the example of Herr Doberman, a tax collector in Bavaria in the late seventeenth century. His area was a province consisting of mainly farmlands and he would go with his staff, in horse drawn carriages to collect taxes. The problem was, after they arrived at the first farm, the farmer would send runners to the next farm to warn them that the tax man was coming. All the other farmers in the area would run and hide in the forests and fields and the taxman and his men could spend days trying to find them without success. Also, some farmers would try and ambush tax collectors and kill them, so his men were heavily armed and also had dogs with them as protection. None of this helped with speedy tax collection. Herr Doberman came up with a great idea, He would create a tax collecting dog, so he took a Rottweiler and bred it with a German Pointer, which is a great tracking dog, believing he would then have a guard dog with great sense of smell. However, genetics don't work that easily. The first litter was a fifty percent mix of both dogs, he bred those pups together, but the result of that was twenty five percent mixes. He bred those puppies together and eventually ended up back with the original dogs, which bred out of the mix. He knew nothing of genetics, but realized that a third breed of dog needed to be introduced into the mix. It took a few years for Herr Doberman to realize this, meanwhile he had destroyed many, many unwanted puppies, he must have been a very cruel and determined man with ice water for blood. He decided to use the Black and Tan terrier to complete his mix. He wanted the Rottweiler for its strength and potential for ferocity, the German Pointer for its great sense of smell, intelligence and slim, streamlined build and the Terrier for its intelligence and shrewd brain power, so Herr Doberman started all over again with the three breeds of dogs. He bred one to the other and then again to the third breed and then swapping males and females and repeating the process. Periodically, as the pups grew, he destroyed all dogs that were obviously misfits and then when they were a little older, he checked to see if they had strong characters, superior senses of smell, were the correct size and had a streamlined athletic build, also with big, deep chests to hold large lungs. He destroyed any dogs that failed the tests. He kept only the dogs that matched his criteria and used many different breeding pairs. Finally had his tax collecting dog as we know it today, but it took many years to perfect and it is said, he even introduced a couple of other breeds into the mix before he was finally satisfied." The General looked at me through narrowed, speculative eyes. "Very interesting DeBeer, but we do not have years, so, if you wanted to speed things up a lot, what would you do?" The answer was pretty obvious to me. "For a short term solution, just use two breeds and keep only the ones that meet the initial specification." He leaned forward. "Let me tell you why you are here." Then he leaned back in his chair and clasped his hands across his midriff. "The jackal cull started me thinking about our border war up on the Caprivi. Swapo, is a banned organization. Their leaders fled the country and now have bases in Angola and Zambia, where they train their members as so called, freedom fighters, we call them terrorists. They have sympathizers and secret members in South Africa and SWA. Their aim is to take over SWA, to which end, the terrorists come across the border at night, sneak across the Caprivi and into SWA where they try to kill farmers and their families and they have had some success. Our troops chase them but get ambushed in the thick bush during the day and at night they can hear the jeeps and equipment coming from miles away and just disappear. I want to get them before they get into SWA, just as they cross the border and are still on the strip or in the area, that is why I found the jackal cull so interesting. I want to breed and train special dogs, terrorist killing dogs that you and your men will train to track the terrorists down and kill them at night, in the dark. That way our men will not be put at risk and perhaps we can stop these terrorist animals coming across our borders once and for all." He paused. "Sir you mean, we may shoot or even kill them if they resist arrest?" "No DeBeer, I mean kill, there will be no arrests, no trials, no bodies, nothing to show they were ever there or that any action had taken place. The terrorists will just vanish and their leaders in Angola and Zambia will conclude they have deserted the cause and just run away, which will make them think again before sending more men and if they do, they too will disappear." I gazed at the General in amazement, "but Sir, we cannot just tear men apart, it's inhumane." General Myburgh rose to his feet and glared down at me. "DeBeer, this is not a debate, you are thinking like a civilized man, you are using logic and emotion, but you will find, out in the bush they have no place. If you were unlucky enough to be captured, they would be happy to gut you like a cheap fish, or hack off your arms or legs with a panga. It will be you and your men or them, you will not have the time for social niceties. I have no intention of trying to force you to do something you do not want to do. So, at any time, if you can come up with a better plan that does not endanger our men, I would be pleased to hear it and use it in preference to this plan, that is my promise to you, in the meantime, have you ever seen the Caprivi?" "No Sir." "You will see it soon enough and you will see there is no normal way to get at small groups of terrorists. The bush is so thick in places, you cannot see through it and even four wheel drive vehicles cannot drive through it. The sand is so soft in places you cannot drive through it without a four wheel drive and even then you may get stuck. Try to engage them in daylight and they will ambush you and shoot you as you pass by. Try to find them at night and you would have to use lights and become a sitting target, but if you can train dogs to find them in the dark and kill them, you and your men will stay safe and you will have saved the lives of innocent farmers, their wives, children, staff and livestock as well, not to mention the local population. You cannot arrest these men in the dark of the bush, they will kill you all if they get the chance. If we are to win this war we will have to play by the rules of the terrorists and that means there are no rules, kill them all!!! His voice rose to a whiplash pitch. "I don't want heroics, I want results and remember, when you want to try and arrest them, there is no hero like a dead one !" I gazed at him, my mind whirling, I was going to get a very close up view of the "Bush War, I was going to have to kill terrorists. My hands went clammy, my heart rate went up and suddenly I could see Auntie's face, whispering about black and white devils, holy shit, I was about to become one of the white devils." The Generals voice jerked me back to reality. "It is now February, dry season in the Caprivi until October, when the rains start. By the end of December, you will need to have the dogs ready to go with the next dry season. You will go from here to the dog unit at Ysterplaat base in Cape Town, your team will arrive shortly afterwards. "You will have six men in your team, with you makes seven, all experienced dog handlers, all have completed basic training and are good with the R4 assault rifle, a talent you may very well need out there in the bush on your own. You, as the specialist trainer will set up the program and guide them through training the dogs to kill the terrorists. Once you get to Caprivi, you will also be allocated a Bushman tracker, who will find tracks and guide you to any terrorists trying to get through to SWA, without him you are lost. You will also have an interpreter from Rundu so you can talk to your tracker, this will all be put in place when you are ready." He paused and took a gulp of coffee. "Now, remember, you do not have a Captain to report to, you will report directly to me alone and if you run in to any officers in the field, just refer them to me, give information to no one and trust no one. You will also carry an ID card verifying you work for this office and also a letter instructing that all assistance be provided to you as needed. That should encourage most officers to leave you alone. I will also give you a telephone number for emergency use, just in case. The password, if you ever use the number will be "Duiwel," just be damn sure it is an emergency before you use it. The phone number will be every alternate number of your police ID, starting with the second numeral. The exchange code to start with will be eight, eight, eight, easy to remember, but secure as hell." He rose to his feet and looked down at me. Pointing a long forefinger at me, he spoke in a harsh whisper, almost hissing at me. "The program will be up and running, operational in all respects before the next dry season, there can be no hold ups, no delays, it must be done, there are a lot of people relying on you DeBeer, do you understand?" "Yes Sir." "Good." So, how do you propose to begin?" I stared at him, he didn't look like he was joking. "Look General Sir, with respect, you cannot drop this in my lap and expect an instant plan of action. I need to think about it before I commit myself and my team to execute it. As I see things, we have in fact got fourteen months to the next dry season. You want the dogs bred, selected and trained by then, so I immediately ask myself some questions. Do we have the facilities and manpower to get it done? You have already told me yes, so that's okay. Now, I need the dogs, bitches in season and plenty of them. I want Bloodhounds and Rottweilers, male and female and an army vet who could get the bitches to go on heat immediately, with the appropriate injections. If you can get this done now, we have an excellent chance to move forwards in time." There was a glimmer of a smile on his face as he said.

"Now you're talking my language, I will arrange it all, you get going and do your planning, I will contact our bases around the country and get you your dogs, also, with immediate effect, I have advanced your rank to Lieutenant. You are a degreed man and have completed your basic training, you will need the rank to get things done. I considered making you a Captain, but you are a little young, so Lieutenant DeBeer it is, congratulations,"

and just like that I was an officer in the army's security police.

He must have pressed a button somewhere, because his secretary appeared through the doorway. The general turned to her. "Get the Lieutenant to his hotel please and have him picked up at eight tomorrow morning." He turned to me. "You can get going now, the driver will take you to the airfield in the morning, there is a transport plane going to Ysterplaat. Most convenient, they can drop you at your new office." He smiled mirthlessly, we shook hands and I left with Hettie, who took me down to the waiting driver. At the hotel, I went to my room and found my new uniforms laid out on the second bed. There was a note attached. "Wear this uniform tomorrow," it said. I sat down on the armchair next to the bed, leaned back and closed my eyes.

Four months ago I was a business man, now suddenly I was a Lieutenant in the army special security police, with G-d knows how many people's lives and safety going to be my responsibility. What the hell did I know about bush warfare? I made myself a vow. Before the dogs were ready to go, my men and I would become bush war specialists and terrorists were going to die, not us. I had room service send me up a sandwich and coffee, then a quick shower and to bed. Tomorrow could take care of itself. I was up at six the following morning, the uniform fitted well. I quickly packed the rest of my stuff and went down for breakfast. At eight, I was collected and driven to a military airfield off the Pretoria, Johannesburg highway, they examined my ID, raised the boom and we drove through, round the back of some buildings and onto the field. The driver obviously knew his way around. A twin-engine cargo plane, was waiting on the runway, otherwise all was quiet. There were some smaller aircraft lined up outside some hangars a fair distance away, but no people that I could see. I got out of the car, said goodbye to the driver and started towards the plane, my kit bag slung over my shoulder. The car drove off immediately and I was alone. The flight to Cape Town was uneventful and before lunch time we landed at Ysterplaat base. There was a car waiting for me and a few minutes later after a drive across the field, I was deposited outside the dog squads' barracks. "You are the first one here sir, the others are only due in after two this afternoon," the driver volunteered. "Thank you, I'll see them then, you can go now." "Yes Sir," and he drove off. Apart from the driver, no one had come to meet or see me. They knew I was there and that was that, I was on my own. Leaving my bag just inside the front door, I went for a quick walk around the training area. It was around three acres in size, stretching north to south. Our barracks occupied the north-west corner, there was a parking area in front of it and a large sliding gate on the right side. On the eastern side was a large building like a warehouse that covered about an acre. There was a running track, about eight feet wide, similar to an athletic track, but it was a dirt track, steamrollered flat and hard, perfect for jogging with the dogs while training them. It ran all the way around the area. The rest of the field was a large open area. I walked across to the building, the door was open. Inside were the dogs' kennels, thirty of them, two rows of fifteen runs, facing each other, gates at each end. There was an oval rubberized track about eight feet wide around the perimeter. Very clever, we could train hard right through winter. Someone had put careful thought into this facility. The rest of it was open area, covered with the same all weather surface. At the far end were some storage rooms. The one was full of dividers to make extra kennels with if needed, the other large room was full of training equipment. Leashes long and short, choker chain collars, harnesses, steps, ladders and other items to put an obstacle course together for advanced training later on, all neatly hung from racks, or stacked ready for assembly and use. I went back to the barracks pleased with my tour of the area. To breed and produce a special requirement dog is a really big undertaking if done correctly." A dog of the kind the General was asking for and to allow only a year to produce them was ridiculous, it would be a hit and miss affair, but I had no other options. Having decided on a Rottweiler, Bloodhound mix, with half the dogs using male Rotties and the other half reversed, using male Bloodhounds, if there were twenty breeding pairs and each litter had an average of three pups, we would have at least sixty pups to start with. If the litters were bigger, so much the better. I wanted the potential of ferocity of the Rottweiler, combined with the exceptional sense of smell of the Bloodhound. They needed the thick dense fur of the Rottie, to protect against the biting cold of winter nights on the edges of the desert, but wanted the longer legs of the Bloodhound, combined with its slimmer, taller build, for running speed and ability to jump high, if needed. A heavily built Rottie would not be able to do that well. I wanted the massively powerful jaws of the Rottie, but needed the incredible sense of smell of the Bloodhound as well. The animals from the Caprivi area hunted by sight, because sand makes a poor tracking medium. The predators picked up prey scent on the wind, followed it to source, approaching from down wind with the scent blowing towards them. Finally, they crept up as close as possible, then attacked. If our dogs were unable to track scent in the dark, the program would fail. I had read that a Bloodhound could smell one scent molecule in ten thousand, so they could follow even a faint scent source. We had a chance of success. The General would not hear of any potential problems, his attitude was "get it done, I don't care how, just do it and don't screw it up." All selected dogs would be coal black, as they would be working and operating at night, which would make them very difficult to be seen, even at dusk, they would look like shadows. We wanted the Rotties half prick up ears for improved hearing ability, otherwise they would have to crop and shape the pups ears, which would take extra time we could ill afford. Naturally, they wanted to retain the keen eyesight of a hunting and herding dog, which they already had. In mixing breeds anything could happen. The pups could inherit the worst characteristics of both dogs and be too vicious and intractable or conversely, be too friendly and easy going to be of any use. The pups could have thin fur, short thick legs, small heads and jaws, or very small bodies and long thin legs. Even worse, they could look perfect, but be useless and this might only show after six months, when they began training. They would all be given basic tests. The rejects had to be put down without a second thought or remorse, there would be no sudden influx of strange dogs onto the open market. The security of the program was paramount. As it so happened we ended up with seventy eight pups, of which forty were obviously no good and were immediately put down. I felt like a Herr Doberman protégé, killer of puppies. A dog's gestation period lasts about fifty three days, so all the pups were born before the end of April. At six weeks old any pups that were obviously wrong, were destroyed as well and finally we were left with thirty four prospective terrorist killers, male and female. The females were all to be injected with drugs at five months, to prevent them going on heat, so they could train with the males and of course go hunting together, simulating a wolf pack, where the males and females hunt together very effectively. The trainers later agreed that the puppies were unusual in that they were very quiet, very little whining or barking, mostly low growls. They seemed content to play in silence, or not play with other pups at all, some, seeming to prefer their own company. They all showed aggressive tendencies at an early age. In my experience, pups that were aggressive loners, tended to grow up with bad temperaments, would have dominating characteristics, make bad and dangerous family pets, but be good as security dogs, owing allegiance only to their handlers after training. I sat down with the six files, time to find out who the General had picked, no, I hoped, rather, had selected for my team.

CHAPTER SEVEN

THE FILES WERE NOT IN any particular order, so I opened the first one. Pieter Smit, corporal, known as Smitty to his friends. Full time soldier, had been in the army since he finished school, passed grade twelve at eighteen. After basic training he had joined the dog training program and remained there ever since. Blue eyes, dirty blond hair cut army style, short back and sides. Thin as a reed, 5'8" and 140lbs. Twenty eight years old. Hard worker, followed instructions well, social drinker only, enjoyed social gatherings. had a steady girlfriend, no immediate wedding plans. Hobbies listed as fishing and hiking. I opened the next folder, Henry Robbins, corporal, also twenty eight, six foot tall, black hair, blue eyes, 200lbs, heavily muscled, small mustache, liked to party, close friend of Pieter Smit. His file was literally identical to his friends, with one exception, there was a note that he was fearless under stress, a good man to have around going into battle, I smiled to myself as I made a mental note. He was single, no steady girl friend, hobby, body building. I could have guessed. I picked up another file. Jack Strydom, my sergeant and second in command. A really big man, six foot four, two hundred and forty lbs. He had been stationed at Katimo Mulilo for the last year, before that was at the army dog unit in Pretoria as a trainer and controller of the men and their dogs. He had been in the army for twenty years, a career army man, would get the rank of lieutenant if our mission went well and I had no doubt he would earn the rank, unlike myself who had been handed it on a plate. Thirty nine years old, tough as nails, a strong leader, could be relied on at all times. Divorced five years ago, no current girl friend, something of a loner. Well educated with a degree in political philosophy and history, majored in South African history. For the first time since my meeting with the General, I started to feel better and more confident. If the rest of the team was as good, we could make it work, we would succeed. Katimo Mulilo, at the Eastern end of the Caprivi Strip, thousands of square miles of bush, crocodiles and hippo infested rivers, this was where we might be going terrorist hunting, get in, kill the bastards and get out, leave no traces. Once the team was assembled, we would brain storm and put a killing plan into practice, then train the dogs to carry it out. I looked over the three remaining files. Three young men, one 23 years old, the other two 24. All three permanent force members, joined the army freshly graduated from high school. Michael van Holt, known as Mick, Bennie Venter and Joseph Jenson, known as Joe. Mick came from the army dog center in Cape Town, the other two from Pretoria. All three were studying part time, courtesy of the army, all three wanted to move up the ladder and start taking the exams needed to get rank, most commendable. All were skilled dog handlers. Lunch time found me in the dining canteen over at the main buildings. I sat back and considered what I had just read. I was the only non permanent force member on the team, the others were all Dutch Reformed Church, I was non denominational, but born half Jewish. It occurred to me that perhaps I had been set up. If the whole thing failed, I could be hung out to dry as the outsider. As team leader and commanding officer, in this instance, I owed allegiance only to my country and deferred only to the General, otherwise, I was on my own, the General had seen to that, the responsibility was all mine. I told myself I was being ridiculous and shrugged off the negative thoughts. My new sergeant was quite capable of handling the operation if I got shot, but I had no intention of becoming a casualty, together with my team, the missing in action label would be firmly fixed to any terrorist who crossed our path. The sergeant was my back up and the two corporals followed him.

The last three, privates, officers in training, completed the team and all would be responsible for training of the dogs. Once that was completed, we would all switch and become handlers and go into the bush with the dogs to carry out our mission, killing any terrorists we could find crossing our border. I locked all the files back in the cabinet, before going for lunch and I was back in my office an hour later. Through my office window, I saw the entrance gate slide open and the army bus carrying the team drove through, it was shortly after two, they had arrived. It was interesting watching them as the climbed from the bus, a little uncertainty in their attitudes as they looked around them and at the drab brown barracks before them, but no signs of nervousness. I got up and hurried to the front door. Outside, they were busy unloading their trunks and belongings, they stopped when I appeared through the door. "Carry on, carry on," I said, "let's get you all settled in and then we can have our first meeting, I'm Lieutenant DeBeer, you have thirty minutes, then you can join me in the dining area. Follow me now, then you can bring your tromels in. I led the way through the entrance, past my office, bedroom combination and into the main area where there was a large round table and padded arm chairs in what was the meeting and dining area, then the six beds with small bed side cabinets, followed by the bathrooms at the end of the building. The floor was covered with linoleum in a medium gray color, the walls were white, a break from army brown. I had my own small bathroom next to my office, the privilege of rank. Each bed had a name on it, the sergeants' first, closest to my room, then the two corporals, the three privates down the other side. The main bathroom was at the end, three showers, three toilets and basins. Six toiletry cabinets on each side of the basins, which took care of the cleanliness issue. I had decided to share my bathroom with my sergeant out of respect for him as second in command, I would tell him later. I left them to unpack and settle in while I sat at the dining table and waited. Coffee and sandwiches arrived from the main building, delivered by a private, driving a small van. I had almost decided that no non-army employed staff would be allowed in this area, not even to clean. We could do it all ourselves. All deliveries could be made by permanent force staff and no blacks would be allowed in the area at all, we could trust no one. The slightest leak of information would put our mission in jeopardy and probably lead to our team being killed when we got to the border, the bastards would be waiting for us. What a disaster that would be, but I was so personally involved, perhaps I was being paranoid, I would put it to the team and see what they had to say.

My day dream was broken by the teams arrival at the table.

I had arranged for food to be brought over after my own lunch. "Sit down guys, anywhere, it doesn't matter." Once they were settled around the table, all looking expectantly at me, I said, "Ok, help yourselves to coffee and food, then we'll begin." While they were busy, I thought again of my agonized thoughts and final decision to tell them exactly what they were going to be doing. If I wanted their total involvement and co-operation, they had to know what was being asked of them up front. Afterwards, if I found any of them lacking, they would be removed from the program and handed over to the General, who I had no doubt would have any such soldier closeted away for the duration of the mission. The rattling of plates and cups stopped, we were ready. "Firstly, I want to remind you that this program and mission are covered by the official secrets act. A transgression in this regard is punishable by the death sentence, if found guilty of betrayal of your country and fellow citizens, so, you may speak to no one about our mission, except the members of the team, no one!! Is that all clear?" I looked around the table, face by face, each in turn nodded and answered "Yes sir." "If any officer tries to extract information from you, just refer him to me." "Okay, this is what you all want to know, we are going to breed special security dogs, then train them to track terrorists to their camps in the bush and kill them there. The dead bodies and equipment will be removed and just vanish." I looked around the table at my team,

I saw expressions of absolute amazement, then excitement. I could see every one wanted to talk at once. I held up a hand.

"Hang on, you will all get a chance, I need to finish first. The dogs will be a Rottweiler, Bloodhound mix and the bitches will start arriving tomorrow. They are being flown in by chopper, each will go in her own pen, next to each other. They were all inseminated in the last week, so the pups are due end March. We are looking for pups as near to completely black as possibly. I have been instructed to destroy any light colored puppies, but I don't know about that, I will reserve my decision on that till later.

HQ found us thirty dogs, some Rotties, some, Bloodhounds, I have no idea how these combinations will work, we will just have to wait and see. If we can average two pups per litter, we will have more than enough dogs to work with, but as you know, some will not have any pups and some will be born dead or deformed, some will just be no good, too small or too stupid. I am hoping to have around thirty good pups to work with. (As it so happened, no dogs arrived the following day, I was informed later that day, that Pretoria would breed the pups and send down them to us at three months old) I looked around the table, "now, any questions?" The sergeant was seated on my left. "Let's go anti-clockwise, Jack, you start." "Ok, what is our time frame, when do we have to be ready?" "Good question, we have about fourteen months. The puppies will be born end of March, so, at five months old, around end August, we start intensive training. At end of November we will start tracking work, obedience will continue. At the end of January they will be ten months old, we will start attack work. At the end of April we head for the bush and they bloody well better be ready, we will not get a second chance." Now there was silence around the table as the men absorbed the information. I cleared my throat, gulped a mouthful of coffee and continued. "While the pups are growing we will plan our campaign and also visit the border and Caprivi to familiarize ourselves with the area, so when the dogs are ready, we will also be, there can be no mistakes. Part of the training will be to get ourselves super fit, so we will be jogging around the security perimeter every night. It is about a quarter mile around and when the dogs are old enough, we will each run with two dogs at a time. During these training runs, at random times, thunder flashes will be set off, to get the dogs used to the loud noises of war, at first, quite far away, then closer and closer. We will encourage them to ignore the noise and remain calm, just follow instructions. There will be many more dogs than us, so we will separate the dogs into two teams, which will run every second day, that way we will all get fit. There is a small gym behind our barracks with running and weight machines. I suggest we start getting fit straight away. We will have more meetings to plan details, this is just an over view. Ok, we keep going to the left, Henry you are next." He looked at me from bright blue eyes. He had a friendly open face. "While we are here preparing and training, what are they doing about stopping terrorists from crossing the border until we are ready?" "There are two army bases in Caprivi, one at Rundu, at the Western end where the strip begins and one at Katimo Molila, the eastern end. There are continual patrols along the strip, with bushmen trackers. When they find tracks, they have to follow them to their source and capture or kill the terrorists. The problem is, you have to track them during day light hours, at night with lights on, they can see and hear you coming from a long way off, so can either ambush you or disappear into the night. It places our men at un-necessary risk and ties up equipment and personnel with no guarantee of a successful_outcome. When we are ready, there will only be one end to each event, in the meanwhile they will continue to do the best they can and we will train on. The war will still go on for a long time, the blacks will continue to try for control of SWA and we will try to prevent that. He nodded and sat back. Corporal Pieter Smit was next to him, now he sat forward. "I see we are sealed in here in our area, for security purposes, but if we have to go up to Caprivi for orientation, who will look after the dogs while we are away?" I turned to him. "I have actually been worrying about our security here and how it should be implemented.

What are your thoughts on the subject?" "Well, what if we opened the gate and just treated the place like an ordinary training center, after all, that is what is has been for years, then we could use extra men from the base to feed and water the dogs while we were away. When we started the final training, we could just order any non essential personnel out of the area, for security reasons, unspecified, they are used to that and it is normal procedure. It would all be seen as just another batch of dogs being trained for army security work and nothing else." He turned and looked at me. I looked around the table. "What do you guys think and remember, these are our lives we are playing with as well? You've got five minutes to consider it, then we will vote, drink your coffee and think? I sipped at my drink as my thoughts whirled by, high security or very little? The base was guarded twenty four hours a day, seven days a week year round, if we just appeared to be a normal dog training squad, the stress on all of us would be minimal and we could concentrate on the training. If I had to explain anything to any one, which I doubted, it was simply a HQ project to try out different breeds of dogs for security and I could refer them to the General if necessary. I glanced at my watch, time up. "Ok guys, let's keep this simple, do we keep it open, or go for high security, hands up for high security?" There were no raised hands. "It's unanimous, we will keep it simple, well done." I couldn't restrain a broad smile, neither could the team, everyone was grinning, a major mutual decision had been made. I raised a hand for quiet.

"We are going to drop all rank stuff while we are here, first names for everyone, we train as a team and I think it will go much better that way, if we are outside in uniform we will do it the official way." I looked around the table and they all nodded pleasant agreement. "You all know each other, I am Rolf. Now to continue, we need to start a regular routine. Up every day at four thirty am, breakfast at five thirty, a meeting from six to seven am while we eat, then start training at seven. Each dog trains for an hour then back to their pen, as you finish with a dog you get the next one in line and carry on.

We take breaks at ten, have some coffee then back to work. We will have lunch at one to two thirty. There are seven of us, so we should be able to get around four sessions in with each dog every day if we have around thirty trainable dogs. The night sessions will be a patrol around the perimeter as I mentioned earlier, with two dogs each, that means each dog will a run every second night. I do not want to burn us out, so I thought on Saturdays we would get up a little later at seven am, do only one training session with each dog, take the rest of the day off, do the perimeter run early at five and be off again. Sunday, we will take off the whole day and just do the early evening run." All the guys were very busy taking notes.

I continued. "Naturally, the routine is flexible, we can change it as needed. One very important item must be mentioned now." They all looked at me. "When we are off duty, no one will drink more than a beer or two tots of anything at any time. Alcohol and secrecy make poor bedfellows, there is no doubt we will all be watched and transgressions will not be tolerated. It would mean instant removal from the program with the disgrace that goes with it. My advice is to forget drinking until we are done. Now, in view of our relaxed security approach to this program, I am going to organize some staff to clean cages, as well as clean and feed the dogs, that will free us up to go and visit the border next week. You can go and finish unpacking and start thinking about how you propose to turn our puppies into executioners, remember, no notes on that subject. We will meet here at five and go for dinner over at the staff canteen, okay?"

The breeding program was underway. An army vet had checked all the bitches and confirmed there were lots of puppies on the way and they would be born in a months time, give or take a couple of days. In order to minimize administration, the General's office had informed me, they would raise the pups in Pretoria and deliver the selected ones to us at three months, so we had until the end of April to prepare ourselves. "Okay guys," I announced at breakfast, "we are leaving for the South West border this afternoon. We will have

Rundu as our base and we are going to have a close look at the strip by air and then by Jeep for a few days. Then we will come back here and make plans, so get ready. Take camouflage uniforms and fatigues, we won't need anything else, we will travel in fatigues and check your rifles and gear, I don't expect trouble, but we will be prepared, just in case. We will meet here at two, sharp, so let's finish breakfast and get it going." The realization that we were about to join the war for real hit us all and there was a subdued "Yes Rolf" response. We completed breakfast in silence and then all went to pack. We assembled in the parking area at two, climbed into the waiting truck I had arranged earlier and a few minutes later stopped at the airfield down the road. The General's name and contact phone number had made it all very easy, after the duty officer, from whom I had requested a plane the previous day, got annoyed and demanded to know on whose authority I was requesting transport. I showed him my letter of authorization on a Pretoria Army Headquarters letterhead, which said "Please assist Lieutenant DeBeer with any requests he may make. Treat all such requests as urgent, to be attended to immediately. From the office of General G. Myburgh. It was stamped and signed. After reading the letter, he became a lot more friendly and very quickly, an army Dakota was made available. There were the usual crates of supplies at the rear of the aircraft, all strapped down, we were at the front, sitting on canvas covered seats, not too comfortable, but we were on our way. The flight lasted around three hours and I was pleased I had got the kitchen to make us some sandwiches and a canteen of coffee. It's true, an army travels on its stomach. We finished it all before we landed at Rundu. One of the guys remarked that it was like a flying picnic but where we were going was not going to be anyone's picnic. This was greeted with groans. At Rundu, we were expected and were taken to a small prefab dormitory, where we would be staying for the few days, beds and a bathroom, army comfort, it was all we needed. The road itself was gravel, just wide enough for two cars to pass each other and looked to be in decent condition, until you drove along it. The potholes in the road made it necessary to drive at way under thirty miles an hour or less, or risk breaking an axle and getting stuck. It stuck out from the northern end of SWA, like an arrow, pointing due east. About twenty five miles wide and around three hundred miles long, ending in a sixty mile wide, arrowhead shaped point. The entire area was covered in bush, from the low knee high type to areas where it was so high, elephants could hide in it and places where it was so thick, even large four wheel trucks couldn't get through, they would have to detour many miles to go around. At the western end of the strip was the town and army base of Rundu. There was also an airfield there and weapons and supplies were flown in and injured or dead soldiers flown out. Natural paths wound their way haphazardly through the bush in every direction. The ground underfoot was soft sand. The entire area was mostly pretty flat with a few small hills and rocky outcrops. The soft sand made for very hard going if you were on foot. There were rocky areas with little or no vegetation and Baobab trees with wide spread branches and thick foliage scattered about the area. High branches and leafy tops, made ideal cover for the leopards that once roamed the area, now all gone, together with all the other wild game, all shot or chased away by the warring factions. So, this then, was the Caprivi Strip. It ended at the Victoria Falls and stretched along the Angolan and Zambian borders on the northern side and Botswana on the southern side. The road ran more or less down the center of the strip from the Begani Bridge all the way to the Victoria Falls. From the SWA coast to the start of the strip was about two hundred miles along the Angolan border, the strip itself was about three hundred miles long, from Rundu to the point at the end near the Victoria Falls. If you added twenty miles on each side of the strip along its total length, the area covered was in excess of twenty thousand square miles of bush and it was in this vast area that the bush war was fought. The surviving animals had run from the war, mostly down south into Botswana, down to the Okavango Delta, where the wild game was protected. It was easy to hide along the Caprivi, dressed in camouflage or khaki. If one crouched in amongst the bushes, you became invisible, blended in with the vegetation. A terrorist could be twenty feet away and you would not know it until you got attacked, which made hunting them during daylight so dangerous. The Generals idea to hunt them at night with the dogs looked like a stroke of genius, born of desperation. The gravel road was not in good shape, but I had originally estimated, if we drive at forty miles an hour, we could get to the eastern side of the strip, from Rundu to the Begani River Bridge in about four hours, one hundred and twenty miles. We would leave at three thirty in the morning, be there around seven thirty am and then drive slowly on to Katima Molilu, another one hundred and eighty miles, to our army base at the eastern end of the strip, doing our first scan of the area. We would spend the night there and drive back to Rundu early the following morning, followed by a last meeting to finalize our operation. As it so happened, we only managed around twenty miles an hour, got to the bridge after eight thirty that morning and had a short break. The visibility was good, the raised road at the bridge looked out over a large area of low bushes, scattered about with lots of wide open sandy areas, but even so, we drank our coffee with rifles off safety. I couldn't help thinking how picturesque the place was and under different peaceful circumstances it would be beautiful and scenic, a natural game reserve, but it was silent and unnerving, not even birds singing, a terrorist imagined behind every bush. Our break over, we drove on, taking the time to examine our surroundings more carefully. The road had been bulldozed out of the bush, then steam rolled flat. After a few years of army transport traffic, it was badly rutted. I had heard it was about to be tarred which would greatly speed up transport and troop movement along the strip. There was a sand verge on each side of the road around three yards wide, obviously a buffer against the bush growing back. The road was just wide enough to allow a car to pass by, if going in the opposite direction. Where the verge ended, the bush started. Mile after mile, low bushes, patches of sandy areas with almost no bush,

bush taller then a man, easy to hide in, with sandy pathways going in all directions. A perfect habitat for the animals that had lived there before they got in the way of the war. The road ran about two miles away from the border with Angola, from Rundu to the Begani Bridge. After that the road ran more or less down the middle of the Caprivi Strip, all the way to the arrowhead point at the common border with Rhodesia, Botswana and Zambia. A hundred and twenty miles further on from the Begani Bridge and we came to the Kwando River, which wound its way through and was part of a vast marshland. This was a great area for crocodiles, hippos and other wild game. It was a natural border, protecting our eastern flank. I couldn't see anyone wading through there at night, it would have been madness. Sixty miles further on and we arrived at Katima Mulilo, it was late afternoon and we were put in a small hut at the northern end of the base, just beds and a bathroom. The army base sat on the banks of the mighty Zambesi River which ran down towards the Victoria Falls, again, a natural border between Zambia and the Strip. Apart from the marshland and swamps, the scenery of assorted sizes of bushes and open sandy areas was unchanged. The army base itself was unusual in that there were no women on the base, not one. Some enterprising officer had created "Piss Lilies." Everywhere you went there were large lilies sticking up out of the ground, large white flowers with green stems. On closer inspection I could see they were made of metal and the flower top was hollow. I was told, instead of walking hundreds of yards to a bathroom and wasting time, a man could simply stop at a "Piss Lily" and relieve himself. The tubes were hollow and went under ground. They were placed all over the base for easy access. We found it all very funny. We joined the guys at the base for dinner, had a quick meeting at which nothing new had occurred to any one and turned in early, after checking our transporter and filling it with petrol. We left at four the next morning with the usual carton of sandwiches, refilled flasks of coffee and water tanks. The drive back was tense, we were going back into terrorist country. The following day we would do the drive to the west along the Angolan border. We had a final meeting late that afternoon, after we got back to Rundu. At that meeting, we initially agreed to concentrate on the southern side of the road, because the terrorists had to cross from north to south, so our Bushman tracker would be able to tell us if he found any signs that men had crossed the road, how many there were and how old the spoor was. While discussing it, we realized, that because of the river running along the border, the terrs would be unlikely to try and get across, if it meant crossing wide crocodile infested rivers at night. Patrols along the road and along the border by troops and also by spotter aircraft during the day, made it unlikely the terrs would travel along the road either, so their best chance of success was to cross over at night near Rundu which would make our lives a lot easier. We would have to concentrate on a sixty mile stretch of the road, going east from Rundu towards the Begani Bridge. Then I had a thought, what if they did not cross the road at all, but stayed on the northern side and just kept moving west until they passed behind Rundu, then tried to cross over into SWA from the Western side or came directly from Angola or Zambia. I voiced this thought to the guys. There was silence, no one had considered that possibility. It meant we would have to extend our patrol into a large rectangle, starting out on the northern side of Rundu, near the Angolan border and going east towards the Begani Bridge, then go South, cross the road and head west back towards Rundu. The following day we would reverse the patrol and start off on the southern side, going east. Three men at a time would follow closely behind our tracker. I thought we would need two protection dogs like German Shepherds or Dobermans, army dogs trained to protect our group, our early warning system. They would go out with us on patrol. The guys all thought it was a good idea and I made a note to organize it when we got back to Cape Town. Once on patrol, the men would swap over every hour, the rest would be in the truck moving along about twenty yards behind the jeep, all guns at the ready to provide covering fire or retaliate if needed. Our bushman tracker, Abe, was going to trot along the sandy path, looking ahead at the ground. He was bare footed, wore only a short loin cloth that looked like it was made from Springbok skin. He was a cheerful soul, always smiling and I worried about him, being out in front of us in the open. If we stumbled on some terrorists, he was most likely to get shot first. Our soldier interpreter from Rundu, Petrus Johannes was his name, said Abe knew about that, but wasn't worried, he was confident we would protect him. The terrorists were killing Bushmen out in the Khalahari Desert if they found them and Abe said he was doing this to try and protect his people. The South African people were outraged that anyone would want to kill these charming, harmless, primitive, bush folk and the army was doing it's best to protect them, but they would not move to protected, enclosed areas, it was not their way, they were children of the land, they said. They had in fact been living a nomadic life in the deserts and bush for hundreds of years. Through our interpreter, I asked Abe if he would prefer to sit on a seat mounted at the front of a jeep, low above the ground, that way, he wouldn't get tired, if he was able to see tracks at about five miles an hour. He had a long conversation with our interpreter, with much waving of arms and pointing at the ground until finally, with a big smile, he nodded. Johannes said he had a tough time explaining the plan to Abe, but it was all okay, he would do it. I was very skeptical, how the hell could Abe pick up tracks of men in the soft sand that was already full of marks. I had the workshop make a chair that Abe could sit on, tilted forwards, just to the side of the right front wheel. It supported his upper body, so he could lean against it and relax, while side wings prevented him from falling off and also acted as a shield. There was an enclosed foot rest, which also shielded his legs. The chair was to be bolted on to the jeep, very securely and be made ready for our first patrol when we got back to Rundu. When we found terrorist tracks, we needed to get within a quarter mile of them before we could release the dogs.

Abe could not tell the time or calculate distance in a conventional sense. What he knew was, how far a man could travel while the sun moved from point a to point b in the sky, so he was shown and actually paced out a quarter mile and so knew how close we had to get to the terrs. He then, would warn us when we were about that distance from them. A very worrying item, was the sandy paths that wound their way in-between all the bushes, or to be more specific, the sand itself. Sand makes a poor tracking medium, it does not hold a scent well at all. I was banking on the old vegetation, leaves and twigs lying on the ground to act as a tracking base. I thought about the animals that had inhabited the area. Without exception, they all hunted by sight and the scent of their prey being carried towards them on the wind, to my best knowledge, none of them tracked their prey. Even the African wild dogs hunted by sight, then I thought of snakes and I relaxed, snakes tracked their food down by following the scent trail made by whatever animal had passed by, until they were close enough to strike. Snakes were plentiful in the whole area, so they must be hunting well and if they could hunt, then so could the dogs, I would find out soon enough. I was also worried about getting the dogs to the right location. If we were going to spend several days at a time in the bush searching for terrorists, we couldn't take the dogs with us, without difficulty. We would need lots of food and water and I didn't relish the idea of all of us carrying an extra heavy load as well as our own combat gear. The ideal way would be to first find the bastards, then call in a chopper with the dogs on board. If they flew in low, offloaded the dogs and took off again, perhaps the terrs would not get spooked and run for the border, I was going to try it and see what happened. There would be a chopper on standby while we were out in the bush, waiting for the call to fly our dogs in with their kennel hands, who would hand them over to us. If we found spoor, Abe our tracker would tell us how many terrs there were and then they could fly in the dogs when we called base. A call sign to base with a co-ordinant, meant we were within striking distance, less than a kilometer from our targets. I couldn't understand how Abe could tell how far away the terrs were, from looking at marks in the sand, but as I found out when we got the program going, he was never wrong. We said goodbye to Abe and Johannes and told them we would see them in April, then we left for Cape Town. After a week of driving around on the strip, it was easy to see why the place was potentially so dangerous to any patrol. You just couldn't see more than a few feet in front of you and where the bush was also thick and tall, even that was not possible. Jack had tried to explain what the strip was like, but nothing could prepare for the actuality of it all. You could be right up close to a man and not see him. Those guys, living in the bush as they did, took on the smell of the bush, while we, washed and shaved could be smelt some way off, our scent carried forward by any breeze. I made a mental note, that if all else failed, when we came back to Caprivi with the dogs, we would have to try living like the terrorists in the bush and hunt them on their own terms if necessary.

CHAPTER EIGHT

COURTESY OF THE GENERAL, I had been given a set of large three foot square aerial photos of the whole strip and vicinity, blown up so every detail was visible. Back at Ysterplaat we could study the area and plan. Our helicopter flights along the strip showed us, that from the air, you couldn't see men on the ground unless they were out in the open, the bush was too thick. The General's idea to attack them at night with the dogs was looking more and more likely as the only sure pathway to success. We had seen several body bags being flown out as well as seriously injured soldiers, for them the war was over. I asked a soldier getting out of a troop transporter one afternoon, what had happened. He told me they had been ambushed in the bush, caught in a vicious cross fire from each side of the path in a densely bushy area on the north-west border, over a hundred miles from Rundu. His Corporal and three of his buddies were dead, the insurgents had escaped back towards the Angolan border. I felt really sad, what a useless waste of four lives. All I could see on the faces of my own men was relief that it was not them, hell, I was also relieved, in spite of my sympathy for them. When we came back to Caprivi, there would be no useless wandering around for my team, there would be a plan in place to fight back. Man, were the terrorists in for a surprise. We had spent two weeks going out on patrols with the troops as observers, orientation was what it was called. Initially I felt overwhelmed by that vast, bush covered area, as well as disoriented. The whole area was flat with only a few hills. There were no landmarks one could use to pinpoint one's location. On all sides, it looked the same, it was bewildering. I carried a compass with me at all times, just in case I should need to find my way in the never ending bush. The smell was all pervasive, a dry, almost sweetish odor, but not unpleasant. After a while we got used to it and it became the norm. We had made a couple of trips down to Katimo Mullilo along the pot-holed dirt road, but saw no one, not even any animals. Back in Cape Town, waiting for the dogs to get to three months and be transferred to us, we started on our training regimen. Up early each day, a five mile run followed by an hour of weight training, then showers followed by breakfast. Then came our daily meeting, at which we laid out our maps and photos and tried to make sense of the area. I had originally wanted to make Katimo Mulilo our base and from there, work our way west towards Rundu, pass it by around five miles, turn around and go back again, but once we had the photos laid out, it was immediately apparent that patrolling all the way from Katimo to past Rundu was ridiculous.

Firstly, there were a number of large rivers crossing the track, but even more important was the distance any terrorists would have to travel to get into SWA if they came out of Zambia. It could easily be a hundred miles or more, during which time they would be exposed to regular patrols and if they strayed over the border into Botswana to the south, they ran the risk of running into lions, elephant or other wild animals and shooting those animals would alienate Botswana, which was a neutral country. Also, they had limited food and water with them, enough for maybe three days, certainly not for any prolonged trek through the bush. They could of course, be killed by those wild animals as well. The easiest route for them was to cross within ten miles to the east of Rundu and go straight over into SWA. The bush was very thick and they could easily make it across into SWA, lying low at night and moving through the thick bush by daylight, ambushing any patrols that had found their tracks, followed and trapped them in the bush. The patrols were really struggling to take them out of the picture without the loss of soldiers' lives and that was where we came in, it would be a completely different story once we were ready. At one of our early meetings, we agreed we would need a jeep and small troop transport truck, both four wheel drive, to use in the bush and soft sand. The truck would have a porthole in its roof, for a soldier to be on guard, with his rifle mounted on a swivel support for more accurate gun fire if needed while the truck was moving. I put in a requisition via the Generals office to have them available when we got back to Rundu. Two months flew by as the team trained and prepared for what was to come. I had requested we be sent two dogs, a doberman and a shepherd from the Worcester dog facility, which was granted and two five month old pups arrived a couple of days later. I called the doberman Jet, he was almost coal black, very few tan markings, the guys called the shepherd Zeebie, after a big ad campaign of the day about trash cans called "Zeebies," but it got quickly shortened to "Zee." We became dangerously accurate with our assault rifles, the daily practice sessions and belief that it might keep us alive, saw to that. What a motivation. The whole batch of puppies arrived early one Monday morning, thirty four of them. All of them coal black, except for one with a small white stripe on a back paw. They were already big and hefty with large paws, which foretold of the size they would grow to, around twenty eight inches at the shoulder and about one hundred and ten pounds in weight. Human contact had been kept to a minimum, I did not want them socialized, we would interact only at the training level, dog and master. They would look forward to their training sessions as a relief from the monotony of being cooped up in their runs and finally, would live for the time they were released to go and kill a selected target. We had two kennel guys who fed the pups four small meals a day, to be reduced to two meals a day from five months onwards. They kept the runs and dogs clean.

We started with house training. Every morning after we had eaten, we released all the pups into the fenced in central open area. Any pup that messed in the area was immediately taken back to its run and shown the litter area near the gate. Then told good dog and then locked in for five minutes, by which time they had forgotten why they were back there, so were released back into the play area again until the next accident. It didn't take long until the pups used their litter area to mess in and accidents became infrequent. The play times were used to start puppy training in the form of games. For example, one would push a pup's backside down until it was sitting and at the same time say "sit" in a firm, yet friendly tone, followed by "good dog." Normally the pup would jump up straight away, but that didn't matter, because by the time they got to five months, they would sit obediently when instructed to, trained by simple repetition, along with down and stay commands. To test their sense of smell, we introduced the pups to minced meat at our afternoon sessions. Each pup was given a very small quantity to eat. Without exception, they all gobbled up the tablespoonful and jumped about looking for more. After doing that for four days, we let one pup into the area and showed it a spot on the floor that we had rubbed with a rag that had been pressed into the meat, then dragged across the floor for about twenty feet. Each pup sniffed its way along the floor, following the trail we had made and at the trail's end was the reward, a teaspoon sized amount of mince. Due to the importance of their sense of smell, I extended this aspect daily, increasing the distance and then even hiding the treats away under pieces of paper or sacking. So far, so good, all the pups showed good tracking skills, together with great senses of smell. At five months old they were all walking at heel, sitting and going down on command. Their smelling ability was just amazing. We had switched them to looking for their handlers outside on the training range and they could find you no matter how hard you tried to hide, so at five months it was time to move on to attack work basics. The first step was to find out if the pups had an aggressive streak in their personalities, so we took them out into the ring, six at a time on leashes and I stood in front of them and flicked them on their noses with a small dish cloth, while adopting an aggressive stance. It took only a few flicks to get them growling and with a little encouragement we had them barking aggressively during the first session, after which we continued with the next batch of pups until we had tried with them all. It was all a prelude to getting them to grab and hang on to the sack, which replaced the dish cloth and eventually the sack would become a throat after all the correct training steps had been undertaken. I was personally disappointed and saddened, that six of the pups failed to show any serious aggression in spite of my best efforts, they just started whining and howling if they were pressurized too much, but not a growl or bark could I get from them. I told Piet to send the six to the Worcester training center. Wouldn't you know it, one of the six and was the one with the small white stripe on a back paw. At five months he was already huge, heading towards being close to Great Dane size, what a waste, but there was no place for pets in the training center, or in the plan to kill the bastards coming across our border. Jet and Zee had been trained along with the other pups, but they were highly socialized, they spent a lot of time with us and were integrated as part of our team. I taught them to sit, stand, down and stay. They learnt retrieving and tracking, they learnt to crawl along on their stomachs under gunfire. We taught them attack work, they would defend us to the death and of course gun fire and grenade blasts made them angry, not nervous. I added in a series of hand signals they would follow if silence was needed. With constant training from the whole team, they became amazing team members, we were really proud of them. We turned the rest of the pups into killers. To watch them in action, tracking their way through a maze we constructed and then tearing the man sized puppets throats out was a frightening experience. We had trained in certain safeguards, to absolutely prevent any accidental attacks. They would need a special verbal and a hand signal command in the right order to set them off, first having been given a scent to follow. There would always be two dogs sent after each terrorist, just in case one dog got shot. They would not attack a man whose scent they had not been given. Years later, I was once asked, "how did you know they were

terrorists and not just innocent people travelling through the bush."
The fact was I didn't know, but I did know!! Our tracker would tell
us how many men there were and if they had boots on. He also knew
if they were loaded down with goods or travelling light. In every
instance the men we killed were carrying AK47's, land mines and
most had machetes as well. They were not innocents. There were
small villages near Rundu, and the villagers stayed close to Rundu
and never wandered into the bush on their own. They knew there
were constant patrols and they could easily be mistaken for terrorists
and get shot." "So you admit you could have made a mistake and
killed innocent people," I was once accused of. "Innocent people do
not go wandering around in the middle of a war zone and there were
no refugees in the area. You need to go over to Angola and see what
those lunatics did to their own people before you point any fingers
at me," I replied. The pups at seven months were ready to start their
final training. The first thing we needed to do was teach them to
grab onto a mock up throat. I had planned it all weeks before, then
sat with the guys and refined it. The throat was made of high density
foam, rolled into a tube about six inches wide, average throat
diameter. It was about eight inches long, longer than a real throat,
but would be shortened at a later date. There were six dowel sticks
around the perimeter to give the neck stability and a more natural
feel when bitten into, like sinews and bone. There was a steel tube
inserted down the center to act as the spine and add some weight
and then whole unit was placed inside a double hessian bag which
was tied closed very tightly. Lastly, a light rope was threaded down
the center tube, so the throat could be hung down from a frame and
swing freely back and forth. Our artificial throat weighed about one
pound. We built a heavy frame at the end of the hundred yard run
and buried the base deep into the ground. The top of the frame was
seven feet above the ground. Each side of the frame had heavy
support legs bolted to it, also sunk into the ground. We used heavy
timber, four by fours, so there was no way a dog could pull the frame
over. There was another lighter frame about ten feet further on, with

ring bolts on the top. A rope was pulled through a ring bolt and tied to the top of the artificial neck. Another rope was tied to a bolt in the heavy frame and also to the top of the neck, so it was hanging at the dogs face height. There were also ring bolts in the sides of the frame at various heights to allow for the height growth of the dogs. The side rope was led through a pulley and back about twenty feet away from the frame, so if you pulled on the rope, the neck was lifted forwards and away from the frame. When you let the rope go, the neck swung down through the center of the frame. The higher you pulled the neck up, the faster it swung down when released. "Okay, let's do a test run, bring me a dog," I said, to no one in particular. All our months of planning had come down to the frame system I had designed and the hours of meetings to define and refine the method we would use. I was so sure it would work, but the proof of the pudding was in the eating and God help me if I was wrong, no one else would. I was in such a state, I don't remember who brought in the first dog. The dog was fitted with a double choke chain I had made. It had two rings to pull on, one at nine and one at three o'clock. The dog was sat in the middle of the frame and the double choker was clipped to ring bolts on the left and right sides of the frame. The side chains were adjusted so the the dog could sit or stand, but could not move left or right or forward or back, so when the neck swung down it would thump the dog on his nose or head. The theory was, that after a few thumps he would get cross and snap at the neck. His handler would then move forward and give him a treat as well as lavish praise. After that we could move forwards with the training. That first dog refused to do anything except sit there, shut his eyes, hunch his shoulders and ignore the repeated thumps from the weighted neck. It took over forty minutes to get the first snap out of him and I had run out of patience by that time. I couldn't understand why a flick on his nose with a dishcloth would get him going, but now there was no response. They took him back to his run and the first notes were put in his log book. I sent the guys to take a break and I went for a walk around the perimeter so I could think it through. If it took that long just to get a first snap from a dog, we would run out of time.

I needed to speed the process up, but how? The puppies had deliberately been raised to that point, in a very calm and quiet atmosphere with few distractions. One day soon, they would run through the bush in silence, at least, that was the plan. What was I missing? I walked on, my mind churning over and then I realized what was missing. The dogs had been raised to be quiet, noise and displays of temper had not been allowed, so now it was quite possible it was working against us, in terms of the violent, but silent displays of temper that would be needed when they were sent to kill terrorists. Having worked out what was wrong, I felt a lot better. I kept walking while I worked out the solution, then headed back to the training area. The guys were all there and I explained what I felt the problem was and how we were going to fix it. They started laughing when they heard the solution and we hurried to get the parts we needed, which were wooden pieces, ten inches long and an inch wide. They were about a quarter inch thick. We pushed the pieces down the center of strips of double webbing straps we had and finally weighted the ends with fishing sinkers, which we stitched into the ends of the webbing tubes. We took the small paddles and attached them, one on each side of our artificial neck by the non-weighted ends, then we were ready. We hung the neck back under the frame and brought back the dog we had been working with. I reminded the guys, we needed silence, no reaction at all unless he bit the neck, then he would get an immediate treat reward and we would repeat the process. As soon as he was re-attached to the frame, I released the neck. The neck as before, banged into his nose, but this time, the two attached paddles swung forwards at high speed and smacked him on each side of his head at the same time. We wanted a display of aggression and we hit the jackpot. The paddles smacking the sides of his face really annoyed him and he snarled a warning. I pulled the neck back and we did it again. This time, not only did he snarl a warning, but he viciously attacked the neck, biting it with serious intent. He got his treat reward immediately and then we did it again with even better results and more aggression, we were on our way at last. It took the whole day and late into the night to go through all the dogs that first time. I hated failure and I took it personally that I had to send six puppies away, but it was the General's direct orders.

The program was moving ahead. We held a meeting that night after dinner. I started the meeting. "Now that we have started the final training, we need to make sure that no one besides us will ever be able to trigger one of these dogs to attack anyone. We need a foolproof set of signals and or voice commands that will send the dog to kill when so instructed. What are your suggestions?" I looked around the table and was met with looks of concentration as the guys thought it through. Henry spoke first. "Look here, normally when a police dog is released there is just a simple word command like, "Vas or Hatz," some guys even use the old fashioned "Sic." I think we should use a completely different word, not usually associated with dogs at all." The guys all nodded. "So, what word?" I asked. Mick piped up. "How about something like hit or zap?" "That's it" Piet shouted, "Zap, it's perfect." I had to agree, it was just right. Not a word used very often by anyone, a single syllable and the dogs would not mistake it for anything else. We were all pleased. I raised my hand for silence. "I have the hand signal we will use first, before the Zap command," I said. "You are holding the leash and release clip with your right hand, the dog is on your left, up close to you. Your left hand is free, next to the dogs face, so you make a fist and flick your forefinger forwards, pointing in the direction you want him to go, then use the dogs name, followed by the Zap command. Then you can release the dog, just remember to show him the correct scent before you release him, or we could lose a team member or two very quickly." The guys chuckled. "We will start using these signals now, right at the beginning, so by the time they are ready, no one will be able to activate them without the name, signal and correct command." On that positive note, we broke up the meeting and got ready for sleep, we were all tired, but very excited by our progress and tomorrow was another day. The training moved ahead in steps. For the next step, we added a large double hessian bag below the neck, filled with sawdust. This was to simulate a body. The rope was attached to the body section, so that the neck would still go first towards the dogs face. The dog's handler now entered the picture. He attached a leash to the dog's choke chain and positioned himself so the dog was on his left, then said the dog's name, gave the hand signal and zap command, then the neck, with body attached was released. The handler encouraged the dog to "kill" the neck and the training moved ahead. The dogs were constantly encouraged and praised as well as being given treats each time they got it right. Then we released the dogs from the side retaining chains, all we needed was the handler and leash. The following day we added a small bag for the head of our "body, then hung the body horizontally, so the whole body would swing at the dog. Once again, with the handler's encouragement, the day went well. Finally, we added arms and legs and let the body swing in low, the legs dragging behind and at last, the dogs were hitting the neck every time. It didn't matter if the body was high or low, crouched or horizontal, even lying flat on the ground, our dogs would hit the neck hard, ripping it apart. We spent a lot of time making extra necks, but no longer had the extra neck paddles, they had served their purpose well. At that point we had been doing the attack training for two weeks and about fourteen hours a day. Each dog had to get two fifteen minute sessions every day and we just kept going until we had completed the days schedule. Now we were entering the final and most critical stage of the training, the dogs needed to attack a selected target. First I went to a local butcher and ordered a couple of pints each, of sheep, cattle, pig and horse blood. We hung two complete dummy bodies next to each other in the frame. The one body on the left side, had some cow blood painted on its neck. The other body had nothing painted on it at all. In that initial phase, we started from only fifteen feet away. We had dripped tiny drops of blood from the start point to the dummy, to simulate footprints to follow, so we could teach the dogs to attack a selected target by following its scent to the source. The handler would show the dog the trail of blood where it started, give it the signals and go with the dog along the blood trail and encourage the dog to attack the correct selected dummy neck. As it so happened, because of the careful training up to that point, the dogs picked up the tracking to the correct dummy with virtually no extra effort. The blood hound genes were really working for us. We used the different bloods to show different scents. We painted dummies with different blood on two or three of them, all hung together and our dogs consistently picked and attacked the correct selected unit. All the while we kept increasing the distance to the dummies. The next phase was to release the dogs and send them on their own, so once again it was back to the start. The handler would give the correct name, signal and command and release the dog from only ten feet away, then move forwards with the dog encouraging it, as it went to "kill" the dummy all on its own. Again, we kept training and increasing the distances from the start position to the dummy until we were at the one hundred yard mark and the dogs would leave their handlers way behind as they sprinted, to go and kill the selected dummy. At last the end was in sight, we had been training solidly fourteen hours a day for four months. Per instructions, I had been submitting regular reports to the General.

He had not replied to any of the reports, but he must have been very pleased with our progress, we were ahead of schedule and the dogs were turning into a very scary pack of executioners. We used the various types of blood to mark a path to the dummies, but the dogs consistently attacked the right target dummy. I bought some syrup and marked a dummy with it, then marked a trail to that dummy in an effort to entice the dogs to attack the wrong target. To my relief, they ignored the syrup dummy and still hit the correct target. I told the guys we were going to take a few days break before we started on the last phase of the training. We went back to running around the perimeter with the dogs twice a day, something we had stopped doing during their intensive training. The rest of the time we spent building a final course for the dogs. The course ran for a hundred yards then came to a t-junction. The left side path was just a decoy and stopped after thirty yards. The right side path went for another hundred yards and stopped where the dummies were hanging. The run was eight foot wide. The side walls were made of compressed board, light and easy to work with, six-foot high.

We scattered old dry leaves on the runway and clumps of bushes, some just small, others blocking the way completely and would have to be jumped over to continue to the end, we even piled up rocks to force the dogs to climb over the obstacle. Having stocked up with the various bloods from the butcher, we dragged a blood soaked sack along the run and finally, wrapped half of it around the dummy's neck, the rest of the sack went back to the beginning of the run. We needed to achieve two things with the new run. Firstly, the dogs were going to start night training, they would run in the dark. Secondly, we were going to let two dogs go on a single scent, something they had not done before. We had built a viewing platform, using scaffolding and hung canvas at the front, so we could see what was going on through slots cut out of the canvas, but the dogs could not see us. Once again it was a perfect kill, the two dogs tore the neck to pieces, seeming to push each other to greater efforts as they worked as a team. All the dogs passed with flying colors as we concentrated on their team work, sometimes hanging four dummies at a time and sending in eight dogs, four teams of two in the dark. In each instance, they took out the correct dummy, the one selected for their team. We were ready. In the little time remaining, we worked the dogs every second day, doing our track training in between, running with the dogs. The days flew by and at the beginning of April we were ready to go. A large transporter aircraft arrived, pre-fitted with cages. We loaded and settled all the dogs, climbed on board and headed for the bush. We were going to concentrate on the southern side of the road, because the terrorists had to cross from north to south, so our Bushman tracker would tell us if he found any signs that men had crossed the road and how old the spoor was. We were starting our first scan of the area west of Rundu the following morning, which was really just a very slow drive going west. We all agreed that because of the rivers cutting across the road, the terrs would be unlikely to try and get across the border if it meant crossing wide crocodile infested rivers at night. Patrols along the border by troops and also by spotter aircraft during the day, made it unlikely they would travel along the road either, so their best chance of success was to cross over at night near Rundu which would make our lives a lot easier. We would start by concentrating on a sixty mile stretch of road, from Rundu going east. I was very sceptical, how the hell could Abe pick up tracks of men in the soft sand that was already full of marks and describe how many men there were, what direction they were going in and if they were travelling light or heavily loaded. In addition, he could tell us how long ago they had passed by and how far ahead they were. We were totally reliant on our tracker and I hoped all the amazing things I had heard about them were true, or our project was going to have a major problem. Our first patrol east was totally uneventful and we turned in early. The sun came up at around seven that morning and we were ready to go.

A few moments later it was light enough to see the road clearly and we drove off into the bush. On the basis that it was just a look and see day to familiarize ourselves with the area, I gave Abe and Petrus the day off. Near the river, was a well worn path, where regular patrols took place and we followed it. Jack was driving, myself as passenger, Jet and Zee were in the back of the small troop transporter with the rest of the guys. We moved forwards at around ten miles an hour. Three hours later we stopped for a break. That was the longest three hours of my life.

The bush around us was silent, still damp with early morning dew. As the sun rose and the bush dried, so the insects came to life and that typical high pitched humming noise could be heard, apart from that, all was silent, not an animal or bird to be seen or heard, eerie and unnerving. I remembered the bush smell, that sort of sharp sweetness, dry and dusty, not unpleasant, but a smell I would never forget. To me it became the smell of death.

Just like the smell of the sea from the beach, fresh with a salty tang or the smell of freshly cut grass, to me, the bush smelt of the dead. Then that day went all to hell. After that beserk start to the program, back at camp all alive and my few days of recuperation over, we went on patrol again. My leg was still sore, but I was alive, so the hell with it, I took a couple of asperins, which helped a lot. This time, Abe and Petrus were with us and we headed east. Abe with the help of our interpreter Petrus, said no one had crossed the track for many days, so after a few hours, we had our break, coffee and a sandwich and carried on. At that slow speed it took all day to get to the bridge and we found nothing. All the guys were really tired. The strain of staring at the bush all day with rifles ready to fire was exhausting. Nerves stretched to the limit, waiting to hear the harsh rattle of an AK and bullets whizzing by if you were lucky, horrible injuries or death if you were not, but nothing happened that day. We set up camp near the bridge and posted look outs. We would change watch at regular intervals, so we all got a turn, then we turned in. While we were driving along earlier, I had made notes of clearings that a chopper could land in if we needed the dogs brought in and numbered them with their positions. Tomorrow was yet another day. Early the following morning, we drove off to the South, crossed the road and turned east back towards Katimo Mullilo, and kept going, heading along the border near the Okavango River, towards the Begani Bridge. I had my note pad out and continued to jot down the positions of clearings we passed by. Jack glanced at me and said. "Rolf, if there were no tracks coming our way near the border, why are we searching again, it's the same route, just further away." "True, but we have only just started to patrol the area, so until we are sure there's no one trapped inside the rectangle we are patrolling, we need to do this circuit. If they chose to move along the road and were not seen before they headed towards SWA, the only way to pick up tracks would be to search both sides of the road, there is no other way at this early stage. Once we are all familiar with the area and are sure it is clear, perhaps we could search only this side of the road, because they would have to cross over to get to this side anyway. We'll have a meeting about it and make a decision, okay?" Jack nodded. "The other little item that I haven't mentioned is a report I read the other day about land mines." His head snapped around to look at me. "What? what land mines?"

"Calm down, there are no tracks, so no mines. If Abe sees tracks we will worry then. It seems that every so often the bastards come across the border, plant a mine in the road and go back again, so just another reason to check both sides of the road until we are sure it is clear. When we find tracks my worry is that the bastards will be behind the nearest bush and ambush us at close range, that's why I insisted that if Abe lifts his arm to signal tracks, we dive out and take cover immediately. After we are sure the area is clear, we go to phase two, hunt them down and bring in the dogs." The day dragged by, there were no tracks and that night we were back at Rundu. We were all really stressed out. Two days concentration, staring at bushes, waiting for automatic fire that hadn't come, was taking its toll of us all, even Abe wasn't smiling so much any more. After a hot shower and food, we had a meeting, sitting around our trestle table. "Ok guys, anyone got any comments, or any suggestions as to how we can improve our patrols?" There was silence, then Henry spoke. "How far is it from the Angolan border, straight across into SWA, across the strip?" "The strip is about twenty five miles wide if you cut across where the strip is defined, but if you cross over near Rundu, technically, you are in SWA immediately." "Why do you ask?" "Well, I was wondering if the Terrs could travel at night, because if they could, they could be several miles into SWA by morning and we would have to chase them." "Henry my man, I think you are on to something. They could travel by night if there was enough light, so when is the next full moon?" One of the guys produced a diary and paged through it, while everyone crowded around him. "Damn, it's the night after tomorrow." They all looked at me." It will be almost full moon tonight, so if we are right, I think they will go tonight, on the basis they will have three nights to travel by moonlight, today, tomorrow and Wednesday. We should find tracks tomorrow morning and I think they will be fairly close to Rundu, because they will want the shortest route into the SWA farmlands, through the very thick, bushy area to our south. That would give them really good cover under normal circumstances, but they don't know about the dogs. Man are they in for a really nasty surprise?" The guys all grinned at each other. I continued.

"Okay, tomorrow, at first light, we will search the area on the south side of the border road and perhaps we will find tracks heading South. They will be way ahead of us by then, so, we know where they are going and I will have the dogs brought in as soon as Abe says we are close enough, then we move. Any questions?" There were none. "Good, get some sleep guys, we all need to be on top form tomorrow." How the hell anyone could sleep, pent up as we were, was another question altogether.

CHAPTER NINE

EVERYONE WAS UP AN HOUR before sunrise, ready to go. A light breakfast and coffee, rifles, ammo and the trucks checked, eight dogs were pre-selected and we were on our way. Everything had been explained to Abe, he did not appear overly excited, but smiled a lot, just another day. We drove to the road and headed east as the sun lifted into the sky. Abe was in his seat scrutinizing the road and sand verge. We crept along, guns ready. I found myself staring at Abe and actually holding my breath. I made an effort to breath normally. We were about three miles along the road, when Abe raised his hand. We crash stopped, everyone dived out and took cover as we had practiced, done in relative silence, but considering the truck could be heard a mile away in the quiet of the bush, no one gave a damn. Once out of the jeep, followed by Petrus from the truck behind us, we crept over to Abe who was already examining the ground. The rest of the guys spread out behind us, rifles ready. A hurried conversation followed. "Abe says four men passed this way, late last night, heavily loaded. They were going that way" and he pointed south. "Okay get up," I told the guys, "gather round, they're gone." Once assembled, I asked them, "How far could they have gone, walking at night, any suggestions?" The general feeling was not more than two miles an hour at best. "The moon came up at nine, so if they waited until eleven to cross the river and got going around midnight, that gave them six hours until it started getting light, about twelve miles into SWA." I unrolled my map and aerial photos of the area and spread them out on the hood of the jeep. "Okay, if we allow them ten miles to play safe, they would be about here," I pointed at a spot on the map. Henry spoke up. "There is a path or track of some sort crossing through there, probably made by elephants in the past." He pointed it out on the aerial photos of the area, if we head along it, we should find their tracks again. They will be hiding in the bush until it gets dark, so we have time to find them." We got back into the jeeps, went a mile back towards Rundu, then turned south again, into the bush. The pathways through the bush wound their way along, twisting and turning. We would have got hopelessly lost without the compasses in the jeeps, I had not forgotten about Abe, but had never seen him in action. It was slow going, but finally, in the early afternoon we got to the path we had seen on the photo of the area and drove slowly and cautiously along it until Abe lifted his arm, we had found the terrorists tracks again. We were out in seconds and waiting. Abe indicated we were within a quarter mile distance from our targets and again, how he knew that was beyond me. Sundown was around six, so we settled down to wait. I radioed our position in to Rundu and also the position of a clearing a couple of hundred yards away. I instructed that the dogs be brought in at 1715 hours. So as not to scare the terrorists into running, the chopper would come in, drop the dogs and leave immediately, hopefully our subjects would stay put. We had a very quiet food break and I gave my dogs water, then we settled down again, it was only just past three in the afternoon. Nothing moved, it was eerily quiet, no birds chirping, not even a breeze to disturb the quiet, just like a graveyard, waiting for its next occupants. It was difficult to comprehend that a group of killers was hidden in the bush just a few hundred yards away as reported by a bushman looking at marks in the sand. A military operation costing thousands hinged on his knowledge. If he was wrong, would we look stupid, not to mention endangering the lives of farmers and their families that we were responsible for. I had no back up plan, one had not even been considered. Sitting in the jeep, I leaned forward and put my face in my hands. I said a silent prayer that all would go well and not be a waste of time. I smiled wryly, a hell of a time to second guess the situation and go religious. There was a soft snort behind me and a wet nose prodded me in my ear. I turned my head and both my dogs were sitting up and looking at me, panting softly. I could almost hear them saying, "relax, it will be okay." I took them out of the jeep and we went for a quiet walk down the path, away from the tracks in the sand. Again, I was struck by the vastness of the place and the silence. Thousands of square miles of silent bush, waiting. I wished I could hear some birds chirping, but that was not on, just the interminable hum and buzz of insects in the bush. A while later, back in the jeep, we settled down to wait out the last forty five minutes. My radio crackled into life, the dogs were on their way. I acknowledged the call, got the guys together and we made our way to the clearing. As instructed, the chopper came in from the north, very low, settled in the clearing and we off loaded eight dogs. The chopper took off immediately and went back the way it had come. The off load had taken only a couple of minutes and I felt should not have overly stressed our terrorists into trying to run. The sun would be going down in about twenty minutes, it was time to get ready. "Ok guys, take the dogs for a quick walk that way" and I pointed down the track. "Be back here six twenty and we will finish this operation." They walked off quietly and I turned to Petrus. "Tell Abe to get ready. When the men come back he must show them the tracks of each terrorist separately, okay?" Petrus nodded. We stood in silence waiting as the sun started going down. A few minutes later the guys came back and in turn each pair of dogs was shown the spoor of one the terrorists. After the four pairs were ready, I looked towards the sun. I had studied it at sundown for several days as it turned into a big red ball and slid beyond the horizon. When it disappeared everything went black, there was no lazy darkening and mellow dusk, it was as though a light switch had been turned off. It took a couple of minutes to get ones night vision going and see a little, if it was a starry night and at least a minute to reorient oneself after it all went black and that was what I had planned.

Let the dogs go about thirty seconds before it all went black, giving them about a minute to get to the terrorists, who would still be disoriented by the sudden darkness. Consequently, they would not be able to fire accurately at the dogs, by which time, it would be too late. The sun turned into a big red ball. "Let them go," I whispered harshly. "Giving them their kill instructions, they first pointed at the spoor with a forefinger, then, "zap,zap,zap" a hand signal and the dogs were released. They took off, running hard down the path and disappeared into the bush in silence, just as we had trained them to do. The only noise they made was a snorting sound as they smelled the scent of their prey, then all was silent. It all went black as the sun disappeared and I started counting to myself, one to thirty. A couple of seconds after I got to thirty, we heard some muffled shouts in the distance, then a burst of gun fire, then the screaming started, shrill and terrified, then it stopped abruptly and it was silent.

"Stay where you are, no one move," I ordered my men. We remained motionless for a couple of minutes. My worrying had been for nothing, it had all gone as planned so far, now we would see what the dogs had done. After my recent very personal experience, we all knew what we would find, but I had not yet seen the end result, having been carted off on a stretcher in the dark. "Okay, into the jeeps guys, Petrus, tell Abe to show us the way to the terrorists." "Yes sir" and he did so. Abe pointed the way from his seat as the lights illuminated the path we were driving along, bush on all sides through the winding twisting pathways. It wasn't long before we arrived at the killing site, a small clearing in the bush. The jeeps' lights and search lights, illuminated the grotesque scene. The four terrorists were lying on their backs, about five feet apart, their throats torn out. I had to turn away and was violently sick at the side of the path, as were my guys. The only dead body I had ever seen was a man they pulled out of the sea, one day at the beach. I was only ten years old at that time. The drowned man looked just like any other man, except he wasn't moving and his lips were a blue purple color. The remains in front of us were a different thing altogether. The memory of my very recent personal encounter with some of these guys' comrades didn't help me, or my men, at all. Their arms were ripped up as well, obviously, they had thrown them up in front of their faces in self protective gestures which hadn't helped them, with two dogs tearing at each man.

They were wearing short sleeved khaki shirts and shorts, now soaked with blood. There was blood everywhere, it looked black in the light from the headlamps. At one side of the clearing were several backpacks, I wondered what was in them. The small transporter pulled up next to us and we all stared at the scene before us. The dogs had no problem finding the terrorists in the bush and Abe was spot on with his tracking. The dogs had turned out to be very efficient executioners and my team, my men, had performed to the very high standard we had set. At last, I had no doubt that the terrorists were going to suffer if they kept coming across our borders, now that we had the proven means to kill them, before they could get at our people in the farming communities. It was not a clean way to die, it was horrific, my guts were still heaving, but screw them, we didn't start it, but we would do our best to finish it. I got out of my jeep, told Jet and Zee to stay and called in a hoarse voice, "Everyone out, get the dogs into the truck, get these four into body bags, then load them up. Check their AK's are unloaded before you bag them, leave the back packs alone they will have to be checked for booby traps by security before they can be taken away. Get finished and we head back to camp." I helped bag the bodies, head first into the bags made it less messy. I noted the exact position of the clearing for army security to get back there and finally left two of the guys on guard with Jet and Zee. "We'll be back soon," I told them and we left for Rundu. Back at camp, I handed the truck over to security, the dogs went to the kennels for washing and feeding and then I went back to the killing site with the security guys to finish up. One of them attached long lines to the six back packs and from about a hundred feet away jerked them hard to trigger any booby traps, nothing happened. The security guys had decided not risk a life by trying to deactivate a bomb booby trap, but there were none. We went back and loaded them into the truck. My two men and the dogs climbed into the truck, while the other guys cleaned the area up. Blood soaked sand was put into bags as well as bushes, so that in a short time there was nothing to show that any event had ever taken place there. One of them said they would come back in the morning and finish up.

I never did find out what happened to the bodies. I had heard they were incinerated, along with any other evidence. In the back packs, we found four land mines, detonators, six extra clips of ammo for their AK's, bottles of water and some food. There were a couple of pangas lying nearby as well. There was no first aid kit, medicine or snake bite serum. It seemed that they really were cannon fodder, totally expendable for their cause. I felt a bit queasy for a moment, then shrugged it off and felt better as I acknowledged to myself that we had saved a lot of lives by stopping the four would be killers. With everyone and the dogs back at Rundu army base, I found my way to the security office and recognized the sergeant on duty. He nodded at me. "Hi Lieutenant, what do you need?" I nodded back and explained that I needed to get a message to General Myburgh. "It's okay Lieutenant, we have already radioed a report to him. He knows your operation was successful, so he may send you a reply later, if he does, we'll bring it to you." I thanked him and left. When I got back to our bungalow, I was starving hungry. Seeing sandwiches on the table, I wolfed down a couple that had been left for me and a couple of mugs of coffee later I felt much better. The guys were all on their bunks dozing, it had been a critically successful day for us, but the stress had tired everyone out. We would have a meeting in the morning, then go back to work. Breakfast over and all the guys around the table, we went over the previous days events. I started the meeting off. "I want to thank you men, yesterday's operation was training manual perfect. I personally cannot see any way we could improve on what we did yesterday, so thanks again." The guys smiled and nodded. "Now we have to go back into the bush and do it again and again until we get instructions to stop. I know we all found the slow drive through the bush very stressful. Waiting to get shot at any second is scary as hell, so we need to ease things a little. There are nine of us including Petrus and Abe. I am going to divide us up into two groups that swap over every day so we get stress relief. When we find spoor, the chopper will bring in the off duty group with the dogs. Petrus and Abe have to go out every day, but they are both protected, Abe by his steel seat and cover and Petrus must always be inside the transporter, out of sight. I will request a second interpreter and tracker, but we may not get them for some time, so in the meantime we will carry on. If there are any large scale incursions, everyone goes on duty straight away. Any questions?" There were none. "We will stick to patrolling the track near the border every day and see how many more we can catch. It's full moon tonight, maybe more are on the way, we shall see. The two groups are as follows, myself, with Smitty, Bennie and Joe. The other group has Jack as group leader, with Henry and Mick. At the end of each week, Joe or Bennie will swap groups, so each group will operate a man short every two weeks. If that proves to be a problem I will have to adjust the schedule, in the meantime we will try it, okay?" There were nods all round. Petrus explained what was happening to Abe, who, as usual, smiled cheerfully about it all. I asked Petrus what Abe thought about the terrorists we had killed the night before. A brief discussion followed, then Petrus spoke while Abe stared anxiously at me. "He says those men would have killed his people if they could and the farmers. They must have known the dangers of trying, with the army protecting his people and the farmers, so we are safe and they are gone. It is much better this way." It was the only time I had seen the little bushman so serious, so I nodded agreement with him and clasped his hand in a friendly way. He smiled broadly and the moment was over. I turned to my men, okay, let's go, the new plan starts Sunday night, we have a few days left till the new week. We filed out and headed for the trucks. Rifles and equipment checked, we drove up to the track near the border and headed east. Abe was in his seat at the front and we crawled along at around at around three miles an hour. We found new tracks a hundred yards further along the track then we had the previous day, also going south. Abe said there were three men, carrying loads. They had passed that way around midnight, so we knew they were traveling under the light of the full moon. That put them on the same time and distance frame as the previous four. After we were sure they were long gone, I called a quick meeting. "When they don't hear from these guys or yesterday's four, I think they will change the river cross over spot as a precaution, they won't know what happened to their men, so will assume the crossover point is compromised. First we are going to do exactly what we did yesterday. Then early tomorrow, we are going to back track and try to find exactly where they crossed the river, just in case there is anything hidden there for their buddies who may follow them, okay let's go get these next three."

My two security dogs were dozing as we drove along, Jack my sergeant was driving, I was in the passenger seat. I turned around and leaned over into the back to pat the dogs and say a few encouraging words. As I did so, Jack's head disintegrated, then I heard the blam, blam, blam sound of machine gun fire. The dogs went crazy, they were making snarling and roaring sounds I had never heard before. The jeep skidded sideways to the left, pointing north and stalled. Jack's body was sprawled against his door. I opened my door and fell out of the jeep, screaming "stay down" at the dogs. With the jeep sideways on, I was hidden from the other side where the gunfire had come from. My assault rifle was still hanging around my neck by its strap, I pulled it off and jerked the slide back so I was ready to fire. I watched the guys erupt from the rear of the truck and dive across the track and down the embankment on the other side. Jack was dead and I was covered with his blood and mess. Then all was silent. As I lay there a figure jumped up from where the guys were hiding, it was Joe Jenson. "We must let the dogs out," he screamed and ran for the truck. It took a moment to realize there was something badly wrong as Joe made it to the truck, I had no choice, I jumped up and tore across to the rear of the truck as well. Joe had already let one dog out and pointing in the direction the gunfire had come from, was screaming, "kill, kill them all." The dog looked bewildered and moved hesitatingly away from him. Joe dived back towards the cages and I dived after him. As he fumbled with the catch on the cage door, I shouted "No" and grabbed his left shoulder. He responded by lashing out backwards with his right elbow, which hit me across the top of my right cheek bone. I felt something tear as I fell backwards, Joe ignored me and went back to the cage lock, I went for him like a mad man, knowing then, that he had actually had some sort of a breakdown and had to be stopped. There was no time for social niceties so I simply smashed his face into the cage in front of him by hitting him on the back of his head. Any normal man would have been knocked unconscious by the vicious blow, but not Joe, he turned towards me, his face a mask of blood and lunged at me. I used a side thrust kick to his chest with every bit of effort I could manage and he crashed backwards into the cages, then slammed down onto the floor at my feet. All the time, he had been making a sort of low key, wailing, gurgling noise, like a wild animal, unnerving, to say the least, but my kick silenced him. I sagged down to the floor gasping for breath and bloody hell, he was starting to move again. I reached behind me and pulled my handcuffs off my belt. My fingers were through the cuff rings, holding them like a bracelet about to slide onto my wrist, but I closed my hand into a fist, turning them into a pair of knuckle dusters, my weapon of last resort, just as the Sergeant Major had showed us during basic training. As Joe started getting up, I hit him on the left side of his head with everything I had left. There was a crunch sound and he went down, lights out. I dragged him over to the side and handcuffed his wrists to a steel retaining ring on the floor, then I carefully sneaked a look out the rear door and saw the released dog lying in the middle of the track.

He had been shot while I was fighting Joe and I had heard nothing. I could feel blood running down my face, but there was no time to check it out. I dived out of the truck, grabbed my rifle and rolled away over the edge of the track out of sight of the shooters on the other side. The guys were all lying in a row, staring at me. I must have looked a sight, covered with blood and gore, Jack's, Joe's and mine. I raised my finger to my lips, silence. Henry crawled over to me with a first aid kit. "Hold still," he whispered and cleaned my face up, it stung like hell, then a dressing and large band aid. "Thanks," I muttered. "Jack is dead, Joe is nuts, I handcuffed him inside the truck." He nodded. "We have to get the bastards on the other side of the road.. Did anyone see where the gunfire came from?" Mick rasped, "it came from about thirty yards away, at the edge of the open ground, where the low bushy area starts, directly in front of us on the other side of the road. They can't go left, it's all open ground and they can't stand up, the bush is too low. They can only crawl, but nothing has moved, so they are still there. I think they will stay and fight." I thought for a moment. "Okay, this is what we do. If Mick is fairly certain of their position, we will each throw a hand grenade at that spot, but all together. If they are there we may get lucky and nail them, but as they go off we will also have a chance to dive across the track into the bush while they are occupied with the explosion. Then we crawl towards them in a straight line, three feet apart, rifles ready.

Petrus must stay behind here with Abe, we can't risk them getting hurt." "Okay Rolf." He crawled away and a few seconds later we were in a line, one yard apart from each other. I was at the right end, Henry at the other end. "Okay guys" I whispered harshly, on the five count." Our grenades had ten second timers, so one, pull the pin, two get ready to throw, three, four, five and throw in an over arm lob, three seconds to get to the target and bang two seconds later. Five grenades sailed into the air together and there was a violent explosion. We were peppered by bits of dirt and bush, then we dived over the track and were immediately hidden by the low bushes. Our rule was, crawl three, stop and listen. Crawl five, stop and listen, then repeat until you got to the target. We started our leopard crawl on the balls of our feet and elbows, rifles cradled across our arms, twisting and slithering forwards. As we finished the five count crawl and stopped to listen, from the bush in front of me rose a black mamba. Of all the things I had prepared for in our crawl towards the terrorists, a large snake was not one of them. I hadn't seen a single snake anywhere since we arrived at Rundu. The guys claimed to have seen crawly things disappear into the bush from time to time, but were never quite sure of what they had seen. I was really very lucky it was a cool morning, because the snake was still sluggish. My rifle, lying across my arms was pointing at the snake and I pulled the trigger on reflex, several times. Each trigger pull sent three bullets on their way from the thirty round magazine and the top part of the snake disintegrated. It all happened so suddenly, I never even got a chance to get scared, the shock set in later. I had Mick on my left, he had frozen when the snake reared up. I shouted "dead snake, dead snake" so the other guys would not start firing at nothing. I ejected the magazine, pulled a full clip from my belt and rammed it home, then I rasped at them, "move, move" and we all started crawling again. My God, I was having a bad day and it wasn't over yet, on the other hand, I was still in one piece, so perhaps it was a lucky day, all things considered. I could see Henry at the end of our line where there was an open space. He looked over at me and gestured we should all stay still, then he suddenly jumped to his feet and ran forwards. He stopped and turned in my direction. "It's okay, they are dead." We all got up and went to look. "It looks like a grenade or two, landed in their hole with them." The three men were badly mutilated and all dead. I took the sight much better that time, just a bit of mild queasiness. "Okay guys, back to the truck and radio in their position. Also get Jet and Zee out of the jeep. The security guys will come and get these three. I had a quick look around and found their back packs a few yards away under some bushes. No doubt there were more land mines in the packs, it was lucky they were not in the ditch with the men when the grenades went off or they would probably have detonated, making a really big mess. It seemed to me that the terrorists were making a determined effort to plant land mines in the area. Both groups we had attacked were carrying mines, but none had managed to bury and set their mines, they were all dead. I noticed Abe and Petrus wandering around, looking at the ground, pointing and waving at each other. I hurried back to the trucks. Jack was already in a body bag. There was another bag with the dead dog in it. Jet and Zee were leashed and clipped onto the back of the truck out of the way, I gave them a quick pat, told them "good boys" and got their tails wagging, they were okay. I looked into the truck, Joe was still lying there handcuffed, just as I had left him, but his eyes were open, staring at nothing, he was unresponsive when spoken to. "I see no point in hanging around here," I said. "Put everything in the truck and let's get back to camp." With everything loaded up and the dogs inside, we had a roadside meeting. "Abe is never wrong, so how the hell did we get ambushed? I asked Petrus. "Abe says there were two groups of men, this group was coming from that side," he pointed towards the south, "so there were no tracks crossing the road, "the other group, the ones we were following are still ahead of us, going that way, south west. They are still ahead of us over there." He pointed. "Did the two groups meet each other?" I asked. "Abe says no, their tracks came from the south east, the others are going south west." (Petrus just pointed out the directions, I did the compass calculations.) "How far away is the other group and does Abe think they heard the gun fire?" After another animated conversation, Petrus turned to me. "Abe says if they are moving at the same speed, they would be about ten miles ahead. They would have heard distant gun fire and may have tried to go faster, but soft sand is not easy to move quickly in, so still about ten miles ahead." "Well, what do you think, guys?" I said, turning to them. "It would take us three to four hours to catch up with them if we left now" said Henry. "It's already past ten" Piet said, "if there is any delay we may run the risk of them getting too close to the farms, perhaps we can call in a chopper and get ahead of them?" That's a good idea," I said. "Let's think it through. If it were us running through the bush, a chopper flies over us, we know they're looking for us, what would we do?" Bennie piped up. "They would want to go back, but would know we were moving up behind them. Going forward would be dangerous, we could be waiting for them, so left or right only, they will not stay in place and get killed. What is east and west of them?" Our photos of the area were quickly rolled out on the Jeeps hood and it became obvious, to the east it was very open country, small, low bushes, no where to hide. To the west was some of the thickest tallest bushy areas in the entire desert, they had to go there if they were to have any chance at all. "We have to get to that bush forest before them to cut them off. Let me think a minute," I said and that's what I did. I had to get my half formed plan crystallized in my mind. "Ok, this is what we are going to do. We know what direction they are moving in, so we will take a chopper ride and half of us off will drop off around the south west side of that bushy area and do that very quickly so they don't realize we are there in front of them. Then we move into position, hide and wait for them to arrive. We could use the sniper scopes on our rifles, they may turn out to be a couple of hundred yards away and in range. After we get dropped off, the rest of you will go with the chopper and jump out a couple of hundred yards behind them. Abe will hopefully find their tracks and you start moving in. Having seen the chopper so close, they will know we are coming to get them and so will run for the bush forest to hide, where we will be waiting for them under cover. Security asked me to try and catch one of them alive for questioning if we can, so we will see what happens. Piet, Bennie and myself will jump off the chopper first and the rest of you will chase them towards us so we can get this finished. If the plan goes wrong and they run back towards you guys, shoot them, don't wait for me and make sure you don't shoot us by mistake." There were sad smiles, this was not a time to laugh.

"Any questions? It will be too noisy to talk on the chopper, so speak up now." There were no questions. We climbed quickly back into our trucks and headed back to base. I radioed ahead to get our chopper standing by, waiting for us. It took us close to three hours to get back to base and another thirty minutes to get ready to go. It was past three in the afternoon when we all got onto our chopper and took off. The flight back took about twenty minutes, our pilot used my map references and said we would fly at high altitude, then drop down behind the thick bush area and we could then jump off out of sight of the terrs and the chopper would keep going. Hopefully they would not know we were there if we did the drop off quickly enough. The chopper would fly back the other way at low altitude and drop the rest of the guys off behind where we estimated they were. They would see that happening in the distance and would know the army was chasing them, hopefully triggering a panicky run for the bush area, where we would be waiting. The chopper dropped down really low, hovered and we jumped out and hit the ground rolling. The chopper lifted and flew back north again. They flew low and slow like they were searching, then the rest of the guys including Abe and Petrus, also jumped out as planned and the chopper flew off towards our base to wait for further instructions.

Mid afternoon in the African bush, wearing combat gear, carrying a back pack and a rifle. It was just bloody hot and with soft sand underfoot and the bush forest behind us, we were sweating rivers. We were not happy soldiers. On the positive side, the snakes in the area would be hidden deep in the shade of the bush, away from the heat and with the sun setting in the west, at least we were in the shade. If my calculations were correct, the terrs would have the sun in their eyes and would not be able to see us. We moved around the corner in a northerly direction and a few minutes later were just in time to see the chopper disappear in the distance. We kept moving along in crouched positions and about twenty yards further along, came across a slight rise in the land. Flattened out on the ground, we surveyed the land in the direction the chopper had gone. It was three thirty, two and a half hours to sundown and we were running out of time. I estimated we were about a half mile from the terrs. In the heat and soft sand, how long would it take them to get within shooting range?

We discussed it in whispers. "Walking normally on a flat surface gets you about three miles an hour, four if you walk really fast," said Piet. "In this heat in the sand, not more than one mile an hour, so somewhere around four this afternoon if we are right and all screwed up if we are wrong," said Bennie. "Let me check with the others" I said, pulling out my walkie-talkie.

"Henry copy" I said into the mike. "Ya, we copy," came the reply.

"What's happening?" I asked. "They are heading straight at you, about a half mile away, over." I replied, "we are hidden and waiting for them. Keep moving up behind them to keep them going. Rolf out."

I clicked the mike off. The next thirty minutes dragged by, then the radio clicked a warning. "Rolf, they must be about two hundred yards from you, can you see them, over?" "Hold on we are checking." I said. "Can you see them?" I whispered. "Got them at ten o'clock, two hundred yards" said Bennie. I clicked on the mike, "Ok we've got them, keep moving towards us, we are going to take them out now." "Ok guys get ready," I said, peering through my scope sight. They had disappeared. "Where the hell are they?" "There must be a gully there," said Piet, "but what direction does it go in, I can't see it?" I groaned in annoyance. "It's all open ground between us and the gully. They could pick us off like ripe tomatoes if we tried to crawl closer. Ok, it doesn't matter, they are going to stay there and wait till dark, then run for the bush, it is their only chance, but they don't know about the dogs." I clicked the radio on. "Henry, they have gone to ground in a gully, we can't see them. Call up six dogs and tell Abe you need to get closer to half the normal distance, hurry up we are running out of time, over." "Will do, over" came the reply. I clicked on, "Our terrorists will run for it the second it gets dark and will be firing at us. We can't fire back, we will kill the dogs, so they need to get there while it is still light. With surprise on our side, the dogs should take them down before they can fire, it is a chance we have to take. Let the dogs go as soon as I let you know I am in position, over." "Ok" came the reply, "they are on the way." I saw the chopper appear in the distance, then it dropped out of sight then re-appeared a couple of moments later going back the other way again. My radio crackled into life. "Rolf, we are ready, any instructions, over?" "We are going to move north-west now, so we will be on the right of the gully and can fire without hitting the dogs or you guys. I will call when we are in position, out."

"Ok guys, lets go." In a half crouch we scurried across the soft sand as fast as we could. I was certain we couldn't be seen with the sun shining straight into their eyes, if they were watching at all, but still, I was waiting for the rattle of gunfire, which didn't come. I breathed a sigh of relief when we flopped down in position, about a hundred and fifty yards from where the gully was. I pulled the radio from my pocket. "Ok Henry, we are in position, let them go now." "Will do," came the reply. From two hundred and fifty yards away, the dogs would be on them in about half a minute. The dogs rocketed into sight about a hundred yards away and we laid down covering rifle fire across the edge of the gully area to keep the terrorists' attention on us and the southern side. About ten seconds later the dogs disappeared.

There was a single burst of gunfire as the screaming started and stopped abruptly a few seconds later. I clicked my radio on.

"Henry, call the chopper back, then move in." "Okay" came the reply. We rose and cautiously moved forwards towards the gully. I stood on the edge and stared down into what turned out to be more of a deep ditch than anything else, running north to south, about twenty foot long and six foot wide, sloping up at the ends. It was deep enough to stand in and remain hidden. The dogs had crashed in at the northern point grabbing the first guy who was standing there and torn his throat out. The next man was about half way down and he gone down next. The last man at the far end was the one who had got off a few rounds just before he too was attacked.

It seemed to me, that the dog he had shot, crazy with pain, had grabbed him by the face and literally ripped it off while his partner had torn the man's throat out. The mens' arms and hands were badly ripped up, no doubt trying to protect their throats, but it hadn't helped them. The injured dog lay near the third man, on its side, breathing very shallowly, pieces of flesh still sticking out of its mouth. There was blood covering everything in the ditch. The other dogs lay quietly along the ditch, muzzles resting on their paws, waiting. I stared down at the ugly scene, my stomach heaved and bile rose in my throat. I managed to control myself, but a couple of the guys had to turn away and were getting sick behind me. "Come on guys, get a grip, better them than us. The chopper will be here in a few minutes and we can get the hell out of here and back to camp." I moved along the edge of the ditch until I was directly above the one dying dog and shot it through its head. The dog gave a little twitch and then lay still, the shallow breathing stopped, it was dead. The other dogs remained motionless. I felt really bad having to shoot one of the dogs like that, but with at least two bullets through its chest I had no option. I couldn't ask one of my men to do it either, it was my responsibility. The chopper arrived about ten minutes later and we bagged the bodies, including the dead dog. The other dogs were wrapped in cheap cotton fabric to stop them getting blood on everything. We gave them some water and then loaded them into the chopper as well. Lastly, we took the terrorists Ak47s and equipment, unloaded the rifles and put it all into bags, then took off for Rundu. The sun was starting to go down.

We got back to base just after five, less than an hour to sundown.

Once there, I handed Jet and Zee over for a good wash and clean, together with the other dogs. They would all get fed a little later. I wrote out a long report on the days events, after handing over to security. They would send men out to the killing ditch to do a final clean up of the area the following day. I put a call through to the General. I actually got through to him and briefly explained what had happened. He seemed shocked and sadly sympathetic. He said he would take care of notifying Jack's family and to keep him informed of any future developments.

Joe was being flown to Pretoria for treatment, so until he had been evaluated, there was nothing else to be done in that regard.

I went back to our bungalow and had a hot shower while I calmed down and then went to the medics' office to get my face looked at. The cut was not that serious, so, cleaned up, with a fresh dressing and some antibiotic tablets, I headed over to the mess hall for dinner. I sat on my own on the far side of the hall and tried to think it through. We had stopped the terrorists from getting through into SWA. We had killed seven of them in our first few days and had not been notified of any that had made it through, so in that regard, we had so far been successful, but my sergeant Jack was dead and Joe was nuts. I lost my appetite.

CHAPTER TEN

THE TERRORIST LEADERS AT THEIR camps in Angola and Zambia must have been very puzzled, seeing as the men they sent across the border had seemingly vanished. None of them had reported back. It was said that SWAPO had spies all over SWA, this being so, they would most likely be contacting them, to try and find out what had happened. When the rainy season started, perhaps we would go spy hunting. I would discuss it with the guys and try to formulate a plan, in the mean time, we needed to do another complete patrol of the area. The ambush had stopped us from doing that, so in the morning we would start again, but near the river, because any terrs coming across, would be long gone from the river area by the time we started our patrol. It was obviously a much safer way of doing things, I didn't want to lose any more men. On that note, I went back to our bungalow, it was empty, I thought about Jack again and was unable to stop the tears. He had saved my life a few days before, but I was unable to save his. Life was turning out to be a real bastard. Soon I was asleep. I was so exhausted, I never even heard the guys come in. The following morning, we were all up early again. I said a few words about Jack, we didn't have the time for anything more formal, we were in the middle of a war. At breakfast Henry said, "You know, if we go nosing around on the banks of the river, we can be seen from the other side. Apart from maybe taking shots at us, if they are watching where their guys left from and we are change of plans." "Good thinking, so what do you suggest?" seen searching that area, it may scare them into a complete "Let's follow their tracks to the edge of the thick bush, without coming out into sight and have a look around." So that's what we did. Abe back tracked to where the bush stopped, around thirty yards from the river. The bank sloped quite sharply all the way to the water, sand and stones. Nothing looked disturbed. Abe had already shown us where the terrorists had stopped in a small clearing, but there was nothing there either, nor had they dug anything up, so we went back to the trucks and carried on with our patrol. The day proved uneventful, we went back to camp and prepared for the following day.

That particular day started much the same as any day for the pre-ceding several weeks. Everyone up at four, washed, breakfasted and ready to go at six as the sun came up. With the Jeep in front and small troop carrier behind, we drove slowly and quietly towards the entrance gate and guard house, as we did every morning. Near the entrance, as we were passing the admin building, we were flagged down by a Corporal at the roadside and that completely changed everything. I opened the window.

"Yes Corporal?" "Good morning Lieutenant, Captain Johnson is taking inventory of all vehicles leaving the camp early morning and wants to see the officer in charge. Please come with me." I groaned inwardly, this was going to screw up our tracking time and distance timetable, but I had no choice. I got out and followed Corporal Visser into the building. I knew all the resident officers, but this was a new one, he must have arrived very recently. The Corporal introduced me. "Sir, this is Lieutenant DeBeer, security police division." The Captain looked me over as I in turn examined him. He was a large man, overweight, brown hair and little piggy eyes. His broken nose veins said heavy drinker, his heavily furrowed brow said stressed and worried, but it was none of my business. In the corner of the office at another small desk sat a private, his back towards me, typing away from a pile of notes, no doubt supplied by Captain Johnson. He paid no attention to me, just kept on typing. The Captain held out his hand. "Vehicle log books?" I handed the two logs to him. His eyebrows rose as he examined them in turn. "You people do a lot of miles," he said. "Yes Sir, constant patrolling will do that." "Don't get funny with me Lieutenant, I'm not in the mood." Yes Sir." "Now then, where do you do all this patrolling?" "From here to Katimo Mulilo, Sir." "What? Why? That's a huge area for a small team to cover." "Sir I follow very specific instructions from Pretoria HQ, from General Myburgh that make the patrols necessary." "What are you looking for?"

"Signs of terrorist activity." "You cannot see much from inside a Jeep, I think you would do better on foot patrols, which I can arrange. You could be dropped off at various points in the morning, do your patrols on foot and be picked up in the evening instead of joy riding around the countryside. We will start today." He glared up at me. "It is not going to work that way Sir, please read this letter." I dug the letter from the General out of an inside pocket and held it out. He grabbed it from my hand and read it. "How do I know this is genuine Lieutenant?" "You could call the General, the phone number is there." I had really had enough of his crap and time was running short. "We are running out of time today, please call him now for clarification." He glared at me. "DeBeer, where will I find the General at six thirty in the morning?" "Sir, he gets into his office by six every morning, he will be there now, I have the number." "I don't need your fucking number DeBeer, I can manage, now get out of my office while I call him and I will bury you if this is all bullshit." At that point, with the Captain shouting at me, the private turned around to see what was going on and holy crap, it was Badenhorst from the train, he had somehow landed himself a cushy job with the Captain. He recognized me instantly as I did him and he smirked at me. Captain Johnson pointed at the door and I left. Man, was he in for a surprise. I leaned against the corridor wall and waited. Men hurried in and out of the building as I stood there. A couple of minutes later the office door opened and the Captain appeared, he was quite red in the face. "The General wants to talk to you." "Thank you." I walked into the office and picked up the phone, the Captain walked in behind me. "Good morning Sir." "DeBeer I have spoken to the Captain and he is going to join you today as an observer, no rank, just an observer. Make sure he joins you for a foot patrol during the course of the day and make him sweat. He needs a new close range perspective as to how you operate and you can tell him anything he wants to know." "Yes Sir, but is this really needed?" "Yes it is, get it done," and the line went dead. I turned to the Captain. "Sir you are coming with us I am told. Please put on combat gear, no badges of any sort, we need to get going." As I started to turn away, he said, "Look here Lieutenant, we possibly started off on the wrong foot, so to say. I need you to get me out of this, I really don't have the time." He smiled with difficulty, it must have been killing him to try and be nice. "Sorry Sir, you have to come along. It was a direct instruction from the General and he will want a detailed report from you on today's patrol when we get back. Your clerk here, is coming along as well, he can make notes, transcribe and type them later, so the General gets a full report. Badenhorst gaped at me, the smirk was gone and I could see he was really puzzled by my being able to give the Captain instructions, because none of my team, including myself, wore any badges or insignia when we were on patrol. The stupid bastard probably thought I was still a private following instructions and hadn't heard my earlier introduction to the captain. "Please make sure he is also in full combat gear," I said pointing at Badenhorst. Suddenly, there was an expression of real fear on his face and to my own shame, I got pleasure out of it. "I need my letter back please." I held out my hand and was handed my letter. "I will meet you out front in twenty minutes, at eight." I turned and left the office. Outside the building, the guys were still waiting. I filled them in briefly as we waited for Captain Johnson and Badenhorst. Petrus translated for Abe, who made no comment. The guys fell about laughing when I told them about Badenhorst and that he was coming along with us. This was not a train compartment full of nervous young guys, these were security cops who lived with the possibility of being killed every day, but had already killed many terrorists and were still here to talk about it. They would happily eat Badenhorst alive if he opened his big mouth the wrong way and I was sure he would do just that. I was most amused at the irony of "what goes around comes around." I thought, "Good luck Badenhorst,"

"you're going to need it." Not long afterwards they came hurrying out to the Jeep. "I introduced them to the guys and we were on our way. Badenhorst went in the truck with the guys, Henry drove the jeep and I moved into the back with Jet and Zee, who were pleased to have me right there with them for a change, although it was cramped. Out of the base, we turned North and headed for the river border track. "Captain, we have a few life savings rules you need to know about. Firstly, if Abe our tracker, seated there at the front bumper, raises his arm, it means he has seen terrorist tracks. We do a dead stop and dive for cover and I do mean dive, your life could depend on it, I cannot emphasize it strongly enough." The Captain did not look happy. God knows how many years it had been since he had done anything at high speed. "Once we are all out, under cover and safe, I will crawl over to Abe and find out how many and how close they are, then we will act accordingly. You will just observe and follow my lead. We have done this many times and my guys are very good at it, as well as being crack shots. Any questions?" There were no questions, he just shook his head and hunched down lower in his seat. I bet he wished he had left us alone early this morning. The expression "what you do in haste you can repent on at leisure" popped into my mind. Damn, I was getting good at summing up situations, but it was also annoying me, I would try to cut it out. Behind us in the truck there was silence as my men stared at Badenhorst, but said nothing, then Mick, always ready for a laugh, spoke to him. He looked decidedly uncomfortable.

"Hey, Geldenhuys, we heard you know the Lieutenant, is that true?" "It's Badenhorst." "Who's Badenhorst?" "Me, I'm Badenhorst." "Is that a fact now?" Mick's voice had taken on a nasty edge. "You look more like a Geldenhuys to me." "Well I'm not, my name is

Badenhorst." Mick's hand flicked out and smacked him right off his seat then he grabbed Badenhorst by the front of his shirt, pulled him up close and stared at him. Badenhorst went limp, all the bravado was gone. Sitting in the midst of highly trained security cops, he had every reason to be nervous. He was way out of his depth. "Now then, Badenhuys, I need you to listen to me very carefully. If we get the danger signal and stop suddenly, you get out of the truck as fast as you can. You will dive over the side next to you and roll into the bush at the roadside as fast as the greased pig you are, your life may well depend on how quickly you get out, do you understand me?" Badenhorst nodded. "Do not forget to take your rifle with you." "I've never done this before," he muttered, "I'm just an office clerk." The guys stared at him in silence. Was this really the guy, the bully who had threatened to beat up the Lieutenant?

"Surely you did your basic training?" they asked. "Yes I did, but I've never been into battle, I don't know what to do." "Just follow our lead, you'll be fine. Remember, if we get an alert it means there are tracks going south, so you get out on the right, the northern side, away from where they might be, got it?" He abruptly changed the subject. "So, we hear you know our Lieutenant?" "What Lieutenant?" "Lieutenant DeBeer, you nit."

Badenhorst looked stunned. "but he had no badges?" "Of course not, none of us have. You can't go into the bush with shiny badges, it would be a death wish. You know, the Lieutenant doesn't like you and neither do we, so listen carefully, you may have only one chance to get out alive today, so I will say it again. If we do get a signal and crash stop, you get out real fast, go over the side and roll into the bush. You do your greased pig routine and don't forget your rifle, it may be all you have between you and dying, got it?" Rather stupidly, Badenhorst tried to get some control of the situation. "You can't call me names, I'll report this." "Mick's hand flicked out at high speed and smacked Badenhorst right off his seat for the second time, then followed through and grabbed him by the throat. "If we get any more crap out of you sonny boy, you won't get a chance to go home, we'll bury you out here in the bush. Thank your lucky stars the "Lieut" is a gentlemen, but we are not, have you got it now?" Badenhorst nodded weakly and Mick released him, then made a clucking noise of disgust in his throat and turned away, as the guys stared and grinned, amused by the scene. Abruptly, losing interest, they took up their viewing positions on each side of the truck as we made our way deeper into the bush. On the river path, we slowed to our usual crawl and waited, while we got shaken about over the potholes and ruts in the pathway. It was eight thirty in the morning, we were running two hours late. Abe was concentrating on the south side of the path, looking for tracks going in a southerly direction, away from the river. Due to the warm weather, the canopy sides were rolled up, as were the front window flaps. The incoming breeze was most welcome. Three miles out of Rundu, Abe's hand shot up and we nose dived to a stop. Henry went out of his door and vanished. I dived out over the side with a shout of "STAY" to the dogs and rolled into the short bush at the path side. The Captain got out much more slowly, lack of practice and exercise showed. The guys had all disappeared, even Badenhorst. Abe was gone, no doubt hidden nearby. I gave a short Bush Dove whistle and Abe appeared a few seconds later. Everyone was on the left side of the path, tracks were on the right, naturally we all took cover on the other side. Petrus was whispering with Abe. After a couple of minutes he crawled over to me. "This is different Lieutenant, Abe says four men came through here around six this morning, not last night, but are now gone, heading south." I raised my voice as I stood up. "Okay guys, they've gone, gather round." We held our meeting around the Jeep, using its hood as a table top, over which I spread our map and aerial photos of the area. "Guys, they came through here around six, it's now just after eight thirty, so, where are they?"

Henry said, "What worries me, is why they would come through so late. We know all patrols were doubled up on last night, so that would have kept them pinned down, but why didn't they go back, why risk it in daylight?" "I think they probably have a deadline to meet some of their buddies further South, so going back was not an option, but we can worry about that later, where are they now?" I asked again. "If we assume two miles an hour, they are about four miles away, near the elephant path," said Piet. Mick and Bennie nodded agreement. Henry said, "If we drive down the elephant path, we may drive right into them or get ambushed." "No, I don't think so. If they've got a deadline, they won't want a fight, so if they are on the north side, there will be no tracks. We will keep on driving down the path for another two miles, then wait an hour and drive back, by then they will have crossed over and we've got them, but I still think they will stay hidden. If they're on the south side, there will be tracks and either way, we will have a choice. We can try to pin them down, wait until dark and send in the dogs, but the pin down may not work and what worries me is the bush area near there to the west. That is some hundreds of square miles of the thickest bush in the entire area and if they get in there it will be a nightmare, all ours. We cannot get our vehicles in there, it will be a search on foot that will be very dangerous indeed, not to mention that the area is snake infested as well. A mamba or cobra bite will become a real possibility, no, we will make for the perimeter in between the two areas and wait for them if they haven't got there yet. Good luck guys, keep your rifles ready, now let's go get them." I turned to the captain. "You see Sir, this is why we cannot do this on foot, it would be impossible." He nodded slowly, the penny had dropped." I had a strange thought as we left, I realized how clever the open frame design of our rifle butts were and that they could be folded flat against the rifle itself. In cramped conditions like very thick bush you could shorten your rifle by about fourteen inches so it would not get caught in thick tangled bush, but could still be used effectively. I made a mental note to discuss it with the guys later on. We climbed back into our vehicles and drove off as fast as was practical. The Captain turned to me as we drove along. "Lieutenant, man, did I misjudge you guys. If this is what you do every day, you really need to be complimented and how the hell do you know there were tracks there, I looked and saw nothing." "We have learnt to trust our tracker, he is never wrong, as you will see soon enough." He nodded and turned away. Thirty minutes later we were on the old elephant path, creeping along at around two miles an hour, heading east, Abe scanning the path ahead, everyone else with rifles at the ready pointing left and right, safeties off. The pathway ran east then south for the most part, with a curve to the left or right every so often, then back to east again. The area we were driving through had bush on either side of the pathway, thick and easily as tall as a grown man. The pathways through this type of bush were much narrower, in keeping with the character of the growth. The area of bush I had discussed with the guys started a few hundred yards to our right, or west of where we were. It was the impossibly thick and tall stuff, even a four wheel drive couldn't get through there. We followed along the path driving very slowly to give Abe a better chance to see any tracks. We crept along swinging first to the right and then to the left, then right again. As we turned a corner, there he was, one of the terrorists standing in the middle of the path about thirty feet away, with his back towards us. Some time later I thought about why he hadn't heard us coming, but at that moment, it all went crazy. Mick was on turret duty, looking out through the port in the roof of the truck behind us, his rifle supported by the cradle, so he could fire, even when the truck was bouncing over the ruts and potholes that we drove over on a daily basis. We came to an abrupt stop, the truck as well. It was fortunate that the trucks' roof was much higher than the Jeep, so Piet could also see the man standing in the middle of the track in front of us and could fire straight over our heads. The man suddenly turned around, actually he spun around in shock as he became aware of us behind him, firing his AK47 as he did so. Bullets whistled all around us as, from behind us came three bursts of gunfire from Piet's R4, bratt, bratt, bratt, three rounds per burst and I was positive the terrorist got hit by all the rounds. He was flung backwards, dead before he hit the ground. "OUT, OUT" I screamed for the guys to hear as I went over the side, "HEEL, HEEL" I yelled, calling the dogs to follow me as I rolled into the cover of the bush at the side of the path, the dogs came flying after me and lay flat as they had been trained to do, bodies quivering with excitement as they sensed my extreme tension. Captain Johnson was still busy falling out of the Jeep and rolling towards the roadside bushes, when two more men erupted from the bush on our left, about fifty yards away, spraying bullets towards us as they did so. They vanished into the bush on the other side of the track. The truck was empty, the guys were all out and hidden in the bushes at the roadside. A hail of gunfire followed the two running men as they disappeared, then silence. I flung my right arm forward in a pointing motion, as I shouted, "sah, sah" to the dogs who took off like rockets, heading for the spot where they had seen the terrorists disappear into the bush. "Guys, stay down, the last one is still here somewhere." I hated sending the dogs after two armed men, particularly in daylight, but the choice was clear, the dogs had to be used before my men could be put at risk. I jumped to my feet and scuttled down the path, almost bent double, heading towards where I had last seen the dogs. I dropped down there and waved for the guys to join me. I covered them while they ran, but the fourth terrorist remained unaccounted for. "Where's the Captain?" No one had seen him. I got a very bad feeling in the pit of my stomach.

"Bennie, you're first aid, go see where he is and hurry man, hurry." Bennie took off. "Petrus tell Abe we need to follow the dogs." He turned and chirped at Abe who immediately took off down the path, we followed. "Shit, Bennie's on his own, Mick, go help him, now." Mick ran off, the rest of us carried on after Abe. About thirty yards further on, we found one of the terrorists dead. From the blood all over his back, it looked like a bullet from our answering hail of gunfire had taken him out. He lay face down in the dirt, his rifle in front of him. I kicked the rifle away from him and one of the guys picked it up. I checked for a pulse on the side of his throat and then from his wrist, there was none, he was dead. Turned over on his back, he was a strange looking man. Very black skin, short black hair, very narrow features, large nose and thick lips. He was around five and a half feet tall. I didn't recognize any tribal characteristics. I motioned to Abe to carry on and we continued down the narrow, winding path. Just around the next bend, we found the dogs and third man, he was also dead, the dogs had killed him, his throat was ripped out. They had jumped him from the back in silence as he ran away. He had no chance against the two big highly trained dogs They whined softly when they saw me. I gave them the stay signal and a quiet "good dogs." They stayed down, but their tails wagged. "We need to get back and see where the fourth son of a bitch went. We'll come back and get them in a little while, they aren't going anywhere, bring their guns with." With Abe leading the way, we headed back again, dogs at heel. "Where the hell is our tourist, Badenhorst?" No one had seen him since the fire fight started and I hoped he hadn't become a statistic. There was still no sign of terrorist number four. At the Jeep, Bennie and Piet had bandaged up the Captain's legs, he had taken bullets through them during his slow exit from the Jeep. "Call up the chopper and get the Captain back to camp, you two go with him, I'll see back there later." The Captain waved a hand weakly at me. I moved closer and leaned over him. His voice was scarcely above a whisper. "You son of a bitch, you and your bloody General, you are responsible for this. Pray I don't get well, because if I do, I will come back to deal with you, you bastard." I answered in a loud voice. "Thank you for that Sir, just get well," and I turned away. From the brief look I had got at his bullet-riddled legs, he would not be walking any time soon, if at all. I moved over to Petrus. "Tell Abe we need to back track and see where those guys came from and remember there is a fourth guy in there somewhere." I waved at the bush behind us. "Guys, where the hell is Badenhorst, we can't leave without him, let's find him now." "With Bennie and Mick looking after the Captain, that left Piet, Henry, myself, Petrus and Abe to find him. As it turned out, he wasn't far away, he had hidden under the truck, a stupid first move, then froze up with fear and just lay there curled up and refused to come out. The guys dragged him out and he cried like a baby. My assessment of him when I first met him was correct, he was a bully and a coward. " Cuff him, put him in the truck and hand him to the MP's when we get back." "Yes Rolf" and they hauled him off to the truck. That left us free to go after the missing terrorist, together with Jet and Zee of course. "Hold on guys, I just need to give the dogs a drink and you need to drink as well. We leave in five minutes." A few moments later, we were on our way, back tracking into the bush the terrorists had come out of. Abe, through Petrus had assured me only three men had come out, where four had gone into the bush earlier that day, so there we were creeping along behind Abe, trying to find the missing man by following his buddies' tracks backwards. To say it was stressful was the understatement of the year, three sets of footprints, none of them from the guy we wanted. We would most likely run into him before we found his footprints, G-d help us if he was lying in ambush, we would be sitting ducks. We heard the chopper fly overhead, heading in to get the Captain. We were about a quarter mile into the bush and we found their back packs but there was still no sign of our missing man, so I called a halt. "Listen guys," I whispered, I'm going to let the dogs go, maybe we'll get lucky." I knew the dogs would find it very strange I was sending them after men that were dead, after all they had seen both dead men and killed one of them. They still had blood all over their fur. They would know they were going the wrong way, I would have to rely on their training and the fact that they were really clever dogs, I had to trust they would work it out, nothing ventured, nothing gained.

At least we would be a lot safer if he was hiding somewhere ahead, the dogs would find him and if he shot them we would be forewarned. I felt sick doing it, but I could think of no other way. I thought of the officers' manual and the instruction which said, "as the officer in command you will not knowingly place your men in harms way without good cause." This was just such a time. Petrus explained to Abe what I was going to try and the guys all moved back behind me. I showed the dogs the tracks, released them and gave them the go get them command. They looked at me and moved hesitatingly down the track. I encouraged them with quiet "good dogs" as I followed them and after a few starts they took off slowly down the path and disappeared into its twists and turns, then all was silent. "I waved a hand at Abe, he took the lead and we moved quickly down the pathway, following the dogs. It wasn't more than five minutes later that we heard the dogs barking somewhere ahead of us and we increased our pace, no easy feat in the soft sand. We rounded another bend in the path and found the dogs standing over a body, but they had not touched it. The man's face was contorted with his death pain, his body all twisted as he lay in the middle of the path. Abe held out an arm, stopping me from going forward and moved to the body on his own. He looked all around then looked at the body. He clicked away at Petrus and pointed at the ground and bush, then looked at me. Petrus said. "Abe says a snake killed him, probably a mamba, he was dead in about an hour, the snake went back into the bush there" and he pointed. So that was that, we had to take the body back with us and early afternoon found us all back at camp writing reports for submission to Pretoria and the General. I wondered how the day would have played out without the Captain's interference, certainly he would not have got shot, but perhaps my men and I would not have been so lucky. We would need to check further south on our next patrol and see if there were any tracks of men coming from the south to meet our dead ones. That was one meeting that would not be happening. The Captain was being flown to Pretoria Military Hospital, I hoped they could save his legs. Badenhorst got off lucky, as an official observer only, he wasn't required to fight and so I couldn't have him arrested and locked up for desertion in the face of the enemy, pity about that. What I did do, was to recommend to the Rundu commanding officer that he be retrained and then returned to active duty with a unit based at Rundu. I believe that was exactly what happened and we never saw him again, I was not at all sad about that, the son of a bitch. At that time we had killed twenty eight terrorists trying to make their way into SWA, plus the twenty five SWAPO troops on our second day up on the strip. The plan to split ourselves into two groups had not worked, the guys worried about each other, when they weren't together, so we scrapped that plan and settled for half the guys staying inside the truck out of sight, while the others scanned the bush as we did our patrol.

We swapped places every couple of hours and that worked well. Only Abe had no replacement, but he did not complain, he was just pleased that his people were safe due to our efforts. We were pleased that none of the terrorists had made it into farm lands, so no one had been hurt, excluding the terrorists, who were dead.

So far they had all crossed the river within five miles of Rundu, mostly around full moon each month and we had got them all.

They moved in pairs with occasional groups of three and there was that one group of four in May. We lost four dogs, three shot as they attacked, but the terrs died with them, terribly savaged before the dogs died and I had been forced to shoot one, that left us with twenty three dogs, plenty to go on with. The summer rains normally started in late October, so there was not much time left before the terrorists stopped trying to cross over into SWA that year. The rain, mud and millions of mosquito made the place virtually impassable during the summer rainy season. I was going to take my men and dogs back to Cape Town and give the dogs refresher training. We would in addition get ourselves super fit again and be ready for the next winters dry season. I decided to do a full patrol all the way down to Katima Mulilo, as we hadn't done one for several weeks, so early the following morning we were on our way, heading East. Henry was driving the Jeep, I was the passenger with Jet and Zee in the back. The rest of the guys were in the small transporter behind us. We drove along at around ten miles an hour, slow enough to scan our surroundings and give Abe a chance to have a look for anything unusual as well. By one in the afternoon we were over half way there and we stopped for a lunch break. I was sore and bruised from the previous days mayhem, but felt better as I moved around and warmed up. We completed our sweep down to Katimo Mulilo and headed back towards Rundu again, so far all clear. It was late afternoon when we got back and I decided to pass Rundu and go a few miles further along the Angolan border, just in case any Terrs were trying to creep across, in spite of a heavy army presence there and for miles onwards towards the Skeleton Coast. Sometimes, late at night the heavy thump noise of exploding artillery shells could be heard in the distance, as the SA army caused havoc in the massed ranks of opposing forces attempting to break through into SWA. My musings were interrupted by Abe raising his hand. We all dived out and took cover, but everything remained quiet. After a couple of minutes, I joined Abe and Petrus. "So, what have we got here?" Petrus passed on the question to Abe, who, with much pointing at the ground and hand waving, answered the question. "He says, four men, heavily loaded, passed this way late last night, heading in that direction." He pointed towards the south west. With the guys gathered around me, I said, "they are heading south west, that is straight towards the farming areas of SWA. This is a change of plans for them, probably to coincide with the coming rainy season, · we are lucky we found their tracks. They have to cross the same old elephant path as the others, further to the west and are probably over it already, so we will go down to the track, starting from the eastern side and see if we can find them." Henry said, "If we don't find their spoor, we will have to come back here and track them on foot, which means camping out in the bush overnight." "Quite right, but let's cross that bridge if we have to, in the meantime let's move it. "We turned around and headed back the way we had come, then two miles later turned south and headed towards the old elephant path.

Once on the path, we headed west and with Abe in his seat started a scan. It was five thirty before Abe raised his hand and some thirty minutes later we were ready. The area the terrs were heading for had some of the thickest, most condensed bush in the whole area and I was very relieved we found their tracks before they disappeared, tracking them on foot to get within striking distance with the dogs would have been a nightmare deluxe. Abe assured me we were at the right place for the dogs, which in his terms was within the quarter mile limit, so we settled down to wait. The chopper dropped off eight dogs, we showed them the four mens' tracks, two dogs to a track just before the sun went down and they were released to carry out their task. As usual, just after it all went black, the screaming started and stopped abruptly about ten seconds later. We moved quietly along the paths after Abe, who led the way, I trotted along behind him with my two dogs as the early warning system, to avoid any nasty surprises and a few minutes later came to a clearing at the base of a rocky outcrop. The scene was as usual, the dogs, lying quietly around the clearing, covered with blood. Four dead bodies, throats torn out lay nearby. Jet and Zee always reacted in an edgy unpleasant manner at the scene of a recent killing and that time was no exception. Their bodies stiffened and they rumbled and growled aggressively as they looked around the clearing. I told them to leave and they subsided, but continued to rumble quietly to themselves, looking into the darkness. I told them to shut up, but they carried on rumbling. I rechecked the scene again. There were four bodies and four firearms, four pangas, four backpacks and four sling bags with more land mines, no doubt. Everything was correct and also, Abe had as usual checked the tracks carefully before giving me a report through Petrus. If there was a fifth man, he would have noticed it, he just didn't make that kind of mistake. I called Petrus over.

"Go over to Abe and ask him if there could have been an extra man that we missed, something does not feel right and the dogs are acting up as well." He had an animated conversation with Abe, the two of them waving their arms in the air and with much pointing at the ground as well. Finally, Petrus came over to me. "He says only if they were carrying a man, there would be no extra track, but the extra weight would show in the footprint marks, there was nothing like that." "What if they were carrying a child?" He turned back to Abe and there was more clicking and clacking. "He says a child would not be noticed, not heavy enough." I thanked him and he went back to Abe. I turned away, I felt sick. The way they looked at each other, I knew I was right, there was a child up in the rocks, or running terrified through the bush in the darkness to get away from us. The kid must have seen everything. I said nothing, I wasn't about to have a child killed for anyone, nor could I start a search, I knew the General would have the kid killed to preserve secrecy, be it a boy or even a little girl, so now what would be, would be. If the kid was from the area, they would know their way around and we were not far from the river either, so there was a good chance the kid would make it back, particularly because there were no wild animals in the area any more. Neither Abe or Petrus would say anything, bushmen did not kill children either, they believed they were a gift from the Gods. There was also the question of why the terrs had a child with them? I would have loved to know the answer to that one. We bagged the bodies and their weapons, then marked the locations of the bags they had been carrying for the security guys. I kept my dogs close to me, I dare not take a chance that one of the guys would accidentally release them and they would take off up the rocky slope and attack the kid if he was still there. Their training had been different in that they were protection for us all and would attack a perceived threat, in this case, whoever was up in the rocks. We waited for the security guys, handed over to them, then went back past the clearing and on to our Jeep. Petrus and Abe were waiting there and we all climbed in and left, Abe directing the way. How he knew the way in the dark, by headlamp light, was just another mystery to me, but a while later we were back at Rundu. I checked on all the dogs and settled my two back into their kennel, then I wrote a report to HQ. I made no mention of the possible child spy. Back at the bungalow, having a late meal, we discussed the days events. I estimated we had at most, two weeks before the rains arrived, the guys agreed. We decided to carry on with our area sweeps right until it started raining, then give it a couple of days before we headed back to Cape Town. Early the following morning, we headed East on our usual run and went all the way through to

Katimo Mulilo. We stayed the night and headed back early the next morning. Late afternoon found us back at Rundu and again we passed it by, heading West near the river. There were no tracks showing and from the radio chatter that we heard, other patrols had seen no evidence of terr activity that day either. Two days later we found new tracks, only a couple of miles or so to the west of Rundu, near to where we had picked up the previous batch. After a quick search of the immediate area, eliminating a possible ambush, we gathered back at where Abe was still inspecting the ground. His whole demeanor was different. He was muttering and mumbling to himself as he walked up and down next to the path and was obviously highly agitated. He turned to Petrus and in the quietest, calmest way imaginable, walked with him along the path, pointing and clicking in that amazing Bushman language, but he was not a happy man. I was walking along behind them and could as usual, see no differences between that sandy path and any others I had walked along. They came back to me, Petrus also looked very worried. "Lieutenant, Abe says something bad is going on. There are the tracks of four men, but the path has been swept clean in front of them as they walked, so only their footprints show, there were other people with them, but he does not know how many. He found a childs footprint at the edge of the path, so there may be more of them that they do not wish us to know about, that were walking at the front." I went back to the guys and told them what Abe had discovered. Everyone looked puzzled and then I realized what was going on. The kid in the rocks must have got back home and this was the start of some sort of retaliation. If they were faking tracks, in the hope we would let the dogs go and kill a batch of children, they were sadly mistaken. "Okay, I think I know what is going on" I said. "It looks like the bastards have taken hostages and are going to set them up so the dogs kill the hostages and not them. Thanks to Abe it won't work. We are going to track them on foot through the bush starting now, let's get going. Check your rifles and ammo, check your water bottles and we're on our way. Abe led the way, I followed with Jet and Zee and the rest of the guys stayed in line behind me. Abe had said they were not far away, that meant further than our standard quarter mile. At least we knew at worst it would be a mile, children do not travel fast on foot. The dogs were tense, sensing the general mood of urgency as we moved along. Ears pricked up, noses twitching, they scanned the bush ahead and around us. They would warn us if they smelt or heard anything out of the ordinary. I had instructed that we move slowly and quietly, just in case the terrorists were close by ahead of us, I didn't want to give them any advance warning. The trail we were following swung gradually to the right heading north-west and I realized we were going back towards the hill and rocky outcrop, scene of the last execution. The last part of that path ran straight into the clearing at the base of the cliff and from around forty yards away I could see figures tied to trees at the edge of the clearing. The dogs were not showing signs of danger stress, rather more curiosity than anything else. Abe glanced at me and I stopped him going forwards with a hand signal. I gestured to my three guys to circle in from the left, while I and the others moved off the path as well, to go in from the right. There were no terrorists there, instead we found the headman from a small local village, his wife and two children, tied very tightly to some trees. Their heads were tied back against the trunks to expose their throats, no doubt to allow the dogs easy access and they had all been gagged with dirty rags, tied around their mouths. Thanks to Abe, it hadn't happened. We untied them, the kids, about eight and ten, both girls, were semi conscious, their parents were not much better. Once we had them lying down and had given them some water, they started to come round and fifteen minutes later were a lot better. I called in a chopper to come and get them while the guys gave them more water and some chocolate bars. With the danger past, they were a lot more cheerful and recovered quickly. They told us how the previous night, four men had come to their little house in a tiny village near Rundu. The village consisted of six huts. They forced them to go to the place where we found them, at gun point. They were made to drag bushes behind them while they walked, to destroy their footprints as the four men walked behind them. Then they tied them to the trees and left. They pointed west, "they went that way." I was getting to know the area quite well, due to our patrols over the past few months and I knew that going west would get them to a gravel road about a quarter mile away, that ran from Rundu going south into SWA. What if the four men had not come from Angola, but from Windhoek and having set up the villagers, were on their way back? Did they have transport? Had they escaped? I discussed it briefly with the guys and then fretted about it waiting for the rescue chopper. Not long afterwards the chopper arrived and the headman, his wife and kids were taken back to Rundu. I instructed the pilot to ensure they got medical treatment and were kept in the camp, hidden away until I got back there. I did not want the terrorists finding out that their plan had failed. With the chopper gone, we reassembled and with Abe leading the way again, followed the terrorists tracks heading west. The dogs stayed in between Abe and myself, alert and watchful. A few hundred yards further along and there was a flash of bright light and a tremendous bang. Abe and the dogs vanished as I was flung backwards by the blast and knocked unconscious. When I came round, my ears were ringing, I couldn't hear properly and I had a tremendous headache. My men had me propped up against my backpack. Some one held out a water bottle and I drank. "Abe?" I croaked. They shook their heads, "you guys?" "we're all okay." "The dogs?" More head shakes. Poor Abe, all he wanted was to be left in peace, together with his family, to go back to his nomadic way of life. The bushmen were helping the army, only to try and ensure their own safety, to stop the terrorists from randomly killing them and now Abe was dead and so were my dogs. I was lucky to be alive, as were my men. I felt desperately sad and also enraged by the incident, the bastards were going to pay, I would see to it. I tried to stand but couldn't. "Help me up," I rasped. Once on my feet, waves of nausea hit me, but supported by my guys, I started to feel better after a while, although I felt like I had been kicked by a mule.

Everything was painful. Just moving my hands was an effort. "Have you called it in?" "Yes," Henry answered, "they're on their way." "We are only about a hundred yards from the road, I want to go and see where they went, but we will go off the path to the right side in case there are any more mines out there. We can have a quick look and come back, let's go," but I found I couldn't just go, I didn't have the strength. "Ok, put me down again and you guys go have a look, I'll stay here, just be careful." Resting against my backpack, rifle across my lap, I watched them fade quietly into the bush. Jack, Abe and my dogs gone, me, almost gone, I had no idea why I had survived the land mine blast, just out of it's lethal range, I guessed. In the distance I could hear the familiar chop, chop noise of the helicopter coming in and then I passed out again. I came round again to find myself being loaded onto a stretcher, the guys were back. "Well, did you find anything?" "Yes, their tracks stop at the road, there are tire tracks down there as well, so they had transport," Henry said. "Check what army transports have been down this road from Rundu, yesterday," I said as they carried me away. I couldn't stop the tears streaming silently down my face, making lines through the encrusted dirt and dust. In the chopper, I passed out again while the doctor was examining me. I woke up in the early hours the following morning, it was still dark outside. I felt sore and bruised, but my head was clear, the headache was gone. There was a drip attached to my left arm and a heart monitor beeped rhythmically behind me, very encouraging. I was dressed in a hospital gown. There was a jug of water next to the bed and I had a glass full then fell asleep again. I was woken by a nurse checking on me, she was filling in the chart at the foot of the bed. "Lieutenant, you're awake, how do you feel." I assured her I felt much better, she took my temperature, checked my pulse and drip and left. I dozed off again. I dreamed of Abe and my dogs and those last moments before the bomb went off, then the scene changed and I was watching a small child running through the bush in terror, that scene faded away and I woke up to find my men standing around my bed watching me. "How are you feeling?"

Henry ventured. "I'm sore but okay. As soon as the Doc releases me, we've got to search the area near the road where those bastards got away, they must have left some equipment behind, their guns for instance. Piet said, "the transport guys told us there was only a truck and a bus down that track yesterday, both going to Windhoek. The troop bus will be back this morning, then we can question the driver." "Good, get going and I will see you guys at the bungalow as soon as I get released, come find me." There was a general "glad you're okay Rolfe," and they left, leaving some clean clothes for me. They looked relieved. The clock on the wall showed 6.15 am. At seven the doctor came in. "Good morning Lieutenant, well, I must say, you look much better." "I'm ok Doc, I just need to get out of here." "Let me check you out first, then we can decide." He gave me a pretty thorough going over and finally gave me permission to go. He took the drip from my arm, put a plaster over the needle hole and said goodbye. I dressed slowly, trying to hurry. I put on my track suit and sneakers and made my way back to the bungalow. I was still sore and bruised, but it would pass. There was coffee and sandwiches on the table and I was suddenly very hungry, a good sign, so I sat down and had breakfast while I waited for the guys to come back. I knew the terrorists had set us up in revenge for our dog program, but instead of escaping back into Angola, which they had plenty of time to do, they had headed off to Windhoek, the question was, why? Thinking about it, I couldn't see them setting off explosives in Windhoek, the place was swarming with police and army and they would run a high risk of capture. On the basis of their behavior so far, they planned ahead, so would have an escape route and then it hit me, in Windhoek they would have the contacts to get a car and as terrorists, they would head back to the farmlands on a killing spree. I had to try and stop them. I left the bungalow and headed towards the army security office, meeting my guys on their way back to me. "Just help me get to the security office, I'll explain later." With two of the guys helping me, we were in the office a few moments later. I requested an urgent meeting with the Captain, who arrived moments later. I mentioned the four terrorists, he knew all about them of course. I told him what I felt they would do, he nodded agreement and grabbed for the phone. Captain Terblanche called the Windhoek office and spoke to his opposite number there, then put the phone down and turned to me. "We were too late Lieutenant, a farm in the north western area was attacked last night, they are all dead, together with their livestock and the bastards burnt the farm house down as well. They are hunting for them, but no luck so far." "You know Sir, I think they escaped to Cape Town." "What makes you say that?" "Well, everything they have done so far has been planned. From setting us up for the land mines, then escaping down to Windhoek, then reorganizing, then back to the farm, then disappearing again. They know, if we catch them they are done. With the whole area sealed off their only chance is Cape Town, where they can vanish into one of the townships, wait for things to calm down and then try to go back where they came from." "You make good sense Lieutenant, I'll pass the information on and also, there's a message from General Myburgh, you must call him. Come through here there's an office you can use." I followed him down the corridor to an empty office, just a desk and telephone. I picked up the phone and told the switchboard woman I wanted to get through to General Myburgh in Pretoria and that it was an urgent priority call. A couple of minutes later I was through to his office. "DeBeer, what the hell is going on up there?" I had expected at the very least, that he would ask how I and my men were, but no such luck. I told him about the terrorist pod we had followed, the village headman and his family we had rescued and how Abe had trod on a land mine which killed him and the two dogs and I escaped with a concussion." "DeBeer this does not make sense, you hunted down four men, then three days later you got set up at the same spot where you executed the previous four. I ask myself, how did the second lot know where the first batch had gone, who told them? From the way they set you up, they had to have known about your bushman tracker, who told them? DeBeer I am holding you personally responsible for this mess,

I want a full report, send it priority." The line went dead. The General was no ones fool, he saw immediately that something had gone very wrong, the facts did not add up. He was right of course, I had left a kid alive and we suffered the consequences, but the last thing I was going to do was tell him. I left with my men still supporting me. By the time we got back to the bungalow, I was feeling a lot better and was walking on my own. "Ok guys, go get our truck while I get changed." One of them hurried away and I changed into my combat uniform. A couple of minutes later the truck pulled up outside, Mick at the wheel. "Where is Petrus?" I asked. No one knew. "Into the truck and lets find him. He is part of our team, he comes with us." We found him sitting forlornly outside the admin building. I called to him. "Petrus, what are you doing here?" He jumped to his feet and hurried over to the truck. "Sir, I thought with Abe gone, you didn't need me anymore, so I am waiting here for reassignment." "Nonsense, you are part of this team, go get your gear, we are heading out and hurry it up." "Yes Sir," his face one big smile, he sprinted towards his bungalow to get ready. A few minutes later we were on our way to the spot where Abe had died. We had discussed it earlier. We all agreed that the terrs must have changed their clothes after laying the land mine trap, so they could get on the army bus, so where were the old clothes, rifles and equipment? We were going to search the area and find the stuff, it was our possibly our only chance to track the bastards down, to perhaps find out where they had gone. They had to have passes and ID as well, which would be checked by the army bus driver, so if we got the records, we could get copies of their photographs, as long as they were genuine, not forgeries. I would check later. A while later we were back on the path where Abe had got killed. The hole had been filled in and the area cleaned up, it had also been swept by security and declared free of any land mines. "Stop," I told Piet. "Let's get out and look around." Once out of the truck, I voiced my thoughts to the guys. "Abe was an amazing tracker, so why did he miss the land mine? How could they dig a hole, bury the mine and leave no trace?" Henry said, "they must have dug a hole under the path from the side, that way the surface was undisturbed." He was spot on, the one side of the path was eroded away, as much as three feet in places. The soil was quite soft, easy to dig a shaft sideways under the path, push the mine into place with a long stick and arm it by pulling on a cord to pull out the setting pin. There were probably two mines, one on each side of the center of the path, because Abe always walked to one side when tracking. The one mine would set off the other when it exploded. That was how I had escaped with my life, because the ground was quite soft, they had to bury the mines quite deep to stop the ground sinking in, so the surrounding earth trapped the blast and forced it up at a narrower angle. I was just out of lethal range, a very lucky escape for me. "Guys, I want a minutes silence for Abe, he was a good man." We stood there, each busy with our own thoughts.

CHAPTER ELEVEN

"OKAY, LET'S CARRY ON, ANY ideas where they would have stashed the stuff?" There was bush all around us, no clues there. To our right was the little rocky outcrop, the small hill. It was the only point of reference in the featureless landscape around us. I noticed we were all looking at the hill. Bennie, who was normally very quiet, said, "that hill is the only place for miles around that they could find again, I bet their stuff is over there." The guys agreed and we headed for the hill. It wasn't really a hill in the true sense, it was more of a bowl shaped depression, higher at the one side. If approached from the south it looked like a hill, from the north the top was flat in line with the land and then dropped away like a shallow cliff. From the east or west, the top angled down to join the flat land below. I said, "We will start by walking up the slope from the west, along the top and down the other side and see if anything stands out." The usual thick bush covered the slope, so it was slow going. It was about fifty yards long from one side to the other, plenty of area to hide something. We stopped at the top and looked down. The only thing that stood out was the dry bed of a stream that ran down into the bowl on the western side and disappeared under the bushes. "You know, I think we have something here. We'll finish our walk down the other end and then have a look where that little river bed goes." Nothing else claimed our attention on the other side and we worked our way over to the dry bed, which started at the base of the little cliff, obviously caused by rain water running down the cliff, pooling at the bottom then running off as a stream. Petrus stepped forward. "Lieutenant, let me go first, I learnt a lot from Abe, I may be able to see if they came this way." "Go ahead," I said. We moved aside and Petrus took the lead. He examined the pathway and looked puzzled, then he smiled and turned to me. "There are footsteps going towards the cliff then going back the other way, that's all I can tell, I can't tell how many there were, only more than two." "Petrus my man, you are terrific, you just saved the day." His face one big smile, he continued along the path. Confirmation that the terrorists had been there was very encouraging and hopefully would lead to something more. Henry said. "Rolf, do you think they mined this place?" "Personally, I don't think so. I think their equipment is hidden here, which means they want to come back and get it at some time. That will be over my dead body, we will kill them first, but to play safe, I will go on with Petrus and call you when we get to the cliff face." I turned and followed Petrus. A few moments later we got to the end of the path uneventfully. I gave a whistle and the guys appeared. Water had cut a crevice into the cliff face and that was what we looked at first. It was clean, nothing was hidden there. Petrus pointed at the ground. "There is loose sand here, like someone was digging, maybe?" Poking at the ground with sticks, showed it to be solid, no signs of digging. The whole area was overgrown with bushes, right up the cliff face, so we continued to poke around with sticks as we searched. A rat jumped out of the crevice and scuttled away, scaring the crap out of everyone, nervous laughter followed. I was quite relieved it was a rat, not a snake. Jumping back in fright, Henry had slashed his stick sideways and it hooked on some bushes above him. He jerked the stick free and some sand showered down. Petrus pointed up and said, "look, that's where the sand came from, they were digging up there." "Get on my shoulders Piet, you're the lightest," said Henry, bending forward. Piet hoisted himself up and Henry stood up. Pulling away the bushes, Piet said, "there's a ledge here and its' hollowed out at the back. There's some stuff in bags, I'll hand them down," and he started pulling them out. There were six bags, all wrapped in black plastic bags. "That's it, nothing else." Henry stepped back and Piet climbed down. "Clever little bastards," I said, "hiding their stuff above the high water mark. When the rains come, this area fills with water and then overflows at the shallow end. The ledge is higher than the high water mark, so their goodies stay safe and dry, now we need to get the hell out of here and back to the truck, let's go and don't drop the bags, there's probably a mine or two in them." Back at the truck, we piled in and drove off back to Rundu again. I couldn't wait to unpack the bags and search the contents. We carried everything into the barracks, unpacked the first two bags and spread the contents across the open floor near the entrance. We found four AK47 assault rifles and twelve clips of ammo. The rifles looked old, but were clean and oiled, there was a cleaning kit in one of the bags. There were two land mines, not activated and two Star 7.62 automatic pistols. All the hardware was wrapped in rags inside plastic bags. We put it all near the entrance and opened the next two bags. There were two fold up shovels, two machetes and a small tent made of brown nylon. There were no markings on anything except the land mines, which had what looked like Russian lettering painted on the tops. We also examined all the bags very carefully, turning them inside out and even checking the seams. The handles were a single thickness of nylon webbing, so nothing could be hidden in them either. Everyone got a chance to check each item, just in case we missed something. Henry turned to me. "Rolf, do you have any idea what we are actually looking for?" "Not really, anything that might be a clue as to where the bastards have gone." "Okay, we've got two more bags, let's hope we find something." I looked up to find Petrus looking at me, he looked away as the guys put the next bag on the table. "Hey, guys, stop for a minute, I want to ask you all something." With all eyes focused on me, I said. "Petrus here, has been part of our team from the beginning, he has risked his life with us and saved our asses today as well. I think he should be in this barracks with us, not on the other side of the camp in the colored section, what do you think, speak up now?" There was a unanimous cheer from the guys and that was that. In contravention of the apartheid laws of the land, Petrus moved in with us later that morning and that was that. We turned our attention back to the bags. Four sets of clothing and four pairs of boots. The boots were filthy and yielded nothing, we even pulled the heels off in case they were hollow. We tossed them aside and started on the clothes. There were khaki shorts, shirts and long sleeved khaki sweaters, nothing else. The clothes were all pretty worn and threadbare in places. We examined each piece of clothing in detail. There were no markings of any sort, all labels had been removed. The pants and shirt pockets were empty, we had not found anything. " Okay, turn the clothes inside out and let's look again, pay particular attention to all the seams" and that was how we found our lead, a small piece of paper, not more than an inch square, rolled up and slid in between the cross hatch stitching at the bottom of a pocket. Piet found it, cut the stitching carefully and handed it to me. "Shit, please let this be something," one of the guys muttered. I very carefully unrolled the small piece of paper and examined it, you could have heard the proverbial pin drop.

There on the paper, very faint, but legible, were two words, Regent and Vanguard. I started smiling. "What, what is it Rolf, what's on the paper?" I handed the paper over to them, they all looked at it, but looked blank, then looked at me puzzled. "It's Regent Road and Vanguard Drive guys, it has to be, get packed, we are leaving for Cape Town as soon as I can get it organized, but we will stop at the farm they attacked in SWA on the way first. Guys, talk to no one about this, not even amongst your selves, These bastards have ears everywhere. We will plan when we get out of here. Henry, let security know we found this stuff and where we found it, they must come and get it. Burn that piece of paper, we will leave nothing to chance. I'm going to the main office to organize a plane. The rest of you go check on the dogs and make sure the kennel guys know they have to look after them while we are gone," so saying I left the barracks, climbed into the jeep and drove to the admin building. I arranged that we would drive down to the farm that had been attacked and continue on to Windhoek afterwards, where an army transport plane would fly us back to Ysterplaat air force base. Being a Lieutenant in the security police, under orders directly from Pretoria, certainly had its advantages. Back at the barracks, my men were all waiting for me outside the entrance, their body language said trouble. I climbed out of the jeep. "What's wrong?" "The dogs and kennel guys are all gone," Piet said. "What do you mean gone?" Together with my bruised body, I suddenly, also had a sick feeling in the pit of my stomach. "While we were out on patrol, trucks arrived with orders from army HQ to take the dogs away. They've all gone together with the kennel guys and there's a message for you to call the General urgently." "Nothing changes guys, go finish packing, we leave at four tomorrow morning." They turned and started inside, I got back in the Jeep and drove down to the security office. They were expecting me and left me in the empty side office to make my call. I called the special private line number the General had given me and on my third try my call went through. His secretary answered. Good day, General Myburgh's office." "Good afternoon, it's Lieutenant DeBeer, I believe the General is looking for me." "Hold one moment Lieutenant." There was a clicking noise and he was on the line.

"DeBeer?" "Yes Sir?" There were no social niceties. "Did you see all your dogs are gone?" "Yes Sir." "I have removed all the dogs from Cape Town as well, it is over. I cannot take a chance on an international incident. You will find the terrorist animals that got away and deal with them, or you and your men will be sent to the Angolan battlefront for the duration of the war. Your only way out is to find these terrorists quickly, before they cause more problems. You have two weeks and if you survive, I will find a reason to put you in military prison afterwards. Have I made myself clear?" "Perfectly." Get going now," he repeated. I said nothing, I wasn't going to give him the satisfaction. The line went dead. So now I knew why they called him "Pigiron," it fitted well. We were on the road at four the next morning and arrived at the farm around four hours later. There was a police caravan parked fifty yards from the burnt out shell of the farm house. We were greeted by two patrolmen. I showed them my security police card and they immediately asked how they could help me. "Any leads on the men that did this?" "There were four of them Sir, they were in an old brown Valiant car. One of the farm hands was on his way home in the early hours of the morning and stepped off the road to relieve himself, when the car drove past very slowly. They never saw him or he would have been killed. He says there were four men in the car, it was just getting light and he saw them clearly. The farm was a mile further down the road and he was still a half mile away when the gunfire started. He realized they were bad men and turned and ran. By the time he got to the next farm, over twenty miles away and sounded an alarm, they had killed everyone on the farm, raped and tortured the women, butchered the animals and set the farm house on fire. We heard they did some really bad stuff to the women before they burnt them alive." I was well aware, that if the terrorists got away, their story would have dire international consequences. "Those bastards are animals, they deserve to die Sir." I nodded agreement. "We will catch them and deal with them. Tell me, how long does it take to drive from here to Windhoek?" "Around three to four hours on the gravel roads Sir." I nodded as I walked off. We walked around what was left of the farm house, a gutted shell only. There was a really bad smell hanging over the area, the smell of burnt flesh. There was nothing to be gained by staying there any longer, so we headed for Cape Town.

I stood in my office doorway and looked around. The bastard was, if nothing else, very efficient. I had been cleaned out. I sat down at my desk and pulled open my file drawer, it was unlocked and empty, all my files gone. The other drawers had also been cleaned out, not even a pencil left. Back in Rundu, after the fiasco in the bush, after my phone call with the General and brief explanation of what had happened, he went crazy, shouting and yelling that I was an inept idiot, incapable of following the most rudimentary instructions and was I aware I had messed up the entire program? I would not apologize and made no excuses. He hung up. I had warned him this might happen, he had brushed that aside, so it became my fault and it really was. If I had chosen to kill the child, none of this would have happened. All gone like magic, old "Pigiron" had earned his nickname, he really was inflexible, single minded and I now thought, evil as well. I had made out a detailed report as requested and sent it off, this was the result. I had never considered myself a fool, so in spite of the official secrets act, I had decided to undertake a little self protection. Many months before, I had been walking down Long Street in the city and I stopped in front of a large camera shop, the windows filled with many different models. I was fascinated by a tiny camera called a Minox B, very small and compact, about the size of a box of matches. It used sixteen millimeter film and the brochure guaranteed crystal clear photographs. It was expensive, but I bought it anyway, a real impulse buy, so I had my own spy camera. I took it out of storage and used it right through our killer dog training months. I had pictures of everything. I took it with me to Caprivi and had a photographic record of the dog squad in action, right to down to pictures of the terrorists remains. Due to the official secrets act, I kept my photography to myself and told no one. Eventually, I mailed it all to an attorney friend of mine with instructions to hold the package unopened until I called for it. If I disappeared, or was found dead under suspicious circumstances, he should open it and read the cover letter, which would explain everything, even the official secrets act. He would know what to do. I sat down and gazed out the window. I had to find the group of killers before they slipped away and there was precious little time remaining. As I looked out across the empty yard, I thought about all the hours and months we had spent training the dogs. What a waste of time and how cruel to dispose of all the dogs like just so much trash, all gone. I had sent the reject pups off to Worcester while we were still training, months before. The twenty best dogs had been picked up from Rundu the day I called the General, then he had got around to removing the others, all gone, now dead I had no doubt, he really cleaned house, the swine. I thought about Gus, the giant puppy with the small white striped paw, exceptionally good natured, I would have loved to keep him. Something nagged at the back of my mind and then I realized I had not seen Gus the morning the reject dogs were taken away, no white paw on that batch of pups, so where was he? The morning after we got back from SWA, we sat down for a meeting and brain storming session. I had done nothing but agonize over the best way to try and find our killers since my last conversation with the "General." I started the meeting off. " Listen here, I have considered their options very carefully. They are not going to be staying in any of the big apartment blocks that filled the area in Sea Point. They are from Angola, speak Portuguese and English. The local Africans speak mainly Xhosa and a little Afrikaans, our man would stand out like a sore thumb. The servants rooms in any of the blocks are not self contained, they all have communal women's bathroom facilities, so no men are allowed to live in the servants' quarters. Any man trying to hide in his girl friends room, would certainly create a disturbance and be quickly ejected, quite possibly with police involvement, something they will want to avoid at all costs." Expanding on my train of thought, I continued, "perhaps they would be avoiding all women, after all, when would they have had the opportunity to form any sort of liason with any women in Cape Town? The work records show they have not missed any days at work in the last couple of years, the first time being a couple of days before, so where does this leave us? Their Zambian masters must have given them a contact name and phone number, but the slip of paper I had found, had Regent and Vanguard written on it. Have they split in two? Smaller groups attract less attention, but that's okay, find one and he will quickly tell us where his buddies are,"

or so I thought at the time. "The more I have thought about it, the more convinced I am that they will be in an apartment along Regent Road. This road is an extension of the main road, only about half a mile long and I am prepared to search every building along its length, room by room if necessary. If they are dressed in overalls and walked into an apartment block looking like maintenance men, no one would give them a second glance. In this instance, the country's apartheid laws are working for us, a black man living in a white area in an apartment would have to remain unseen or complaints would be quickly heard from that paranoid section of the population who saw black danger at every turn. These terrorists must have had a pre-arranged date and time to meet someone, so would have to leave their hiding place to do so, the question is when?" Suddenly I realized what I had missed and it all fell into place. The son of a bitch needed a phone to contact his people in SWA for instructions and help if he was ever going to make it home and I was just the bastard to make sure it didn't happen. My guess was he was in an older apartment block, small apartments, no servants quarters. These blocks would have lots of privacy, people coming and going quite freely, now all I had to do was find him. Big joke, only a half mile of apartment blocks and we would need to search them all. "As I see it, we have no option but to start at each end of Regent Road and go block to block, talk to as many people in each block as we can and see if anyone has seen any of our terrorists, we have their army photos of them to show, so if they are here, some one must have seen them," said Piet. Mick raised a hand. "Do you know if police security will have a list of all apartment blocks without maids quarters, if so it will save us a lot of time because they will not want to be where the girls will start talking about strange men on the premises." "That is a great idea man, I will check now, before we go hunting," I made some phone calls and found all roads led to Police Security Headquarters in Pinelends and Colonel Archie Bakker. I decided to call the Colonel and ask for help. The Colonel's reputation preceeded him. His men were all devoted to him. He was known as a no nonsense leader, a man who supported his men at all times, a man who led from the front, going into dangerous situations with his men time and again in the fight against drug running, terrorism, vice, organized crime and matters of state security. "How the hell can you see what is going on from an office miles away" he had been heard to say. A big man, well over six feet tall, black hair cut short, blue eyes, wide shoulders, he had worked his way up the ranks from patrolman to Colonel, over twenty five years of service to the community. It was rumored he was in line to become the youngest General the police force had ever had. On the basis of the information, I called him. I told him what was going on and he immediately agreed to help. "You know where my office is?" "Yes sir." "Get your men together and be here at two this afternoon, we will get it all organized." "Yes sir, thank you sir." He was already gone. Shortly before two that afternoon, Mick, Henry, Piet, Joe, Petrus and myself presented ourselves at security police headquarters in Pinelands. There were two armed guards on duty outside that I could see and probably others that I could not. I parked and led the way through the double glass doors and yet another reception desk. They were expecting us and after examining all ID cards, we went up to the fourth floor and our meeting with the colonel.

The room was about twenty foot square, with a wide worktable that ran the length of the room. There were chairs all the way around the table. The Colonel sat at the far end of the table with a thick, opened file in front of him. He did not get up. "DeBeer ?" "Yes sir." " Come sit with me, you men go to the carton down there marked Regent, open it up and find the roll of photos showing both sides of the street and the photos taken from overhead. Pin them all along the wall, then we will begin."

"There was a "yes sir" chorus and they got busy. I sat down next to him. "This file has the names, addresses and phone numbers of everyone who lives on Regent Road, broken up into pages for each address on the street. So we have a list of people for each apartment block and what apartment they are in, the same for businesses. There are no houses on the street, makes things a little simpler. When we have the photos up we can eliminate any buildings that do not match your profile." I nodded. I couldn't help thinking was this legal or was it some sort of invasion of privacy of the Regent Road people. I shrugged mentally. Too bad, their loss was our gain.

The guys finally got the rolls of pictures pinned to the wall and we examined them. The colonel said, "We will start at the corner of Regent and Queens Roads, then work our way towards St,Johns Road, so look at that first block facing down the street and tell me what you see?" We all stared at the photos, there was silence. The colonel started talking. "No security doors, just an open entrance, the same at the back of the building and the side entrance from the parking area. No elevators, just stairways front back and sides for the three floors. Municipal rules say four floors or higher have to have an elevator. Anyone can come and go as they like from this block, so we mark it yes, got it?"

Everyone nodded, we got it. The Colonel looked across at one of his men. "Call the municipal office and tell them they will be starting refuse collections at nine am only, I don't want them getting in the way." His sergeant hurried out to arrange it. Two hours later we were done and had eight blocks on the list. Any blocks with security doors and elevators were omitted. A black man would have stood out like a sore thumb trying to get into any of those blocks. "Okay, we will meet at Sea Point station at five tomorrow morning, everyone will be in uniform with bullet proof vests. I will have extra men from security here to help us." He turned to me. "DeBeer, the one marked block is where you have an apartment, so you and your men can inspect that one."

Yes Sir." He continued very quietly, "DeBeer, I made some enquiries and found you have made a dangerous enemy, I am sure you know what I am talking about?" "Yes sir." " Everyone speaks highly of you, with that one exception, which you will have to deal with later, in the meantime we will go get your terrorists, okay?" He gave me an encouraging grin. I smiled back. "Thank you sir, much appreciated." He turned back to my men. "We will keep it very simple, you men will search the very first block we discussed earlier, then the Lieutenant's block. My teams will search the other six blocks, they have done this before, so will be quicker than you guys. Each block will have my men at each entrance and on each stairwell, also in the alleys at the rear and sides and lastly on the street at the front, all in twos, no one on their own.

A lone black man will stand out like a sore thumb. No one will be able to get in or out without passing them. I want to impress on you all, that my main worry is not a couple of black men, if they are there we will find them, my worry is what else we may find while searching these apartment blocks. Anything is possible, from drug running, prostitution or even kidnapped children. These people will be armed and ready to shoot. I don't want anyone getting hurt, so take care and be aware at all times. Got it?" There were nods all round. "Good, get going and we will meet in the morning. I will lead one team, Lieutenant Jansen will lead the other and Lieutenant DeBeer the third." We left and headed back to our office. Not long afterwards, back at Ysterplaat, we gathered round our table again, armed with our list and photos. We re-examined the photos again, trying to burn all details into our memories. Nothing new came of the exercise and we packed the pictures away. I turned to my men. "There are six of us including Petrus, he can go with Henry. Petrus nodded. When we get to my apartment block, I will take it on myself. I will change into a suit and tie, you guys will position yourselves on each floor, the colonels' men will have the block sealed off and I will visit each apartment. It is a small block, only ten apartments, so will not take long. If I see or feel anything strange, we will visit that one again together and take it to pieces. Okay guys, that's it, until five tomorrow." We went off for dinner in the canteen, then sat around chatting for a while before turning in, we were all pretty stressed out. If we didn't find our fugitives in the morning, the General would eat us alive.

We arrived at Sea Point Police Station before five the following morning and found the Colonel already there, with his two teams. "The rest of the men are already moving into position. We will begin as soon as I get the ready call, probably around five thirty." I nodded.

"Are you men all clear on what you are doing? Any questions? " There were no questions. "You are team one, I will call you T1 on radio, my guys will be 2 and 3. You can go and get into position now. I would park just around the corner from the first block on Victoria and wait till I call you." "Yes Sir, thank you." He smiled and walked off. We got back into our car and drove off down the Beach Road. The road block at the bottom of Queens Road let us through after I showed my ID and shortly afterwards we were parked and ready. We had spent hours waiting over the last couple of years. Hours and hours up on Caprivi waiting for terrorists almost daily, always in silence, waiting and listening. Sitting in a car for thirty minutes was a breeze. There was constant voice traffic from the radio as the colonel's men finished moving into position and around five thirty the radio crackled into life."T1 go, copy?" "We copy, T1 out." "Lets go guys, good luck." We left the car and as we rounded the corner we saw a large crowd of people outside the block on the sidewalk. A woman rushed up to me. "Thank goodness you're here officer, the noise is driving us crazy." I could hear loud music in the background, coming from somewhere in the block. "It started a couple of hours ago and they won't turn it down," she continued. "It's number 2D, a young girl lives there, always having parties and loud music, but this is ridiculous." I turned to Piet, "come, let's get this sorted out quickly, then they'll all go back to their apartments and we can finish up, tell the guys." I turned to the woman, dressed in a pink dressing gown, brown hair in curlers. "Show me where the apartment is madam. She led the way up to the next floor complaining all the way about inconsiderate people and having been kept up half the night. I remained silent. Outside 2D, the noise was very loud indeed, no wonder the residents were all awake. "Get these people away from here" I shouted at my guys. Very quickly they were chased away, but remained on the stairway at the end of the corridor. There was a steel security door covering the front door. I tried holding the door bell down and could hear a faint ringing. I next started hammering loudly on the door and also kicked the steel door, shouting "Police, open up." I wasn't worried about announcing our presence, the loud noise gave good reason for it.

I was starting to think we would have to break the door open, when the handle turned and it swung open. Standing there was a young blonde woman who looked to be in her mid twenties, she was stark naked. She was obviously under the influence of something, her eyes were wide and staring, her pupils were pin pricks. "Yesssh," she said in a very slurred voice. "Open this gate," I shouted at her, "police visit, open the gate now." She turned to a small hall table that had a bunch of keys on it, picked up the keys, turned back to me and collapsed onto the floor unconscious. "Shit, she's got the damn keys. Piet, you've got long arms, try reaching in and drag her closer so we can grab them." Piet indeed had very long arms and just managed to get hold of a wrist. He pulled her towards the door like a wet fish. I managed to get hold of her other hand with the keys, took them away and unlocked the security gate and rushed inside. There was a young man unconscious on the couch in the lounge, he was dressed in jeans and a tee shirt. The offending stereo system was on a stand on my right and was blasting out music by "Chicago". At any other time I would have enjoyed the whole fiasco, including the good looking naked blond, it was more like a comedy routine, but as it was, it just added to my stress, the General was waiting. I jerked the plug and wires out of the wall and the noise stopped. The silence really was golden. There was a phone on the hall table. "Piet, call 10111 and get an ambulance here, tell them to use Colonel Bakker's name to get through the roadblock. "Tell them two people, both white and unconscious on narcotics and liquor. Wrap the girl in a blanket and wait for the ambulance, while we check out the block." Everyone living in the block was wide awake. We told them we had been instructed to do a security check while we were there and did just that. We never found our terrorist, just a lot of highly irritated people whose night and early morning had been ruined. We left quickly, the Colonels men vanished. One down, just my apartment block to go. We drove the quarter mile there and parked around the corner, out of sight on Regent Road., it was six forty five am, the sun was rising.

My apartment block sat on the corner of Regent Road and Argyle, a narrow side street in the heart of Sea Point. It was a neat looking building, painted white, three floors including the ground level, which was the garage level, they opened onto the street. On the Regent Road side, was a driveway around the back of the building and more garages. The apartments sat above the garages. The entrance was near the corner, no doors, just an opening into the building, stairs on the left or straight through to the garages at the back. Mailboxes lined the wall on the right. There was another staircase at the far end of the building, there was no elevator. The floor and stairs were concrete, painted a dark red color like blood. I hoped it was not an omen for the near future. I climbed the stairs to the first floor and walked slowly and quietly along the landing towards the apartment at the end. On my left I looked down into the parking area and back wall of the shops that faced the main road. There was a staircase at the end, going down to the car park. Apartment 101 would be my first search, my apartment was 102. I went quietly into my own apartment and changed into a dark suit, black shoes, white shirt and red striped tie, the picture of a civil servant. My pistol was holstered under my jacket, out of sight. The whole block was sealed off by the Colonels men, who had been joined by the police from our first search. The block was really closed off tighter than a mouse's ass hole, I thought. I closed my door quietly behind me, locked it and turned towards 101. I rang the bell. The door was opened by a blonde, skinny woman in a house coat, a cigarette drooped from the corner of her mouth. She fitted my idea of poor white trash, hair in curlers at seven in the morning, feet in slippers, no make up, very pale skin and watery blue eyes. "Yes?" she asked. I flashed my I.D card at her, the top line on the card, printed in bold black print, said Police Special Branch. Before I could say anything, she said, "Come in, come in" and stood aside. I went in, there was a small bathroom on my left, it looked dirty, then came the kitchen, open plan with a one bed roomed lounge, dining room combination. Furthest away from me was the bedroom area. I was standing in the dining room, lounge area on my left. The whole room was about thirty feet long. There was a cheap, unmade pine box bed under the far window, on my right was a small couch and armchair, covered in a blue fabric. On the left was a small round wooden table and chairs. In the middle of the room was a man in a wheel chair. Slicked back black hair, dark eyes and a pallid unhealthy complexion, complete with pock marked skin. He was however, cleanly shaven and wearing a blue toweling dressing gown and brown slippers. I could see the bottom part of his legs, they looked wasted away and skeletal. "This man is from the Railways, Piet." she said. He said nothing. I remained silent, waiting to see what game she was playing. She turned to me. "Sir, as you can see, he's still in the wheel chair, his legs are never going to get better. I've got a letter from the doctor and a hospital report to show you, if I can just find my glasses." She turned around and started rummaging around in a cupboard. I realized she had not read my warrant card, she couldn't see it clearly without her glasses, she just knew it was official and thought I was a "Railways" man. She turned with her glasses in place and examined me for the first time. If it wasn't so serious, I would have been most amused. She held out a letter, I took it and read. it was from a Doctor M. Andrews at Groote Schuur Hospital, dated a week earlier and stated that Mr. Piet Kemp, of the address I was then visiting, had been examined and found to be paralysed from the waist down due to an accident at the railways goods yard in Cape Town the previous year, in which his spine had sustained severe damage. The injury had healed, but in spite of intensive treatment, the extent of the spinal damage was such, as to make it unlikely that Mr. Kemp would ever walk again. Further enquiries could be made by contacting the doctor. The report contained a lot of technical information, to back up the letter. I looked up, the woman was staring at me intently. I handed her back the letter. "Please Sir, don't take his pension away, it's all we have, we will starve without it."

"Now, now, calm down, I'm not here for that, what I need to know and the reason I came to talk to you, is to find out if you have seen this man." I decided to improvise a little. She still thought I was from the railways office, so I used that as my opener. " Look, there was a problem at the goods yard and we are now looking for this man. We were told he was seen at this apartment block." I held out the photograph, she took it and examined it. "Yes, he's upstairs in 204, what did he do?" You could have knocked me over with a feather, I got such a shock. Who could get that lucky? Aunties' face flashed before me, score one for the white devils. Before I could answer, Piet in the wheel chair suddenly spoke up, in a raspy, whiny voice. "She would bloody well know where every man in the block is. Since I got hurt and being half a man, she gets the hots for anything in pants. She'd screw the postman if he would have her. She drools over the balcony wall at the young guy next door every chance she gets. She lets the dog's ball roll through the drain pipe onto his balcony, so she has an excuse to climb over to get it, oh yes, she knows all right." "That's not fair." she shouted. "I'm sociable and you're miserable all the time. I understand why, but it's not my fault you had an accident and I also have needs you know. I would go and get a job, so I would have some spending money, but you're helpless with out me, so I'm stuck here all day with you, you misery and you blame me for trying to find a friendly face I can at least talk to and I won't put up with any verbal abuse from you either." Her voice had risen to a loud, high pitch, then in silence, she glared at Piet, then at me. I wondered why she had not recognized me, probably her glasses. I hadn't really glimpsed her more than a couple of times, so it looked like he was lying. I said as calmly as I could, "I'm sorry, I didn't mean to create a situation here, but I really need to know if you are absolutely sure that the man you saw, was this man?" I pointed at the photo she was still holding. "Yes, I'm sure," she said. "he's with that thin skinny guy, Mr. Phillips. I was surprised, because black people are not allowed to stay in white homes you know, but I thought maybe they're gay, so I said nothing." "When did you last see him?" " Yesterday afternoon, I was taking Binky for a little walk around the floors and Mr. Phillips was just coming out of his front door, the other guy was closing it. I just said hello and walked on towards the stairs." "What does Mr. Phillips look like?" "He's about your height, but very thin with thick glasses in a brown frame and brown hair, do you know him?" "No, he doesn't sound like anyone from my office, I wonder what he does?" I was of course hoping for more information, but nothing else was forthcoming. Apart from my neighbours, I didn't know anyone in the block, I was rarely there. Piet was sitting in silence, staring at the floor. What a life these two had, living off his disability check. He needed her and she, with little education lived off him. Just enough money to get through the month, nothing to spare. What the hell would become of them in years to come. If the ANC came into power, they would probably cancel the white folks pensions if they could, what a disaster that that would be, but who would blame them if they did. I turned and headed for the door. "Thank you for your time, I must get back to the office and report this" and that's how I left them, him staring at nothing on the floor and her glaring down at him, in silence. I hurried back across the street to the restaurant, to wait for Henry. We had agreed to meet there. I used my walky-talky to call him. Hey Henry, he's here, I found him, come to the restaurant." Five minutes later he arrived with Petrus. He was also blown away we had got so lucky. "He's on the top floor, 204. His partner is a white guy, about six feet, skinny, brown hair, thick lensed glasses, name of Phillips. Get parking across the street and arrest him when he arrives, he should get home sometime late afternoon, I would think. Do it quickly and quietly with Bennie and Mick, then drop him off at the security office in town and come back here. Then we will go and get the other one. The arrest of the first terrorist turned out to be a simple affair. I reported to the Colonel so he knew what was going on, he gave me the go ahead, I had two guys at each end of the passage, then myself and Mick together with two of the Colonels men and we were ready. We moved to the door in silence, there was no sign of any other tenants at that time. I did a no nonsense savage kick on the door, it flew open and we rushed in. My man was standing in the middle of the room and I shouted at him, "stand still," as I waved my pistol at him. "Henry handcuffed him and we hustled him out and down to the car. The security guys took over the apartment and started searching it, the garages would be searched next, as well as all the other apartments just in case anything was hidden there. "Leave nothing unsearched or unchecked" the colonel had said, "that way you will not have any regrets or guilt later on." We took our man off to Sea Point Police Station where I had arranged to have him jailed for the next few days. He was listed as prisoner X. There was no reading of rights or such nonsense, he was a terrorist killer, he had no rights, he was from another country and in practical terms did not exist. He was put in cell eight, I thanked the duty officer and we left. He had remained silent throughout and would not answer any questions, so leaving him on ice for the moment seemed a good start, also I had an idea of how I could get him to talk, I prayed I was right. I had dismissed the guys and sent them home for the next day, to meet at the office the day after. They needed the day off, they had earned it. I went to see the Colonel, who had dismissed all his men and gone to his office. They had found a drug operation going on in one of their searches. Three men had been arrested and locked up with no gunfire or resistance. The two drugged idiots I had found were in hospital under guard. They had a large stock of the drug mandrax in the apartment and would appear in court once they had recovered. The road blocks were gone and life in Sea Point had returned to normal. I thanked the Colonel profusely for his help. I could never have done it without him. "So DeBeer, what now?" "Sir, the captive doesn't exist, he is a ghost who will help me to find his friends and then it is over. I am following the General's instructions, I have no choice in this matter. I intend to have the whole affair complete in the next two days." He nodded. "Good luck DeBeer, if you need more help, call me." We shook hands and I left. What a great guy and officer he was. I went back to my empty office to think. Back at my Sea Point apartment, the guys were waiting for Phillips to get home. He got home at five thirty and was promptly arrested and handed over to security. It was nearly over, but I needed to see Phillips' apartment first., so I drove over to his block and climbed the stairs to the first floor and walked into the apartment, the door was open. There were a couple of technicians busy fingerprinting the whole place. I had already pulled on a pair of surgical gloves to avoid getting my own prints on anything. The layout was the same as my own apartment, bathroom, kitchen, dining room and lounge with a small balcony on the left, bedroom area at the far end. The first thing I noticed was a painting about two foot square, of P.W.Botha, hanging on the wall in the lounge area on my right. I moved closer to the painting. It was indeed an oil painting with the artists initials JD at the bottom. There was a small brass plate on the frame at the bottom edge with the engraved message, "PRESENTED TO A.PHILLIPS FOR 25 YEARS OF SERVICE TO THE NATIONAL PARTY." I turned to the two men still busy examining things. "I'm taking this painting away, do you want to mark it?" "It already has a tag Lieutenant, just sign the log." He pointed at the table. I signed the log book next to the painting entry and took the painting off the wall. I took it to my apartment, stood it up on a chair and stared at it. So, Phillips was a staunch member of the National Party and had been for years. This discounted him as being any sort of terrorist, it made no sense, there had to be something else going on.

I sat at my desk and did some brain storming. When we had first started training the pups, Mick had fallen in love with the puppy with the paw stripe. We had all trained hard, but my mind kept coming back to Mick. He had to be the one who had saved the puppy, if not I was in desperate trouble. He was always busy with Gus, doing basics and obedience and became very attached to him. He was devastated when Gus failed the tests, perhaps, just perhaps he had decided to save the dog, I was going to find out. My files were gone, but they had left the phone book and I knew his parents lived quite close to the base. I couldn't ask Mick for his address, what I was about to do had to come as a complete surprise. I couldn't remember the address, but if I saw it, I would recognize it. I feverishly grabbed the book, but my hands were shaking and I dropped it. I cursed out loud and forced myself to carefully pick up the book and open it to V, after all, how many Van Holts could there be? The V's went on for pages and pages, hundreds and hundreds of Van this and Van that, more than Smith or Jones, amazing. I paged carefully through from the beginning and there it was, I recognized the address. I made a mental note only, nothing in writing and hurried out. Idiot that I was, I then remembered they were all waiting for Phillips. They called me just after five thirty, they had arrested Phillips and handed him over to security. I thanked the guys and sent them home, we would meet at my office at eight the next morning. A while later, at seven, I drove slowly past the house and parked around the corner, out of sight. I got out, locked the car and hurried back towards the house. It was one from the corner, white walls and red tile roof. The path from the gate went straight down the middle to the front door. There was a thick green hedge about eight foot high, right around the garden, affording some privacy from the neighbors. There was a narrow flowerbed around the edges of a neatly mowed lawn on each side of the path. There were windows on each side of the front door, probably a lounge and main bedroom. It was fairly normal layout for homes built in that area. There was a bell push set into the wall on my right side and I pressed hard against it with my forefinger. I could hear the chimes coming from inside, followed by footsteps. The door swung open and there stood Mick. It was no time for polite conversation, I was feeling very stressed. "Okay" I rasped, "where is the dog?" I had guessed right, his face went white with shock as his eyes widened with recognition. "Sir I" and then there was silence. "Well" I snapped. He tried again. "Sir they were going to kill him, so I had to save him. He's such a nice dog, not a mean bone in his body, loves everyone. I took him out in the trunk of my car, they only search the cars coming in, not out, so he's alive and all the others are dead by now." His voice trailed off into silence as I stood there glaring at him. "Are you going to arrest me?" I was so excited I could have hugged him. "No you fool, you accidentally saved us, let me in." He moved away and ushered me into the room on the left, the lounge. His face was a picture of relief. "This is what's going on." I said. "The one we caught is not talking. If we can get him to believe that Gus is one of the dogs that killed his friends and we are going to feed him to the dog alive, I think he will tell me everything I need to know. So, we are going to teach Gus a trick. When I flick my finger at him, he will show all his teeth and snarl, expecting to get a treat in return, just a show, but our friend, I believe, will think his time has come. I need his leash, choke collar, a dishcloth and some dog treats, have you got them here?" "Yes Sir, I have, I'll go get them." "Wait, where are your parents?" "They're in Beaufort West, visiting mom's sister, they'll be back tomorrow night." "Okay, good, get the stuff." He turned and left. I looked around the room. The floor was mostly covered with an imitation Persian carpet, in colors of beige, brown and maroon. There was a large black wood display cabinet against the far wall. The right side had a lot of miniatures of different breeds of dogs on the top shelf. The lower shelves were filled with silver cups and trophies for athletics. I could see Mick's name engraved on them. The left side was full of books, mostly novels and detective stories. There was a coffee table in the same black wood in the center of the room, covered with gardening and home décor magazines. The lounge suite was a comfortable looking, padded suede three seater and two single armchairs. My examination was disturbed by Mick coming back. He was holding the equipment. I took the stuff from him and said, "Right, let's get this going, where is Gus?" "Follow me." He led the way down the passage and through a small but well equipped white tiled kitchen to the back door. He pulled the door open and there stood Gus, tail wagging a welcome. I patted his head and scratched behind his ears, got my hand licked in return. What an impressive dog he was. He looked almost as tall as a Great Dane, covered with shaggy black fur, he had a huge head and massive jaws, a fairly short furry tail, wagging enthusiastically and one white striped paw in strange contrast to the rest of him. With my hand resting gently on his head I looked around the garden. It was a duplicate of the front garden, but no path through the middle. At the far wall there was wooden post sticking up about five feet high. "What is that post?" "Oh, there was a garden faucet on it, but the pipe burst, so dad cut it off and moved it to the wall of the house down there" and he gestured to my right. "It looks perfect for what we need" I said and I walked over to it. "Put on his choke chain and leash, then tie him to the post on a very short leash about eighteen inches away only." Mick did so, then looked at me, Gus, tied up short, looked anxious. "This is how it works. I am going to flick his nose with the dish cloth and irritate him until he shows his teeth and sounds a warning. The second he does so, you move forward, give him a dog treat and make a big fuss of him, then we will repeat it a few times, got it?" " Yes, but Sir, what if he won't respond?" "We'll worry about that then. We need to be more worried about getting savaged if we piss him off enough. I knew of several cases where that happened, with tragic consequences. We don't have the time to use the nicely, nicely, huggy, kissy method, this is the fast track use it or lose it system, are you ready and stop calling me Sir, it's Rolf remember?" "Okay, let's do it," he said. "Move over to the left a little Mick, out of the way, but so he can see you, then remain quite still so as not to distract him, you only move in with a treat if he responds." " Okay," he said, moving out of the way. Gus was looking quite alarmed, he wasn't used to this kind of treatment. I moved forwards without crouching or threatening body language and expertly flicked Gus on the nose with the dish cloth. At the same time, I flicked the fore finger of my left hand out towards him in a pointing movement. The sting on his nose made him jerk his head back in shock and before he could recover I did it again and again and kept on going. Gus jerked to the left and right, tried pulling his head back, but of course nothing helped, he was on a very short lead.

I remained apparently calm and relaxed, no aggression at all, just kept flicking his nose. My arm was getting very tired and sore as was my forefinger but I had to keep going, this was the only sure way I would get the information I needed. After around ten minutes of effort my arm felt like it was going to fall off and I was starting to feel desperate, when suddenly a break through. After a bout of almost strangling himself by pulling and lunging back and side to side in a effort to get away, Gus finally lost his temper and snarled in rage, showing all his teeth to me. I moved back and Mick jumped forwards, showering Gus with praise and giving him a couple of his favorite snacks. Gus looked as amazed as a dog actually could, he was being rewarded for showing aggression, very puzzling. Mick moved back again and I moved forwards. I flicked my finger and as I raised the dishcloth and Gus snarled in apparent fury, he had recognized the finger signal, not a stupid dog at all. My G-d he had big teeth. I moved back and again Mick moved in with treats and praise. We tried another few times with equal success and that was enough. I put the dishcloth down and cautiously offered Gus a treat, he accepted and licked my hand, we were still friends, it had worked. I rubbed his face, neck and nose gently to show him I was still a friend and got licked again in return, a gentle giant indeed. "I'm going back to base now," I said, "I'll be back at six, be ready in uniform, we will pick our boy up and take him up to the forest, tie him to a tree so he cannot move and pretend that he is going to die just like the people he set up in Caprivi. It must work, I am convinced it will." "Rolf, that was bloody amazing, I can see why the General had to have you, we are going to be okay. Once we have taken care of the other three we are home clear." He was clearly elated. "The rest of the team will be blown away." " Ja, well we can celebrate later." On the way out I used his phone to call base and I booked a small prisoner van to transport my pet terrorist to meet his fate. Back at the base, I signed for my van and parked it outside my office, ready to go, then I went over to the canteen for a quick snack. I nibbbled at my food, no real appetite, had a cup of coffee then went back to my office bedroom. I lay down to have a nap, setting the alarm for five, that would give me time to get ready and go get Mick and the dog. Technically, I was on a three day pass, if I wanted to sleep then that's what I was bloody well going to do. I woke in good time, got ready and was at Mick's just before six. I left a message for the rest of my guys that I had to go to a meeting and might be late, they should wait for me. I did a quick test on Gus, he passed with flying colors and we were off. I led the way, Mick and Gus in the old army Ford behind me. We made it to the police station in Sea Point around five thirty and parked in front of the charge office. I got out and went over to Mick. "I'll be awhile, stay here and look professional, this is serious business." "I'll be here," he said. I went in. The charge office was really a very big room, around forty feet wide and thirty deep. There were four desks centrally positioned, each flanked by filing cabinets. There was no one manning these desks, probably out on patrol. On my right was a large recessed area barred off from the office, the holding tank. It too was empty. Against the back wall was another desk, the duty sergeants', more filing cabinets and a large steel safe. I stood at the reception counter as the sergeant moved towards me, a large man, well over six feet tall, built like a side of beef, sandy hair, a small moustache, pale complexion and the badge on his breast pocket said "VISSER" He looked me over, "Good day Lieutenant, what can we do for you?" I produced my document requesting release of prisoner X, cell eight. I had elected to keep him nameless, political prisoners had no rights, more so if no one knew of their existence. After scanning the document, the sergeant went over to his desk and made a note in a large ledger book, then brought it over to me for signing. He compared the signatures, while I produced my military police I.D. card and he examined that. He noted the number and name in his ledger, then he looked at me and said, "this is all in order, bring your transport to the side gate on your right as you leave the parking area, I will wait for you there." I went back outside to the van, first telling Mick I was going inside to collect our guy. I stopped at the high steel gates, one of them swung open to allow me into the yard. I drove in and stopped in the center of the yard, the cell block was on my right. As I got out of the van, I noticed the heavily armed guard checking that the gate was locked correctly. He had been there as I drove in, out of sight on the left, just a safety measure, good security.

The sergeant led the way to cell eight and produced a large ring of keys, selected one and unlocked the door. The door was very wide, at least four feet and about four inches thick, covered with a steel skin and reinforced with steel ribs, the doorframe was also steel, set into concrete. It was painted black and there was a large number eight painted on it. No one was going to break through that any time soon. The cell was around twelve foot long and eight foot wide, but four feet into the cell heavy iron bars went from floor to ceiling, creating a safety zone, so it was quite safe to open the door and step into the entrance section. The ceiling was very high, I thought about fourteen feet and there was a small window, heavily barred set up near the top, above the door. The light was recessed into the ceiling also with a barred cover. At the back wall was a low steel bunk, bolted to the floor and next to that was a small steel basin and an enameled hole in the floor, which was the toilet. It was all painted white, the floor was plain concrete. My prisoner sat cross legged on the bunk, looking at us. I turned to the sergeant. "Please give me five minutes alone with him before you unlock the cell." "Certainly Lieutenant, five minutes it is." He turned and left.

CHAPTER TWELVE

THE PRISONER WAS STILL SITTING on the bunk looking at me. "Get up, turn around and walk backwards to me, do it now!" I snapped at him. He did as I had instructed. "Put you hands through the bars." He did so. With his hands through the bars I handcuffed him to them so he couldn't move away, or turn around and kick me, then crouched down and handcuffed his ankles as well. The ankle cuffs had a little longer chain to allow prisoners to shuffle along. Once that was done, I reached up and uncuffed him from the bars, just cuffing his wrists behind him. "Turn around now," I said. He turned and faced me. About my height, short curly black hair, dark brown skin, very dark eyes. He was very thin. He was wearing dirty, stained khaki pants and a khaki shirt, equally dirty and stained. His face was expressionless. "This is your last chance to tell me what you know, otherwise I will take you away from here and kill you, you will be of no further use to me, but you will die the hard way, in pain, it will be pay back you bastard, I owe you." His eyes widened and his body stiffened, I had succeeded in scaring the crap out of him, but he remained silent. "Okay, your choice, we will get it done now." I could hear the sergeants' footsteps coming back. He stopped next to me. "Ready?" he asked. I nodded. "Step back from the gate," he said to my prisoner, who did so quickly. The gate swung inwards.

"Come out." I stood aside and he shuffled out into the yard. "Wait there." He stood still. The sergeant locked the cell and then the outer door. "Ok, we can load him in the van now," he said and I pushed my prisoner towards the back of the van. He turned towards the sergeant. " Sir, please do not let this man take me away, he is going to kill me." The sergeants' reaction was instantaneous, he slapped the man so hard across the side of his face that he knocked him off his feet and he landed flat on the ground, stunned and groaning. "You dare talk to me you black bastard," he roared in fury. "You dare ask for help? If he kills you, he will be doing us all a favor, now get up and get the hell in the van before I kill you myself." The suddenness and ferocity of the assault left me momentarily numbed, then I remembered, he was part of the group that had slaughtered a family, their staff and all their livestock, not to mention Abe and my dogs. Any humane feelings I was harboring, vanished. The man lay motionless. "Shit Sergeant, I hope you haven't killed the idiot, I still need him." "No, Lieutenant, I promise he's still alive, you can kill him later for real." So saying, he reached down and picked the man up by one arm and a leg, carried him over to the open van and dumped him inside where he lay groaning. I slammed the door closed and locked it, turned around and shook hands with Sergeant Visser. "Thank you, I may see you later, depends on what they decide down town." " I'll be here until six tonight, then Terblanche comes on duty." "Ok, maybe later then." I climbed back in van and started up. By the time I had turned around, the gate was open and I drove through, the guard nodded to me. I drove into the parking area and stopped next to Mick's car. "Follow me, we are going to the forest above Molteno Road." I drove off with Mick and Gus behind me. We drove towards the city, then at the outskirts, turned away to the right up Buitengracht Street, which went up towards the lower mountain slopes and forest above the city. Not much later, at the top of Molteno Road, I branched off along the rangers road into the forest and finally stopped at a clearing a half mile along the road. It was starting to get dark. I jumped from the van and went over to Mick. "Leave Gus in the car for the moment and come and help me." "Sure Rolf." Now that we were in the forest proper, there was a strong smell of pine from the trees and the thick mat of pine needles scrunched softly under foot. This was the forest I had literally grown up in, living as we had, right on the edge of it and I felt strangely comforted by the familiar surroundings and sounds of the forest.

We went to the van and I opened the door. "Out you get," I said to him, "quickly now." He was awake and slid himself towards the door. I grabbed his feet and slid him out of the van, he was still groggy. We picked him up and carried him to the other side of the clearing, where I selected a sturdy looking pine tree. Mick held him against the tree and I tied him to it very securely, hands, ankles and waist. He remained silent. "I have brought a friend of yours to see you." His eyes widened in surprise, but still he was silent. I nodded to Mick and he went off to get Gus, this was it, all or nothing. I don't know who he expected to see, but it certainly was not the dog. He was facing away from the car, I was standing a little to one side so the dog would be in front of me, facing my prisoner. The huge dog was suddenly standing in front of him, looking at him, but actually watching me. He yelled in terror. I flicked my finger and was rewarded with a vicious snarl and showing of that very large set of teeth. My prisoner became incoherent, I couldn't understand a word he was saying. I motioned to Mick to back off a few feet, which he did, giving Gus his treat at the same time, then we all stood in silence for several seconds, waiting for my prisoner to regain his composure. As the terrified gasps subsided, I stepped in front of him and said very quietly. "I see you were not very happy to see our friend, I can't say I blame you. You will now tell me what I need to know or I will strap your head back against the tree so the dog can get at your throat, then I will blindfold you and gag you and leave you here all on your own. Later on, I will let the dog go and you will die like your friends and those poor people from the village that you murdered. (My captive didn't know the villagers were very much alive) If you tell me what I need to know, you stay alive and I will take you back to your people in Rundu, they can deal with you themselves. That's the deal, what do you want to do?" There was a shuddering exhale of breath as he finally gave in to his terror and said, "just take the dog away and I will tell you what you want to know," his voice had a completely defeated note. I tried not to let my elation show, as I asked him, "where is the rest of your group?" Mick hurried away with Gus. "If you go down the Vanguard Drive from the Eastern freeway towards Goodwood, the Langa township will be on your left side. There are some big electricity pylons there on that side, just before the turn off on the right to Epping Industrial Area. The pylons are on the road side of a deep drainage culvert. On the left side of the pylons are some shacks. As you drive down the road you will see those shacks on your left, one of them has the edge of its roof painted red. You can only see it as you drive towards it from about fifty yards away." Mick had come back without Gus and was also listening in silence. "The men are in that shack. I am supposed to pick them up there at three in the morning the day after tomorrow." Damn, I was right, I had nearly missed them, thank G-d for Gus. The thoughts rushed around my head. "How were you going to pick them up?" "With a stolen car, they showed me how to steal a car in the camp in Zambia, we were going to drive back to South West along the back roads, through the farms, I know those back roads well. The roadblocks are gone by now." "What are the names of the people that trained you in the camp in Zambia." "They called themselves Mike, Joe and Harry, I do not know their correct names. Everyone used false names for security reasons." "What is your correct name?" There was a slight hesitation, he knew I had his ID tag from the army base at Rundu and that by now, I knew it was a false name. "Albert Nangano." "What is your home town." "Windhoek." Mick was busy writing it all down in a little note book, by the light of his flashlight, I hoped he would be able to read it later. It really was an unreal scene that played out there in the Molteno forest by the light of Mick's flashlight. I asked about the people he met in the camp in Zambia. He said they all used only first names, so no one knew who they were or where they came from. He said some were from South West, he could tell by their accents, but that was all and the men in charge were all unknowns, again, first names only. Mick was still writing it all down, I hoped he could see what the hell he was writing. Once I handed Albert over to our security guys, they would get the details out of him. I asked which camp he had trained in, so he assumed I knew about the training camps and told me, without realizing that I knew nothing about the location of training camps for terrorists in Zambia. Had he been to any of the other camps, I asked and yes he had, so I had the names and locations of two camps. The security guys would be very interested in that bit of information. "What happened that last night in the Caprivi Strip, before you went to the farm?" There was silence as he took a deep shuddering breath. It was quite dark by this time, a light breeze whistled eerily through the branches of the trees and bushes around us. There were the forest noises of the night, crackling in the bushes as some rodent scurried by, a last call by a Guinea Fowl as they settled in the branches of trees for the night and the smell of pine trees around us. Normally I loved the forests I had grown up in, now I couldn't wait to get away, but we were not finished yet.

"A child was up in the rocks on the hill when the dogs came and listened to my friends dying, it was horrible, their screams as they died and the snarling and moaning noises of the dogs from hell. The child has trouble sleeping, he wakes up often, screaming. He is only seven years old. He thought they had been attacked by wild beasts, not dogs, so lay still so as not to attract their attention. It was only minutes later that the army men arrived with their jeeps and trucks with bright lights and he saw the dogs being taken away and the remains of my friends put in bags and also taken away. They cleaned the place so well, not a trace remained and then they all left. He ran back towards the border and by the time the sun came up was back in Zambia and safe, it was only a couple of miles. When he got back to the camp and told them what happened they were furious. The following day, I was called in and introduced to the other three men you are looking for and given a plan to carry out. We were to go back into Caprivi to the village near that hill and take the headman, his wife and two children and tie them to wooden stakes in the ground like you have tied me here. Tie their heads back to keep their throats exposed, then blindfold and gag them so they could not cry for help. First we made them walk from the road carrying our bags, while we walked behind them, brushing the ground, so our tracks covered theirs and were fresh. It was so close to Rundu that we knew you would find the tracks very quickly, which you did and your dogs killed them that night.

We thought you would get the message that this was indeed revenge for killing our people and you would take the dogs away. While you were busy with that, we hid our belongings and hitched a ride to Windhoek on an army transport, the driver thought we were on a pass from the army base, because I worked at Rundu and the others worked at Swakopmund and we all had the correct ID with us. At Windhoek we found a place to get some food and that night we stole a car and headed for the farmlands. When we reached that farm in SWA in the very early morning, the others went crazy, they wouldn't listen to me and attacked the people on the farm. Instead of just shooting them as instructed, they did terrible things and finally killed them all and burnt the place to the ground, then we left and made our way through to South Africa along back roads. I swear I took no part in the torture, I cannot prove it." He stopped and his body shook and trembled. After a few moments he continued. "I dropped the other three off at Langa and continued on towards Sea Point. I left the car on a vacant lot at the back of a place called Paarden Eiland and walked through to Sea Point in the dark, to the apartment you found me at. They gave me the instructions in Zambia before we left, that's all I know." His chin dropped onto his chest and there was silence. "Why do I not believe you?" I asked. I took a cloth from my pocket and tied it firmly across his mouth, I did not want any loud screams echoing out of the forest. His were wide and staring, I walked around behind the tree again and he tried to turn his head to see what I was doing, I picked up a little finger and bent it backwards until it dislocated at the knuckle. The strangled howls and gasps coming from behind the gag told me it was horribly painful. I suddenly jerked the finger forwards and it clicked back into place. The noises turned to groans. I moved back in front of him and stared into his watering, bloodshot eyes, then removed the gag. I looked down at him and said, "You need to listen to me very carefully, I do not have the time to play around with this. I am going to ask you some more questions. What ever you answer we will write down and then act on the information tomorrow. If you have told the truth you will go to prison and that will be the end of it. If you lie, it will all go wrong and then I will come and get you and bring you back to this tree for special punishment. The little finger bend was only a sample of what I will do to you. I will have two pliers and a hammer with me. I will use the pliers to hold your fingers and I will break every finger joint on all your fingers of both hands, then I will do the same to your toes. If you are still alive, I will break your knee caps with the hammer and then crush your nose and break your jaw. You will feel the pain of hell gone mad. Finally, I will bring the dog and let him tear your throat out. Do you understand me?" He gave a small nod, his body was shaking. "Good, the Corporal will write it all down." Mick nodded to me. "What is the phone number you have to phone tomorrow?" Mick started writing. "What time do you have to phone? What if there is no answer? How will they answer the phone? Are there any passwords? What do you reply with? Will they give you instructions? Will you ask for help to go back? How do you end the conversation? What language will you be using on the phone call? I got all the answers and finally I asked if there was anything else I needed to know? There was not. The phone call would take place in Shangaan, an African language. We had what we needed to catch the SWA connection. It was quite dark by that time as I stared at my prisoner, trying to think if I had forgotten anything. After a few moments I said to Mick, "okay that's it, let's go." We untied him and took him back to Sea Point Station. "Remember if you lied to me, I will come back and feed you to the dog, you bastard." "Sir I promise it's all true." "We shall see," and I left to go back to my office, Mick went home for the night, to be back for our meeting in the morning. I called the special number for the minister and had him on the line a couple of minutes later. "Yes Lieutenant?"

"Good evening Sir, I have this very urgent information for you."

I gave the minister the SWA phone number and all the information I had got from my prisoner. "Thank you Lieutenant, I will now arrange it all, we will collect them tomorrow. I will speak to you again after it is done, good night." The line went dead. I was at my desk by seven the following morning and waiting. The morning dragged by, all I could do was drink coffee and wait. Finally, around two in the afternoon the phone on my desk rang and I scooped up the handset. "Lieutenant DeBeer, good day." A pleasant women's voice enquired if I was Lieutenant DeBeer. I assured her I was. She asked for my security I.D. Number, I recited it to her. "The Minister will be coming to see you at nine this evening, please wait for him." "Yes I will." "Thank you Lieutenant, goodbye." The line went dead and I hung up the phone. I was amazed, I had spoken with the minister the evening before and now he was coming to see me. I had thought he might send for me, not actually pay me a visit, so mentioning international scandal and the national secrets act had really moved things along. The guys all arrived and I filled them in with the latest events, they were elated. It was only just after two in the afternoon, so we all went for a late lunch. I let Mick tell them what had happened the previous afternoon. It looked like it was finally over. The guys all wanted to stay with me to see what the minister wanted. I could hardly send them away after all we had been through, so a very tense day dragged on, waiting for the visit from our Minister of Defense, not something that happened more than once in a blue moon. Near nine, I positioned myself at the main entrance and waited. A short while later, a long black limo drove into the car park and stopped near me. The driver stayed in the car while two very large security men exited from it, one from the front, the other from the rear, they both wore dark suits. They looked me over. "I'm Lieutenant DeBeer," I volunteered. The one closest to me held out his hand. "ID please?" I handed it over and he examined it, comparing it to a photo he had taken from a jacket pocket. My opinion of these guys went up, they weren't just gorillas in suits, talk about being careful. I wondered how many photos of me there were in various government offices. The inspection over, he handed the ID card back to me and only then did the minister get out of the limo. A big man, over six feet tall, dark suit, white shirt with a dark red patterned tie. His black hair, greying at the temples was combed back smoothly. Permanent frown lines etched his forehead above a longish face. He looked a little over weight. Dark eyes, a strong chin and a surprisingly open face smiling at me. "DeBeer, it's Rolf, is it not?" "Yes Sir, it is." I smiled back as we clasped hands. He turned to his men. "Park the car and come and find me at the Lieutenant's office." They didn't look happy, but the Minister had already turned away and was heading for the entrance. I hurried after him. "Okay Rolf, show me the way?" A few minutes later we walked into our small office area, where my men had gathered, waiting for instructions about our coming terrorist hunt. When I walked in with the minister, their eyes widened with excitement and they scrambled to their feet. "Relax men," this is just an informal meeting between the Lieutenant and myself." I stepped forwards, "Guys, go to the canteen and have coffee, I'll call when we are done." There was a general chorus of yes sirs and they were gone, looking very curious indeed. He pulled a chair out from the table and sat down with a sigh, then he motioned me towards a chair and I sat down facing him. The Minister of Defense looked at me quizzically, "so Lieutenant, we have taken the SWA connections into custody, it all went very smoothly. How you got the information is a wonderwork. I have no doubt you have saved many lives, well done my boy." I breathed a sigh of relief, my prisoner had not lied, I would not have to punish him, not that I would have, after all, it would have achieved nothing but he did not know that. "Now, you said national security was involved, tell me what is going on." I told him what we had been up to for the last eighteen months, omitting nothing. When he heard we were going to get the terrorist team that night, he asked if I was confident that we had identified the right men and did I think there was any chance they might get away. " None at all," I said, it is a case of surrender or die, we cannot afford to take any chances with these men, they are the ones that committed the atrocity on that farm in SWA a few days ago. He sat in silence for a while, then said, "You know, with all the evidence destroyed, he will deny all knowledge of the terrorist killing program and even if you and your men all testified to its existence, where is the proof?" I smiled at him as I reached under the table and produced the envelope I had stuck there. "Here is the evidence Sir, photos, documentation, names and notes. He will not be able to deny it and there are even the registration numbers of the vehicles used to transport the dogs." "Why did you prepare this dossier, what made you distrust his motives?" "He threatened my men and myself. He said if we screwed up his operation, he would hang us out to dry, demotion and transfer to the border as privates was mentioned and he said he would ensure I would do duty on the front line for the next two years. I had already pointed out things that could go wrong with an operation like that, but that was disregarded, resulting in the death of the headman of that village near Rundu, his wife and children, except it didn't actually happen, they are all alive and well." The Minister's eyebrows lifted and he stared at me. "Really, what actually happened?" "That afternoon when we found the tracks crossing into SWA, so near to Rundu, we were quite worried. At first we thought it was the beginning of a new phase in their plans, perhaps they were planning an attack on Rundu, or just having a look, spying on the place preparatory to an attack, we started following them, I had to stop them and quickly. Our tracker, Abe, stopped after only a few steps and went back to where he had started from and began examining the ground closely. He was visibly upset and chattering away to himself. He turned to Petrus the interpreter and there was much waving of arms, pointing at the ground and loud chattering as he explained why he had stopped. It turned out, that our clever terrorists walked behind their captives and brushed away their tracks as they went. The terrorists were the only ones leaving tracks for us to follow, but Abe was amazing, he could see the ground underneath had been swept clean and it made him suspicious, then he noticed a childs foot print at one side, that had not been swept and it confirmed what he was seeing.

I did not call up the dogs, but I was worried we were walking into an ambush, so I brought up my two special protection dogs, not from the killer squad, but a Doberman and a German Shepherd I had specially trained for just such an event and let them lead the way behind our tracker, if there was anyone waiting for us, I felt they would give us a warning in advance, we could not afford to wait. We found the village headman, his wife and three children, tied to trees, gagged and blindfolded. The terrorists were gone. The village headman and his wife were exhausted, the children were hysterical as you can imagine. I radioed in our jeeps' position and told them to come and get them, which they did. We gave the unfortunate headman and his family our rations and water and some chocolate for the kids, got them calmed down and off they went to Rundu where the doctor examined them and then we put them in a small disused hut at the far end of the camp. I had told them to keep the family there until I came to get them in a few days, so they are still there." I took a deep breath and sighed, then continued. "We carried on tracking the terrorists after the chopper left and I watched our tracker Abe and my special squad security dogs get blown to pieces when Abe triggered a land mine." The minister cluck, clucked sympathetically. "I don't know why I survived the blast, just plain luck I guess. The chopper took me back to Rundu as well and when I woke up, I saw the camp commander and explained that terrorists had kidnapped them, we had released them and they needed to be kept hidden until we caught the terrorist bastards, or their lives would be in danger. He agreed with me and is having them looked after. When we finish with the terrorists tomorrow, I will have the headman and his family released, so they can go home to their village. Once we had them settled at Rundu, I put through a call to the General to tell him what the terrs had tried to do. He misunderstood me, it was a bad line and he thought the villagers were dead. He went crazy, screaming and yelling that I had ruined his plans and he would have me severely punished for dereliction of duty, failing to follow orders and being responsible for the deaths of innocent people, but first, I had better go and catch the missing terrorists before they got the information out and created an international incident. If I failed, I would be arrested and jailed and he would deal with me when I was in prison. I realized I was in serious danger, so I just said I would certainly find the terrorists and stop the story from leaking out. In the meantime the terrorist group had made it into SWA and slaughtered everyone on a farm, including the animals, then they escaped into South Africa and made their way to the Cape Town area. I was not sure you had been given all the details about it yet, but I will make damn sure they are finished with by this time tomorrow. I contacted you because I believe the General is out of control and you most certainly will end up with an international incident if he is not stopped."

The Minister looked very thoughtful and said, "You are right, I need to stop this, the question is how?" He held up a hand, "just let me think for a minute." He gazed off into nowhere while he thought. His face brightened suddenly, "Thank you Lieutenant, I believe I have the answer, I will be back in Pretoria in the morning, call me at this number," he handed me a card, "tell me the terrorists have been dealt with and I will deal with our General." I didn't ask what he was going to do and he did not volunteer the information. "By the way Lieutenant, are there any more photos and documentation." It was my turn to look surprised, "No Sir, why, do we need some extra copies?" "No, no, not at all" and he rose and extended his hand. "Call me tomorrow Lieutenant." "I will Sir." His two large assistants were waiting at the door, ushered him to his limo and he was gone. I allowed myself a small smile, thinking of the other batch of photos, being kept by my attorney. The Minister had let me know, he knew I had another set, but left it at that, a clever man, he had impressed me and I found myself liking him a lot. I felt I could trust him, so I left it at that and began to prepare for my showdown with the terrorists.

The Minister gone, I went over to the canteen to get my guys and soon we were assembled around our table. They were all curious as hell about the Ministers visit. "Look, guys all I can tell you is, it was a visit about our future here in the army and it looks good. I will know in a few days and so will you. Now we need to plan the take down of our three missing terrorists. We know they are in that shack at the top of the drainage ditch, the shack with the one roof edge painted red. You all saw it from Vanguard Drive, on our left on the drive past, right on the corner of Langa Drive, almost under the massive electricity pylons. This is what we are going to do. The people living on the edge of Langa in those shacks, are mostly migrant workers who will do almost anything to earn some money. They have to be out of there by around three thirty in the morning to get to the collection points where the construction people pick up cheap labor. There are still people up and about until after midnight, so our time is two in the morning, when the place goes quiet for a while. From two thirty, they start getting up and getting ready to go to work. Just after two, my man will play the part of a drunk wandering around trying to get into that shack. After he comes out, if he walks straight past me, that would be the signal they are there, if there's a problem he will pull my arm and I will follow him away to a safe distance to find out what is wrong. I'm pretty certain they are there or we are in deep crap, remember these bastards are serious killers and if they're not there, we have a very serious problem on our hands. Three murdering bastards armed with AK47's running around loose, but let's forget that for the moment, it's not very likely." The guys agreed with me. "Okay, how do we take them down?" "By the way," said Henry, "Who is the guy who is going to look in the hut?" "Just a guy I know, who is helping me out, he speaks a few African languages and looks like a young Xhosa guy, his identity must remain secret or his life will be in danger. He will arrive in a separate car, then go and find out if our three guys are in the hut, after he confirms they are there, he vanishes, okay?" They all nodded.

"As soon as he is gone, Henry and Smitty and I could dive into the shack, one center, one left, one right and either they surrender immediately or get shot if they resist, we have no other alternative. We have silenced pistols, I don't want to start a riot in the camp, we need to ensure the safety of the other people in that area, but in thinking it through, that's no good at all. We would be silhouetted against the doorway as we went in and would get mown down, so thinking further I remembered that in poor, violence prone areas where gang fights are commonplace, when gun fire starts, nobody shows their faces, everyone hides. No one wants to get involved and take a chance on getting shot, so the noise will actually help us. This is what I propose. As soon as I get confirmation that our guys are there, I will toss a couple of stun grenades into the shack, that will knock them senseless, then we enter the shack safely, handcuff them hand and foot, deliver them to army headquarters and it's done. We will have three of us at the front and two at the back just in case they go through a wall or try to run for it before the grenades go off. If that happens, shoot to kill, is that understood?" Everyone nodded. "Have I missed out anything, let's all just think for five minutes, we can't afford any mistakes." A couple of minutes later I said, "Okay, times up, any comments or suggestions." Henry looked at me. "That shack is only nine or ten foot square, don't you think two stun grenades will be a bit of an over kill, you could end up hurting other people in the vicinity." "Good point, so one grenade it is." "Mick spoke up. "The door ways into those shacks is too narrow. To have three men there is a waste, I think we should rather have three men positioned along the rim of the ditch and only two at the door way." "Good point, one near the pylons and the other two further off to the left, outside the line of fire if we have to shoot them, but if they come out through the back wall, they will turn left, back into the camp, because right side are the pylons and barbed wire around the base. They would run straight into you guys on the left and I repeat, shoot to kill, we cannot let them get away. Anything else?" There were no other comments or questions, so we went through the operation a few times to make sure everyone was on the same page. Just before I ended the meeting, I repeated we would be using an old panel van which we could put the three bodies in when we finished and two unmarked cars for the rest of us. Everyone would have walkie talkies with ear pieces, so we could all stay in touch. I stood up. "Okay, we are all ready to go.

Go and check the equipment, we don't want any breakdowns tonight and check your rifles as well, combat gear everyone, this is an army security operation and will be conducted as such." There were serious nods and yes sirs all round. "Dismissed guys, go get lunch, we will assemble here at ten tonight, ready to go."

I went back to my office bedroom, sat down on my bed and thought it all through again. Tony, was at first was very reluctant to help me when I called him. "Jeez Rolf, you know my history, how can you ask me to help the police?" "You will be saving lives. These men have killed plenty of black men, women and children as well as whites, if they get away they will kill a lot more. Your people don't need these men around to kill them, you've got to help me, I'm asking you?" I understood his being torn between what he saw as his duty to his own people and his loyalty to me, but I really needed his help. Finally he agreed to meet me on the corner near the shacks at two am. He would arrive in another car and vanish as soon as he had confirmed the right three guys were in the shack. I was very relieved he had agreed, I did not want to go in blind. I dozed off and woke up at five, I was hungry, time for dinner. I made my way over to the canteen and had a decent meal. I thought about Rikka while I ate. I wondered how she was doing back in Pretoria. After tonight was over and I knew what my future looked like, I would contact her and see where that went. I blinked and put her out of my mind, first things first. Dinner over, I went back to my room and started getting ready. I laid out my combat gear, then checked everything.

I stripped my pistol down, cleaned it carefully, then re-assembled it and loaded it. Nine millimeter parabellum FN Browning automatic with a fourteen round magazine and one up the spout.

A muzzle velocity of 1750 ft. lbs per second per second, guaranteed to knock down any assailant. Basically, it meant that a bullet weighing around a quarter of an ounce, would leave the barrel and travel 1750 feet in that first second as it accelerated, providing it did not hit something. In addition, the bullets' weight, multiplied by the muzzle velocity, gave the bullet an impact weight of about 440 lbs as it left the barrel, more than enough to flatten a close range terrorist. I said a silent prayer that it would all go well and we could get back to normal army life, not that being a security cop could be considered normal by any ones' standards. The guys were also all busy with their equipment in the dorm, almost time to go. Nine pm and we were ready. I handed out the walkie talkies and supervised the installation of new batteries. I could almost hear the Sergeant Major at base camp saying, "DeBeer, leave nothing to chance, that way you won't have regrets later on." I couldn't control the crap that happened in the bush, but this I could and we would take no chances. I was not about to lose any more men, two was enough. We tested the radios and ear phones, everything was working well. I personally checked all their rifles and handed out the ammunition I had drawn earlier that day. Five clips each with thirty rounds per clip, the rifles to be set on auto, which was three rounds per trigger pull. That was the setting for the new R4 assault rifles. I made them turn the radios off, we didn't need any flat batteries. We had decided to leave at ten and get there before eleven, park against the curb a hundred yards up the road and watch the shack through binoculars, just in case our beauties decided to leave early. I told the guys to all go to the bathroom, there were not going to be any toilet hold ups on this trip. They laughed, they said I reminded them of their mothers, but they all went anyway, myself included and then we were on our way. The old truck and cars attracted no attention parked against the curb on Vanguard Drive. Small convoys like this were commonplace, going back and forth to the Transkei, taking people to a visit their families, delivering goods and bringing back more people and parcels. It was around eleven pm and apart from light traffic down the road, all was quiet. The weather was good, the moon was up, so visibility was good too. I could see the shack with the red edge facing us, but all was still. I had a good look at the shack through the binoculars. I thought I could see a dim light showing through at a join in the wall at the near corner, but I wasn't sure. "Here, have a look at the shack, nearest corner to us, it that a light showing through?" I handed the binocs to Henry, sitting next to me. He had a good look. "I'm not sure, it sure looks like it, but it could be a trick of the moonlight." "Okay, we'll just have to wait, we've got three hours, so settle down. I'll take the first watch, you guys can doze if you want, when I get tired, Henry can take over." We all settled down and our wait began. I had called the station commander at Elsies River police station earlier that afternoon and told him we would be carrying out a top level raid in the Langa extension squatter camp that night. After he had checked on my credentials, quite rightly, he called me back and offered assistance. I explained that seeing as the guys did not officially exist, it fell under the heading of a security operation and I could not involve him at all, those were my instructions from Pretoria. I informed him we would be in and old truck and two cars and gave him descriptions and numbers of the two cars and truck. I told him they would be parked near the corner of Vanguard and Langa Drives from around eleven pm that night and please to let the police on duty know that we were to be left alone. He said he would make sure we were not disturbed and not to cause a riot in Langa, get in and out quietly. Just in case, he said he was going to put the riot squad on standby from midnight to three am. I thanked him and assured him I would try not to create a situation for him and that was that. In the half hour we had been there two patrol cars had passed by, but had not even slowed down, so the Commander had kept his word. I had a look at the shack every so often, it all looked very quiet. The hours dragged by, I handed the watch and binoculars over to Henry about twelve thirty, leaned back and closed my eyes. That didn't work, I was too stressed, so I just rested my head against the seat back and stared out the window. The traffic had eased off a lot and there were almost no pedestrians, just the odd guy hoofing it down the road towards Langa. Apart from a glance or two at the cars, the passers by ignored us. There were patrol cars coming and going at irregular intervals, some were regular police patrols, others were flying squad and all of them in that area were based at the Elsies River Police Station. I allowed myself a private smile. The station commander had increased patrols in the area, he was really worried about a possible riot. I was certain it wouldn't happen. If there was gunfire, everyone in the area would snuggle down as low as possible and stay quiet, no one wanted to get shot by some lunatic settling a score or carrying out a robbery. No, there would be no riot. I dozed off. I woke around one thirty. The road was very quiet, just the odd car now and then. "Anything happening," I asked Henry. "No change, all quiet." "Good, we move at two, not long to go. Where's that coffee flask?" I had a small cup of coffee, it went down well. "Check the guys in the truck, will you?" The walkie talkie chirped as they replied. "Get ready, we move in ten minutes." We all checked our radios and we were ready to go. I started the car and drove slowly and quietly down the road, crossed the intersection and parked against the curb about fifty feet past the shack, the truck pulled in behind me. "Lock the truck when you go," I said quietly into the radio, then we were all out and crossing the drainage ditch, there was a horrible stench. People had been using the ditch as a toilet for a long time. We went quickly up the small slope, I headed for the path behind the shacks, Henry followed me. The other three spread out on the road side of the shacks, one to the left at the base of the pylons, the other two over to the right, about fifty feet away, out of the line of fire. Once on the path at the rear, I glanced at my watch, two am exactly. As if on cue, I heard Tony coming my way, singing drunkenly as he staggered along. He stumbled about, banging into the sides of the shacks as he came closer. No one came out to shout at him, I was right about that. He appeared around the corner of a shack about thirty feet away, with the moon up, the path was quite brightly lit up. He continued to sing in Xhosa while he fumbled around at the doorway of the terrorists shack, then almost fell inside. I said a silent prayer for his safety, I must have been mad to risk his life like that, what the hell was I thinking and that he had agreed to do it for me, showed a bond as strong as brothers, that I had not realized was there. I had taken it for granted, I must have been mad and now it was too late to stop it. I heard his drunken voice raised in surprise to find himself in the wrong shack and then what were obviously apologies and he stumbled back out onto the path muttering and mumbling to himself, what a performance. He headed towards me and passed by without a word or a glance at me, the signal that they were the right guys. He stunk of cheap booze, I wrinkled my nose up as he passed by and then it all went to hell.

"Rolf, Rolf." My ear piece crackled to life. "Jesus, the bastards are coming out of a hole into the ditch," a voice shouted. "Lay down your weapons and hands up." Then suddenly, gunfire, the crack, crack noise of AK's, answered by the blam, blam sound of R4's, then more R4 fire, then silence. My ear piece roared to life with a shouted warning. "Two down, one runner your way." A dark figure sprinted past behind me, a couple of shacks further along and disappeared along the path heading into the depths of the squatter camp. I sprinted after him, pulling my pistol out of its holster as I did so and clicking off the safety catch. I snapped at Henry as I ran, "go left and up, we'll try to corner him further down. The months of hard training paid off as I sprinted after him catching up fast, he was running for his life, but out of shape and weak from bad food, he couldn't out run me. The moonlight was good, I could see him clearly. He turned right and disappeared behind a shack, I sprinted round the corner and went flying, I had slipped on a piece of plastic bag lying on the ground. I crashed into the ground, dropping my pistol, but automatically rolled to minimize the shock. As I started to my feet, the muzzle of an AK47 was jammed against my chest, my terrorist had come back to get me. I froze. He stared at me from behind the rifle. "Now you die white man," but he never got to pull the trigger, suddenly he was flying sideways away from me, as a steel bar smashed viciously against the side of his head. I have no doubt he was dead before he hit the ground. I jumped to my feet in shock, turning to see which of the guys had saved me and there was Tony, he had not left, he had stayed to see what I was doing, as I had stayed to watch over him years before. I bent over the man on the ground and checked his throat for a pulse, he was dead, the side of his head caved in. I turned to Tony and was stunned to see he was crying, big tears rolling down his cheeks. "I have killed a black brother to save my white brother, in this white country which says I count for nothing, how could this happen?" he whispered harshly. "You are my brother, that's why, now get the hell out of here before the others arrive." I pushed him and he turned and disappeared among the shacks. I picked up the steel bar, it was an old rusted piece of building rod, the one end very bloody. Henry came rushing around the corner and stopped when he saw me and the body on the ground. "Are you okay?" "Yes, I'm fine, help me carry this guy back to the truck." All was said in harsh whispers, standing there in the middle of a black squatter camp. "Hold on a moment, I dropped my pistol." I pulled a small pencil flashlight from my pocket and found the automatic a few feet away. I put the safety back on, tapped it against my leg to shake off some sand and holstered it. "Ok, I'm ready, let's go." I laid the iron bar and his rifle on his chest, then we picked him up by the arms and legs and made our way back to the truck. The other two were already in the truck and we slid our body in next to the others. "Have you searched the shack top to bottom?" "Yes Rolf, also under the plastic sheets on the floor and in that tunnel, it's all clear." "Good, now let's get the hell out of here." Everyone seemed strangely unmoved by the dead men, only a few moments earlier, living and breathing, now nothing. I wondered if anyone was worrying about them, where they were, if they were okay? I stared down at them. We drove quietly away, down to the National Road, turned off at the Brooklyn bridge and were back at Ysterplaat about twenty minutes later.

The roads were all virtually deserted at that time of the morning, I didn't see more than two or three cars on the road all the way back. We left the cars and truck with the bodies and their belongings parked outside our barracks, keys in the ignition and went inside. "Organize some coffee while I call this in," I asked, then we'll have a debriefing session." I dialed the special phone number and it was answered after two rings. "Yes," a voice said. I gave the code number and the voice said "Go ahead." I said, "They are finished, I have them here in the truck." "We will collect," said the voice and the line went dead. I next dialed the number the Minister had given me. A woman's voice answered the phone, totally expressionless. "Yes." "Good morning, it's Lieutenant DeBeer, the Minister is expecting my call." "Ah, yes Lieutenant, ID please?" I recited my ID to her. "Hold a moment."

Her voice had warmed up marginally. "Yes Lieutenant," the Minister was on the line, sounding remarkably wide awake, I wondered when he ever slept?

"Good morning sir, it's done, they are dead. They would not surrender and we had to shoot them. "My boy, I am glad this is over. "Thank you Sir." "Lieutenant, I will come down to Cape Town after I finish here tomorrow, I will make arrangements to see you when I get there, the office will notify you a little later." "Yes Sir, I will be here." "Excellent, see you tomorrow" and the phone clicked off. I put my phone down and went out into the dorm. The guys were all sitting around the table, having coffee, talking quietly amongst themselves. They looked up as I sat down at the table. "Well, we should know sometime tomorrow what's happening to our squad, in the meantime I need your reports on last night, but first I need some coffee. "The coffee was ready and I sat down at the table. The guys were in high spirits, as was I. We had got the terror cell, they would not be doing any more killing and we were all safe, no one got hurt. "Listen guys, before you write up your reports, I would like to know what happened when I went around to the front of the shack." "Piet said, "well, we were spread out along the road side of the shacks, down towards the bottom of the ditch, just as we planned. With the moon out, it was quite light, we heard the drunk singing, then some shouting, then it went quiet. We were waiting for the grenade to go off when the men started coming out of a hole in the side of the ditch. I shouted a warning and they stood up and started shooting, so we fired back. I thought we had got all three, then one stood up and ran like hell. I warned you and that's all we know." It was my turn to tell my men what happened. "I ran after him and I sent Henry around to the left to cut him off if he turned that way. As I ran round a corner, I slipped on a piece of plastic bag and fell over. I rolled as I hit the ground and found my hand on a piece of steel pipe. The son of a bitch came back to get me. He leaned over and told me, now I was going to die, that's when I hit him with the pipe, he dropped his rifle and staggered back, I was on my feet and I hit him again this time using both hands. He fell down and lay there, that's when Henry arrived. We checked him, he was dead.

I found my pistol a little way away, then we carried him back to the truck. If I hadn't fallen over and landed with my hand on that steel pipe, I would now be dead. Perhaps there is someone up there looking after us?"

"We can all be thankful for a successful operation and we all got back safely." The guys all nodded and smiled agreement.

We wrote our reports out, I collected them and headed for bed, it was already past four in the morning. "We can meet here at two in the afternoon, get some sleep guys, well done."

I woke up around noon and checked the yard. The car and truck were gone, I breathed a sigh of relief and was washed, shaved and dressed an hour later. I badly wanted to go and see Tony, but I could not go out yet, I had to first wait for the Ministers'

call, also, I was ravenously hungry after the past days of stress, so I went for lunch then back to my office to wait. The guys were all up and about, also waiting to hear what was going to happen to them, now that we were off the hook. The phone rang just after two, I snatched it up, my squad crammed themselves into my small office, I could hardly throw them out under the circumstances. "Good afternoon, Lieutenant DeBeer speaking." It was the Minister. "Good day Lieutenant, there has been a small change of plans. I have good news for you. Our friend has gone on early retirement, effective immediately, so that relieves the stress you have all been under, there will be no reprisals for doing your duty, rather effectively I would say. Anyway, your remaining team members will stay on at Ysterplaat and carry on training security dogs, you on the other hand, I want you to come to Pretoria and go back to school at the Police College where you can complete your studies, which will enable you as a professional police detective. You will leave college with the rank of Captain. You have proved yourself as a resourceful detective and leader of men out in the field under extremely stressful conditions. We need men such as yourself and additionally you will be able to earn an excellent living once you are qualified. I don't want you to say anything now, I need to see you personally and discuss the future with you, so stay where you are for the moment. I will be in Cape Town in two days time, I will call you and we can meet then, okay?" "Yes Sir." "Good, I am expecting big things from you Lieutenant, well done." "Thank you Sir," the line went dead.

CHAPTER THIRTEEN

"**YOU'RE ALL GOING TO STAY** here and run this training center, well done guys, the General has gone." They all burst out in shouts of happiness, shaking hands and slapping each other on the back.

After they calmed down, I continued. "Henry, as the senior man here, you are now in charge, you will report to the base commander and get things going smoothly again. It appears I am going to be transferred, I will know in a couple of days, in the meantime I'll be coming and going until I find out what's happening to me, so that's it. We all shook hands and that was that, no fanfare or party, life moved on." I couldn't tell them anything else, so they left my office and gathered round our table to start planning the restart of the training center. I headed for the city, I needed to see Tony. At that time of the afternoon, in heavy traffic, it took me around thirty minutes to get to the city and another thirty minutes of circling before I found parking. I fed the meter, then crossed the square to the office building, waited impatiently for the elevator and was soon at my office door. It was not locked and I went in. Tony was sitting in an armchair facing me. He rose to his feet and we shook hands in silence. "What the hell," I exclaimed and grabbed him in a bear hug, he did not resist. "Come on Tony, please sit, we need to talk." "Yes, we do." He sounded sad, his voice a monotone. I spoke earnestly to him. "I cannot change what happened last night, if not for you, I would be dead, so I'm really glad you chose me over him. In any other place in the world it would just have been one man against another. Here, with our unique situation, it is black against white, white against black or brown. Black against black in a political situation here in our country, I know this is a real gut wrench for you, but I would have done the same for you if things were reversed, because for us I know, the man has become more important than his color. So, now I owe you my life and I have to repay you with a life." He had been looking at the floor, now his head jerked upright and he snapped at me. "My G-d, you're not thinking of killing yourself are you, that's just crazy." "No I'm not, calm down and listen. I have one terrorist still locked up, the one I arrested last week, I am going to give you his life in exchange for mine, I am going to let him go free."

His eyes opened wide in surprise. "You can do that?" "In this case yes I can." "But how?" "All I can tell you, is that the circumstances of his arrest and detention are so unique, it makes it possible for me to release him, he will be a free man. Will you accept his life in exchange for mine?" There was no hesitation. "Yes, for you I will." "Okay, when I leave here, I will go and get him and we can get on with our lives. I realize it's not a perfect solution, my hope is we can still be friends, we have a long and good history together." He smiled at last. "We have been through the mill, haven't we? You're a good man, I'm proud to have you as my friend." We shook hands and I left to collect my prisoner.

Back at Sea Point Station, I showed my authorization to collect the prisoner in cell eight, signed the register, then drove into the yard once more. In the cell, I handcuffed his hands behind him and his ankles as well, then added a chain from the handcuffs to the ankle chain, short enough to prevent him from standing up straight. I led the way to the old Valiant and pulled the front door open, he hobbled along behind me. "Get in." He moved backwards into the doorway and when he felt the seat at the back of his knees, sat down and then wriggled himself into the car, ending up sitting sideways, facing the doorway. I closed the door and walked around to the drivers side. "You're going to let him ride in front?" the duty sergeant asked. "Sure, the way he's chained up he's harmless and I can keep an eye on him." He nodded and waved to the gate security to open up. I drove through and headed for the road up the west coast. We drove in silence, my prisoner remained slumped sideways against the seat, facing away from me. About an hour out of the city, we were getting close to Langebaan, a small village with a fish factory, small harbor, fishermens' cottages and lots of holiday homes. He twisted to turn towards me a little. "Where are you taking me?" He sounded nervous and I couldn't blame him, after all, our last outing together into the forest, had scared the crap out of him, now he thought I was going to kill him for real.

"Relax, we are nearly there and I have good news for you, I am letting you go free, you can go home." "This is a trick, a white mans' game, you are going to kill me, I know it." His voice rose in panic, I had to shout at him to get silence. "Shut up you fool, no one is going to hurt you. Do you think I would drive you all this way if I wanted to kill you, just think damn it." "Why, why are you doing this?" "Your friends are gone, you are of no further use to me, so killing you is not necessary. What you need to remember is, that I have your photo, I have your fingerprints, I know what village you came from, I know who your family is, so for you, this war is over. When you get home you will not go back to your terrorist friends or I will let it be known that you were the one that gave us information about them and they will torture you and you will die badly. My advice is to stay in your village and go no where until the war is over, however long that may take. If you choose to go back to your Zambian masters and if they take you back again, when I find out and I will find out, we will hunt you down and there will be no escape, I will feed you to your friends, our devil dogs. Do you understand me?" He shuddered but said nothing. We drove on in silence and a few minutes later I saw the Langebaan turnoff coming up on my left.

I passed it and pulled into a parking area a little way further along. I parked at the back of the area and turned off the car.

"Stretch your legs towards me so I can unlock the chain." He did so and with his legs free, I unlocked the handcuffs as well. I kept my pistol on my lap, just in case he decided to get nasty, but he remained passive. "Climb over into the back, your bag and clothes are there. You can get changed, then you can go. I have some money for you, so you can get on a bus to Windhoek and go home. Your ID card from the army camp is in the bag as well, so it will get you through to Windhoek." He slithered over into the back of the car, unzipped the kit bag and started changing into the army overalls he had been wearing, before he left the Caprivi. We had found them buried in Caprivi only a few days before. He suddenly started talking to me. "You know, white man, you are not really giving me a choice by letting me go. If I go back to the army base, they will fire me and the staff will know I am back. They will talk and Zambia will find out. They will send men to kill me. Same thing if I go back to my village. Who will protect me?" "You should have thought of that before you became a terrorist. If I was you, I would go to Angola, join up with UNITA, it will give you a chance and who knows, it may all be over soon and you could go home." He didn't answer me, just finished changing in silence. "Leave the prison clothes on the seat, you can take your bag and belongings with you." I got out of the car, putting the car keys in my pocket. My pistol was back in it's holster. I went around to the other side of the car and waited for him as he got out. There was a path from the back of the car park heading towards the Langebaan road. I pointed at the path. "You can walk into Langebaan and try to get a ride heading towards SWA or you can stand by the side of the Main Road and try to thumb a ride from here. There is two hundred Rand in your bags' side pocket, that's enough to get you through to Windhoek. He turned around and looked at the path, then knelt down and fiddled with his shoe laces, at least that's what I thought he was doing. I moved a pace to my right to see and that's when he flicked a handful of gravel back at me, but having moved to the side, it mostly missed me. He spun around and came for me. I noted the glint from his left hand, held low and assumed he had a knife. My years of training clicked in. If you were attacked with a knife in this manner, you had to wait until your attacker was totally committed to his lunge, too late to change direction and then you countered at that moment, that small window of opportunity was your chance to turn the tables. In this instance, at the last split second, I did a small shuffle to my right and brought my left hand down towards his wrist in a semi circular movement, at the same time, I slid my right hand across his chest and up under his chin across his throat until my forearm was hit by his throat as he continued to move forward. As that happened, the edge of my left hand had slammed down on his left wrist and my fingers curled around his wrist, pulling him in the direction of his lunge, but seeing as his throat had slammed against my forearm, his forward movement had come to a dead stop. My right arm continued to move him backwards while my left hand pulled him forwards. The force twisted his head backwards and to the side from the pressure of my right arm and there was a snapping sound as his neck gave way. It sounded like a piece of bamboo breaking in half. His body went limp, he was dead. The entire attack and retaliation had lasted less than a second. I dropped him and he slumped to the ground.

Strange thing, I hadn't realized he was left handed. I bent over and checked for a pulse in his throat, then I checked his wrist. There was nothing, he was dead. The parking area and road were deserted at that late afternoon hour, so I hurriedly opened the cars trunk and slid and rolled the body inside, then his bag. The knife turned out to be one of those short blades that was part of a belt buckle, but honed to razor blade sharpness. The blade part went into a small metal sheath inside the belt, the small handle was part of the buckle. I pushed it back into the belt and clipped the buckle together. If he had succeeded in getting me with that, it would have sliced me open like a hot knife through butter. I took back my money, banged the trunk lid closed and glanced around the deserted car park, got into the car and drove slowly away, heading back towards the city. I felt numb, my motions were almost robot like and it was some time before I calmed down. I had certainly misjudged the man, I had believed him when he said he had not taken part in the torture of the farmer and his family, now I was not so sure. I had kept my word to Tony, I had let him go, he had elected to rather try and kill me, now he was dead. Could I have used some other method to subdue him? Perhaps, but in that kind of situation you do not have time to weigh alternatives, you just react. Your subconscious mind takes over and you carry out an action appropriate to what is happening at that time, afterwards, you could dissect it and in hindsight consider other options, but it was too late, he was gone.

Was I a murderer? I didn't feel like a murderer, I really felt relieved, but at the back of my mind would always remain that little niggling doubt, had I done the right thing? He wouldn't be hurting any more women and children, that was certain and with that thought in mind, I actually felt a lot better. As I drove on towards Cape Town, I couldn't help thinking about the past months since I was called up for army duty. I had set up and executed a dog training program, then put it into practice, with the sole purpose of killing terrorists out in the bush at night. In spite of my misgivings, we had killed, no, torn apart about thirty of them, I had lost track. Perhaps more than one had got away, who could tell? I had lost three of my team, one dead, the other insane, as good as dead, and one blown to pieces. The doctors did not hold out much hope of a recovery for Joe. Then there were the three recently deceased at the squatter camp and lastly the one I had just killed. That made about thirty four. That was my crowning achievement over the past two years, thirty four lives snuffed out and I felt somehow responsible for the lives of all the dogs that were now also dead. I would have to live with it for the rest of my days. Perhaps it would drive me as wacky as the rest of them. I would see the Minister tomorrow and perhaps get a new start, I could certainly do with one. A while later I was back at my office, it was only six in the afternoon, the dorm was deserted, my team was probably out celebrating. I dialed my special phone number, gave my code number and a voice asked what I needed. " I have the last one with me, it is in the car outside my office." "We will collect, leave the keys under the drivers seat," the voice said. "Yes," I answered, "I will." As usual, the line went dead without a goodbye. I showered, changed and went for supper. None of the guys were there, so I ate alone, a rather small meal, my appetite had gone again. Back at my office, I got ready for bed, I needed to be ready to leave at six the next morning. I turned off my lights and sat in the dark, looking out of the window, just in case the car was collected early, I was curious to see who the collector was. Around eight, I was struggling to keep my eyes open when an army car pulled up outside. I had left my car over to one side, away from the lights. A man got out of the passenger side and walked over to my car. As he turned sideways, I recognized him, he was one of the staff at the base's car pool, so that was his cover, he was actually army security. He opened the car door, retrieved the keys under the seat, went around to the rear and opened the trunk. He glanced briefly inside, shut the trunk, then got in and drove away and just like that it was over. I fell into bed and was asleep as my head hit the pillow, it had been one hell of a day. I was woken at six by the high pitched beep of my alarm and by seven I was ready for breakfast. Afterwards, I called Tony. He was a lot more cheerful. "So, did you let him go?" "Yes, I did, at Langebaan." "Good, so what now?" "I think we should visit Auntie." "What makes you ask that now?" "Well I was thinking about her last night and I just felt she would like to see us?" I heard the hiss of a hastily drawn in breath. "That's very weird," he said. "What is?" "I got a message from Auntie last night. She said she wants to see me and definitely to bring you with. Can you get off duty this afternoon?" "Yes." "Okay, I'll pick you up at your main gate at twelve. I'll wear my white coat and you climb into the back." "Okay, will do, see you later." I never did tell Tony what happened to the last terrorist, what was the point? It would just have upset him and he probably would have blamed himself. The simple truth was, life is full of choices and the terrorist made his. It could just as easily have been me that died and disappeared.

I was ready and waiting near reception at twelve. Tony pulled up and I climbed in. We stopped at a supermarket a few blocks away and I went in to buy a few things for Auntie. I decided basics were best, things like sugar, salt, tea, powdered milk, coffee, jam, honey and soap. I had quite a load when we got back on the road. Tony had taken off the coat and we drove in silence for a while. "Are you nervous," he asked at last." "Not yet, perhaps when we get there?" We drove on in silence as the miles slid past. "What made you want to see Auntie?" he asked at last. "I think, now that the whole mess is finished, I need to know if we have got rid of our devils. On the one hand I feel stupid, a white man in our modern world, asking a "Sangoma" of the primitive world to explain what has happened to our lives. I worked out what Auntie tried to tell me and she was correct, I just don't understand how she knew or could see the future, but she did, so I want to know what else she can tell me? I have another year of army to go, maybe she can give me a little peace of mind, or if not, forewarned is forearmed." "What did she mean last time we saw her?" Tony asked. "Well, the black and white devils referred to me and the white army, the black devils referred to the terrorists and Auntie saw both groups as evil. I think the main devil she referred to was my boss, the General and she also saw the whole incident at the squatter camp as it really happened and tried to warn me. I thought she was just being nice, when she said we would need each other and to look after each other, but she already knew about your gang and my chase through the camp before they happened, so now I have to trust that the information she gives out is accurate, but she scares the crap out of me." Tony nodded slowly as he absorbed the information.We did the rest of the drive in silence and got to the farm a short time later. The small parking area was unchanged and Tony parked in the same spot. We carried the goods we had bought up to the cottage and knocked on the open door. The same high pitched voice called come in and in we went. Auntie was dressed the same way as previously, only the colors were different. Outside, only the chirping of birds could be heard, all else was quiet. This time, there were two chairs facing a single chair, set up in front of the fireplace, where a small fire was burning. "Put down your parcels and come and sit with me," Auntie instructed us, so we did and she sat herself in front of us. "Tony, how have you been and how is my sister?" she asked. "All is well with us Auntie, thank you." She turned in my direction. "So, white man, how have you been?" "Well thank you, no complaints." It was unsettling to be referred to as "white man" and I was reminded of the day I met Auntie and she had started screaming at me, which made me even more uneasy. "Tony, give me your hands," she said. He reached forward and placed his hands on hers. She remained still and silent for a moment, then spoke. "Where there is no intent, there can be no guilt, defense of a loved one is not a crime, more of an obligation. To do nothing when honor and concern dictate otherwise, would be the crime and you would then have to live with your conscience. Live in peace, your ghosts have gone." This was all said in a harsh whisper, I could see Tony's hands shaking, my turn next. She released Tony's hands and he sat back, obviously stunned by what he had just heard. "White man, sit forward, I wish to look at your face." I found that a bit strange, seeing as she was blind, but I leaned forward into her waiting hands and was shocked, her finger tips felt like ice, I almost jerked away. When I first met her, her touch had been pleasantly warm. After running her hands over my face and jaw, she sat back with a deep sigh, almost a groan, her hands dropped limply into her lap and all was silent for quite a while. She suddenly sat forwards, wrapping her arms around herself, like she was hugging herself. She gave another high pitched groan and began to rock her back and forth, then started to speak in a high pitched voice, a total contrast to the harsh whisper she had used speaking to Tony. "You carry the blood of many on your hands, white man, all victims of the violence you helped create, so much blood, yet none seek revenge, they believe the devil will take care of their suffering and you. What you do not know, you cannot fear, you did not see and you did not hear, now time grows short, you cannot wait, if you wish indeed to resolve that state. The choices made dictated the outcomes," her voice got louder, "but your devil walks with you, she will not easily let you walk away, your blood for theirs. You could not avoid your duty, a day of reckoning must come and you will once again need a war dog, keep him close, he may be your only hope." Her voice tailed off as she shook and shuddered, then all was quiet. We sat motionless, frozen to our seats. It was like I was in a thick pea soup fog that I couldn't move through. She groaned again, her hands clenching and I heard her mutter, "the hatred, the hatred, so many dead," then she was silent, we remained motionless, waiting. After a couple of minutes she stirred and sat up straighter, when she spoke, her voice sounded soft and weak. "You must go now, I am tired, thank you for the gifts." She gestured gently in the direction of the door. Tony suddenly spoke to Auntie, it must have taken real nerve, knowing how scared he was of her. "Auntie, please, what must we do?" "You can do nothing, it is this white mans' problem, only he can solve it, I see the problem, not always the solution, now go." She again gestured towards the door and thanking her for her time and wishing her well, we left on unsteady legs, just as before. In the car, heading for Cape Town, Tony spoke. "Jeez Rolf, what the hell went on up on the border, how many men have you actually killed?" "I didn't personally kill anyone up there, there's a war going on and it's kill or be killed. It's all done by the army as a whole, they cross the border to kill us, we try to stop them and either they die or we die. I took responsibility for my unit, as the officer in charge. It wasn't fun, I can tell you, but I can't discuss any of it with you, its all privileged information. Now I have to work out who wants to hurt me, I will need to make some calls when I get back to my office. At least you're okay, that's a relief." We drove on in silence for a while. "What war dogs was Auntie talking about?" Tony asked. "I'm not sure, I've had contact with lots of patrol dog and police dog units and on the border as well, I'm not sure which ones she was referring to, probably dogs I have personally trained. I will need to think about it." We drove on in silence.

In the meantime, I was pretty sure Auntie was referring to Zee and Jet, I would have to get myself a dog at some point, but was the General still out to get me, was he the Devil she referred to? It seemed likely, after all, I had brought his little empire crashing down, old "Pig Iron" would want revenge? He had men under cover all over the country, did they still follow his instructions? Would he send a couple of them to get me? Keeping the dogs close at hand started to make sense, personal protection was indeed what I needed. When I got back to base, I would find an excuse to talk to the guys at the motor pool and see what their attitude was like, perhaps I would learn something?

We were getting close to the air base and I slid over into the back seat, Tony pulled the white coat on that's how we arrived back, driver and passenger. I showed my ID to the guard and was waved through. As I got out I said to Tony, "Thanks much, my pal. I'll call you and let you know how it's all going." He replied, "You take it easy, you hear, don't do anything stupid, I know you. If you need me, call me." I nodded and Tony drove away.

What the heck, I thought, no time like the present and I made my way over to the garage and motor pool. The two men I recognized were on duty. Close up, the one who looked in the trunk of my car when he took the terrorist's body away, was a large man, overweight, with pock marked cheeks. Puberty had not been kind to him. He greeted me with a grin. "Yes Sir, can I help you?" I just came to thank you guys for your help over the past few weeks, much appreciated." He smiled again, "we were just carrying out instructions you know. Actually, we should thank you, we heard you got rid of old "Pig Iron" all on your own." I was really surprised, I had no idea the news had spread that fast. I tried to keep my face neutral. "It was not such a big deal, I was just lucky" He gave me a big grin. "You wouldn't know it, but he stuck Arnie and me" he waved a hand in the general direction of his partner at the other end of the garage, "in this place as a punishment, three years ago, for some minor problem that we could not fix for him. I was a Lieutenant like you, Arnie was my Sergeant and just like that, rank gone and undercover here in the garage doing odd jobs for him like the other night, instead of police work like we studied and trained for. Now, thanks to you we are going back to the security offices in Pretoria at last and getting our ranks back as well. We really owe you." " No you don't, I was also following instructions you know." He moved a little closer to me and spoke very quietly.

"Here's a bit of information I think you need. The blonde girlie from office reception, was put there to keep an eye on you, she's his daughter and a real snake. She comes across as sweet and nice, but if you cross her up, she turns into the bitch from hell. She was going out with a guy, Muller, based at the Potch army base, a Captain no less and he dumped her, that was about four months ago. Only a month later his rank was reduced to Sergeant and he was sent to the border by daddy. The poor bastard is dead, he didn't last a month. The guys in Pretoria call her "The Devil's daughter." I was so shocked by the news, I just stood there, my mouth opening and closing, but no words emerged. "Sorry Lieutenant, I see you're shocked, but you needed to know and as I said, we owe you big time." I coughed and cleared my throat. " Thanks for that, I really had no idea, geez, you really knocked me out of the park with that one, but I'm grateful man, good luck when you get back home, maybe I'll see you up there sometime." "That would be good, anytime Lieut." I turned and left, Arnie waved from the other side of the garage, I waved back.

With the last member of the terrorist cell dead and gone, I wanted to see what had happened to the man we had arrested for hiding him, "Arthur Phillips." He was being held in a small three floor building, one block up from Darling Street, near the "Castle." It occurred to me, for no particular reason that it was a sad name for a street near the prison and courts of justice. I parked my car in yellow lines, one of the perks of having a police car, put my "On Police Business" card on the dash and walked the few yards to the front door. I pressed the large button marked "door bell" and a small panel in the heavy looking door opened. I was examined by one brown eye and a voice said. "Can I help you?" I held my warrant card up for inspection and said, "I'm here to see Lieutenant Mostert." The door opened and I went in. The door swung closed behind me and I was in a small reception area. One brown desk with the large man in a dark suit, now seated behind it, on duty. I assumed he was the owner of the eye that had recently peered at me through the door peephole. Facing him was a row of six brown chairs with padded seats. On the left was a staircase going up and also down to the basement. "Have a seat Sir, I'll see if the Lieutenant is available. I sat down while he dialed a number. There was a plexiglass screen in front of the desk, which afforded the duty man some voice privacy. He muttered something into the phone, then his expression lightened and he replaced the handset in its cradle. He stood up and looking down at me said, "Sir, he will be with you now." I thanked him and settled back in my seat. I had met Mostert a few times out at the base, when he had come out on security business. He was a little shorter than me, with very wide, powerful shoulders, pale skin and black wavy hair. I never saw him smile, which I found a little odd, but it was not my business to do a psychological profile, so I let it go at that. He appeared quite suddenly at the bottom of the stairs, having come down very quietly. He was also wearing a dark suit and there was I, in jeans and a sweater. I was starting to feel out of place. "Hello DeBeer," he said, offering his hand. We shook and I asked how he was? "Well enough," he replied and turned back up the stairs. I followed, thinking "Well enough for what?"

We went up to the second floor, then turned right down the corridor and in at the third office. "Have a seat DeBeer and tell me what I can do for you?" Mostert was obviously not one for small talk. I sat on a chair, the same as the ones downstairs, while he sat down at his desk. "Have you got anything interesting out of Phillips?" I asked. The "General" wants this entire affair finished with and the files closed. He gave me instructions to attend to the terrorist group very urgently and report back to him, which I have done. Phillips is the last loose end. I can tell you that Phillips' buddy gave me the locations of a couple of terrorist training camps and some names, probably false, which I have passed on to Pretoria. I believe the bases are marked for removal, if they have not already been wiped out, together with all their occupants? Couldn't happen too soon." "Where are the three terrorists you caught," he asked in a quiet voice? "They all died in a shootout at Langa." "Aah, so that was you guys, interesting, go on?" "The forth one, had a bad accident and is also dead." Mostert chuckled. "So, he had this accident after you got the information you needed from him, yes?" "Yes, it was most unfortunate." Mostert roared with laughter. "You sly son of a bitch, how did he die?" "I believe it was a broken neck, which happened when he tried to escape."

Mostert laughed on uncontrollably, finally stopping when he had a coughing fit. A glass of water from the flask on his desk and he calmed down at last, his face red and his eyes watering from his exertion. Still smiling broadly, he said, "You bastards out in the field, have this holier than thou attitude, Pretoria's blue eyed boys who can do no wrong. I've had you rammed up my nose by Pretoria several times as an example of how things should be done and there you are killing off your prisoners faster than we can arrest them, some example you are." I stared at him in silence, it became clear to me, I was the "white devil" together with my men, all devils, all killers. "You're right, but I never set out to be an example to anyone, I just carried out my orders as best I could and what happened, happened, so now we must move on, we have to let Phillips go." Mosterts' face was a picture of horror. "What, why?" "The General wants the entire affair finished with. No loose ends, nothing to say anything ever happened, so your prisoner goes free." "But he's a terrorist, he must stand trial. He was arrested while hiding one of the gang that committed that atrocity on the farm in SWA." He stood up and glared at me. I tried to remain calm as I said, "if you were stupid enough to try and put him on trial, the prosecutor would ask you for evidence, so, what evidence do you have?" "Well, the black man in his apartment, you chased him and his gang all the way from SWA, you and your men know all about them, you are witnesses." Mostert was now glaring at me. "Sorry, I and my men know nothing and will not be witnesses to anything and where is this gang you are referring to?" "You said they were all dead." "Did I now, my memory is not too good, perhaps I was mistaken, in any event you have no proof of anything and there is no documentation. If you want to ruin your career, the General will eat you alive if you try and countermand his instructions. You have no witnesses, no dead bodies, no documentation and one skinny white man who apparently knows nothing." I stood up and pointed a finger at Mostert. "This affair ends now. I am ordering you on behalf of the General to close the books on the idiot in your cells unless you can tell me here and now that you have got valuable information from him. Well, have you?" He was silent. "It will say you picked him up on suspicion of harboring a black man in his apartment and released him when no evidence was found. He knows if he as much as sneezes in the wrong direction, you could always pick him up again and will certainly not want a repeat performance. Go get him now, give him his clothes and belongings and bring him to me, I'm in a hurry." Mosterts' face was a picture of bewilderment. His vision of some sort of fame and glory for bringing a terrorist to justice had just vanished. He stood there, his mouth opening and closing as he searched for something to say, but couldn't find the right words. "Hurry up man, I'm waiting" I shouted at him. He turned without a word and hurried out, I followed him. I wondered how long it would take before he found out the General was dead. It didn't matter, if I had to I would call the Minister, he would quickly set Mostert straight. There was a heavy steel door at the top of the stairs, the top half was barred and an armed guard sat behind the door. "Open up Smitty," Mostert snapped. "Yes Sir" and he produced a large key which he used to unlock the door and then still had to punch some numbers into a key pad as well, before the door swung open, high security indeed. On our right was the security office, then six single cells, all similar to the cells at Sea Point station, but a bit narrower, separated by thick partitions, probably steel panels, cement covered.

At the very end was the bathroom, two showers, some toilets and washbasins. Phillips was in the last cell, all the others were empty. He lay motionless on his bunk. Next to his cell was an open area, about twelve feet square, with a small brown wood desk and chair on the left and three chairs against the opposite wall, the interrogation area. There was a window on the left looking out at the rear brick wall of the next building, about twenty feet away. Mostert turned to Smitty. "Get him out of the cell, clean him up, get him dressed in his own clothes and give him back his belongings, he is leaving." "Yes sir," came the reply and he started unlocking the cell door. I sat down at the desk and waited. Mostert sat on one of the other chairs and looked across the room. "Why is the General doing this?" he asked. "I don't know, I can only guess that he wants to avoid any publicity, but that's just a guess, I just follow his orders and question nothing and he likes it that way. In this instance, the Justice minister also gave approval for Phillips release, so let's not screw it up, okay? I'm going to take Phillips home and that's it, it's over for us all." He nodded and we sat in silence and waited. About ten minutes later, Smitty came out of the bathroom with Phillips, who was now dressed in his own clothes. They looked too big for him and I realized he must have lost a lot of weight during his time under arrest. He kept looking at the floor and would not look directly at us, neither did he speak. He just stood there shivering slightly, symptoms of intense fear. The man was obviously terrified and I wondered what the hell Mostert had done to him. "Smitty, help him down the stairs please," I instructed. "Yes Sir," came the reply and taking Phillips by the left arm he led the unresisting man towards the stairs. He had to actually support Phillips by holding him around the waist, or he would have fallen down the stairs. At the front door I took over. I said nothing to Mostert and he too was silent. On the sidewalk, I held Phillips' arm, and the door banged shut behind us. I helped him into my car and he sagged against the door after I closed it, still silent. I drove slowly away, turned right onto Sir Lowry Road and drove towards the bridge, which led down to the freeway. Once on the freeway, heading west towards Sea Point, I spoke to him, trying to keep my voice calm, neutral and a little friendly. "Tell me," I said? He jerked upright and gasped with fear as he stared at me wide eyed. "Relax Mr. Phillips, I'm taking you home, it's over. I was just curious. You are not a stupid man, just the opposite in fact. Why would an intelligent man like yourself, get involved with a bunch of terrorists, it makes no sense?" His voice was a harsh whisper as he replied. "I tried to tell them but he wouldn't listen." "Who, Mostert?" "Yes him. He kept punching me in the stomach, telling me I was lying. When I collapsed, they threw water on me and then tied me up and gave me electric shocks. It carried on for days. They kept asking me where the other terrorists were. I didn't know he was a terrorist, they threatened to kill me if I didn't do as they told me to, what could I do?" Tears ran down his face. He took a deep breath. "I used to go into the gardens at the top of Adderley Street on my lunch breaks and sit there while I ate my sandwiches."

"About two years ago, an African man sat down on the grass near the bench where I was sitting and smiled at me. I smiled back, he ate his lunch, I ate mine. The following day he was there again and every day from then on. I assumed he worked in a nearby office building like myself. We never spoke, just nodded at each other. After about six months, one day he greeted me and I returned the greeting. The following day he sat much closer to me and greeted me again, then struck up a conversation. I don't remember what we talked about, just everyday things. No politics or serious stuff because he was black and I was white but the lunch hours passed quite pleasantly. Then one day he started telling me about himself, where he came from and how difficult and sad it was to live under the apartheid system. He said he lived in a corrugated iron shack in the Nyanga township, he was not allowed to live in a white area. Until that day I had never even thought about it. He pointed out that even in the gardens, he couldn't sit on a bench at lunch time, the benches were reserved for whites only, each one had a "whites only" sign on it and I had not noticed them, I just took everything for granted. There were signs like that everywhere, all over the city, at the entrances to parks, some offices, on water fountains, at movie houses, public transport and taxi ranks as well. Where ever one went there were signs, "whites only" or "blacks only, it was the law of the land." Phillips voice became a bit stronger. "He called himself David Ntoli, but I suspect now it was a false name. After he pointed out he was not even allowed to sit on a park bench in a public place at lunch time, I became so embarrassed, I got off the bench and thereafter sat next to him on the grass and we became friends. He asked about my life and I told him. As humble as my life was, it was palatial in comparison to his. More than a year went by and then he rang my doorbell one Saturday afternoon. I was very surprised to see him. He apologized for the intrusion and I invited him in. He told me he had to see if I had been truthful about my humble lifestyle because he needed my help. He said sometimes he had to hide political refugees from the police and there may come a time when he would ask me to help him. I said I really did not want to become involved in that and he said you are already involved. Then he opened my front door and two very large African men hurried in. David said if I did not do exactly as he told me to when I was needed, these two men would come and kill me. If I called the police or told anyone, I would be killed and they would be watching me from then onwards. The two big men, their faces were covered with scars in a zigzag pattern, jabbed me with their forefingers as David spoke, to emphasize the point. I was terrified and agreed to do what they wanted. David said I had been selected because I had no family and only a few friends. If they had to kill me, no one would make a big fuss and I would be quickly forgotten. I had never known such fear. Finally they left and I was alone with my terror. Later that evening I calmed down enough to go to bed. He was right, I was too scared to tell anyone, so I just went on with my life. A year went by. I thought they had forgotten me and actually relaxed, then a few days ago a message was pushed under my door. It said I would get a visitor the following night and he would be staying for a few days, look after him or else. What could I do, they would have killed me?

He arrived the following evening and moved in with me. Two nights later your men burst in, took him away and locked me up, so now you know it all, I am just a stupid man and I should have known better, but fear is a strong motivator, so I have been punished a thousand times over for my idiocy." He lapsed into silence, tears running down his face. He made no effort to wipe them away. We were already in Sea Point, driving along the beach front, so I pulled over to the sidewalk and stopped. "Mr. Phillips," I addressed him and he stared at me. "Sometimes we become victims of our own making. Decent, quiet living, calm, sensitive people become targets for extortion because they become fearful of the consequences as you did. If you had originally contacted the police you would have been fine, but your fear got the better of you and now you have the results, it's really a shame. I can't take it away but I can give you a new start." He looked interested, "What do mean?"

"I visited your employer at your work. I showed them my credentials and told Mr.Young your manager, that you have been working under cover for us, and was sworn to secrecy. We have now arrested the terrorist cell, these men had approached you to help them with financial arrangements through your bank and you became suspicious and contacted us. Following our instructions, you were instrumental in having them arrested and can now return to normal civilian life because your service is no longer needed, in fact, you are something of a hero, putting your life at risk in service to your country. Your job is waiting for you when you go back in two weeks time after you have a small vacation." Phillips face was a picture of amazement as I continued. "I have had your apartment renovated and painted, the door has been replaced and a steel security door added on, so you will be safe. Now then, please open the glove box in front of you." He hesitatingly pressed the lid button and it fell open. "Take out the big brown envelope and open it."

He did so and out fell a bunch of keys and a smaller envelope.

"The keys are to your apartment doors and there is R5000.00 in the smaller envelope so you can pay your accounts and rest up for the next two weeks. Your refrigerator is full of food. I have given you your life back and you are expected at work in two weeks. You are covered by the official secrets act, so you cannot discuss anything with anyone and so will not have to answer any questions about anything that took place while you were away. Any questions?" He shook his head. "Good, now lets get you home." I started the car, drove away and some five minutes later stopped outside his apartment block.

"Good bye Mr. Phillips, we will not meet again." He climbed unsteadily out of the car, closed the door and walked shakily away. He said nothing, not even goodbye. Not that I really expected him to, you don't get gratitude for tearing a man's life apart, even if he brought it on himself. At my last meeting with the Minister, I had asked for arrangements to be made to save Phillips and set him free. He had agreed to my idea and had the money delivered to me at my office, together with a voucher, which would allow the maintenance division at the government buildings to fix and paint the apartment. Now it was done and I could get on with my life. Back in my office at last, I sagged into my chair and stared at the floor. It had all fallen neatly into place, so what was I to do? I could just leave Rikka alone, but what If I met her at an army office in Johannesburg, I wouldn't invite her out and I didn't want to be alone with her, so she would become suspicious anyway, no, far better if I stamped on it straight away. I got up and walked over to the garage. Reyneke was there as usual. "Hi again, I wonder if you have the General's home phone number for me. I need to call his daughter and put a stop to everything now." "Sure I've got it, I'll write it down for you, but listen man, I just got a call from Pretoria, the General died last night, it seems he had a heart attack and that was that.

You know of course, that his daughter will blame you, do you still want to phone her?" "Yes, I must, to do nothing would be worse. I will try to extend condolences, if she slams the phone down, at least

I tried." "Okay, here's the number." He wrote it on a slip of paper and handed it to me. "Thanks man, I'll see you later." He nodded, we shook hands and I left and headed back to my office. I sat at my desk and stared at the phone, I wasn't looking forward to making the call that would prove that "Auntie" was right again, but I had no choice. I picked up the phone and dialed the number on my piece of paper.

The phone was answered on the third ring. "Hello?" I recognized Rikka's voice immediately, even though it sounded strained. "Hi Rikka, it's Rolf, I'm very sorry for your loss, I just wanted to extend condolences." Whatever I thought she might say, she surprised the hell out of me. "How did you get this number?" she shouted at me, so I answered the same way. "I'm a security cop, remember, I just made a call and was given the number. By the way, while I was up on the border at Rundu, I met a Sergeant Muller on his way to the Angolan front," I lied to her. "It seems he knew you quite well. He told me a rather sad story I had trouble believing, but once I found out you're the General's daughter, it all made sense." "This is all your fault, you bastard," she hissed at me. "You killed him, you killed my father." "No I didn't, he did it all on his own with no help from me." She hissed again. "You will suffer for this, you son of a bitch, I will make sure of it." I felt as though something inside me twisted at that moment and as I spoke, my voice came out all hoarse and raspy. "Do you have any idea how many men I have killed, following your fathers' direct instructions? If I was in any way responsible for his passing, he became just another face etched on my personal wall of death." The harsh breathing from the other end of the line, said she was listening. I continued. "The only thing missing from the wall is the face of a woman. I never killed any women, not one, so perhaps you are what is needed, to give me and the wall peace at last. Maybe the Devil needs his daughter and long before you come looking for me, I will find you and you can join him on the wall. You were his willing partner in life and I could rejoin you in death, you stupid little bitch!" I chuckled emptily into the phone and was rewarded by a gasp of horror as the phone went dead. So "Auntie" was right again, Rikka was the one, but I doubted I would have any more problems with her. I had seriously scared the crap out of her, she would not want to take a chance I was being serious, but if she did try to harm me I would just have to deal with her in a similar manner. Who knew what time would bring to the table? I wasn't the nice young guy who went off to war. I knew all the killing and the horror of it, had changed me a lot, just how much I would find out later, in the meantime I was out of the war and going back to school. I am reminded of what Auntie said to me as I was leaving her cottage, Tony had already left. "A cobra may grow old, even unto death, but her poison remains just as deadly long after she is gone, beware, your cobra is still out there and she is restless, go now." She pushed me out of the door and I followed Tony to the car, I did not look back. So that was that, it was all over. My army discharge papers had arrived, releasing me from further service, I could go home. I packed my trunk, put on my uniform and then wandered around the base saying goodbye to the staff I had got to know over the past months. The last person on my list was the base commander. His secretary ushered me into his office and he rose to greet me. Shaking my hand, he waved at an armchair and I sat down. "So, you're leaving at last are you?" he said. "We're going to miss you around here my boy, we haven't had this much excitement with the dog school for years." I smiled broadly. "Thank you Sir." He continued. "I believe you're off to the Academy in Pretoria for a while, so I'm not going to say goodbye, I have a feeling we will be seeing you again one of these days, so let me wish you all the best, make us proud Lieutenant." "Yes Sir, I will do my best" and with that, we shook hands again and I was on my way. There was an army car and driver waiting for me at the entrance, my few belongings already in the trunk. I did not know the driver, so we drove in silence. He took me home to my parents house, off loaded my cases and was gone. My folks were understandably excited, mom made a special dinner for me, after which we sat down and over coffee I told them as much as I could about the previous couple of years. We chatted on till late that night, finally heading for bed. When I woke up it was already after ten in the morning. I got up and found the house deserted. Mom had gone shopping, Dad had gone to supervise the packing up of my apartment. I couldn't go back there in case Mr. Phillips or the strange couple on the first floor saw me, there could be serious consequences, so dad went for me. He was going to pack my personal belongings and clothes into some suitcases to take home, the rest of the apartment was being packed up and taken to Pretoria by a moving company, to be placed in storage. When I had my new Pretoria address, the contents of my old apartment would be delivered there. I bathed, got dressed, had a leisurely breakfast and then went to sit in the lounge and read the paper. I settled back in the armchair and opened the paper. I had not even begun to read when the doorbell rang. I muttered a curse of annoyance, put down my paper and went to the front door. Through the frosted glass, I could see a single figure standing there. I opened the door and said "Yes." Too late, I recognized Rikka, her blonde hair now grown long and shaggy, covering most of her face and simultaneously noticed the gun in her hand, pointing at me. All she said was "Bastard!" then pulled the trigger. I didn't hear the bang, all I saw was a flash, and then it all went black.

END The year 1890 in Cape Town, South Africa, marked a turning point for anyone who owned a dog at that time. The village had grown into a large town of many thousands of people, stretching forty miles along the coast and inland as well. Many people had acquired dogs as pets, with the consequence that dog bites were commonplace and mostly the dogs were free to roam about as they wished. The dogs often formed packs that ran about playing and generally having a good time, chasing each other, or cats, horses or cows, which were also plentiful and allowed to roam the fields which stretched across the various communities. The authorities, inundated with complaints from outraged citizens who had been bitten, or had their livestock savaged, called a meeting of the town council, at which time a law was placed in the statute books, which stated, "Ye shall not suffer a vicious, un-muzzled dog to roam free." To this was added various penalties, which included fines and even the putting to death of a repeat offender dog. The problem was, the good men of the council failed to define what constituted a vicious dog, which meant in essence that a dog would get at least one free bite or even more if bitten people did not file a complaint and even if they did, the onus was upon the complainant to prove that a particular dog was responsible. As poor as the law was, it met with a certain success, in that many people were fined and the general public took much better care of their pets, which largely, were not wandering the streets any more. It was not until 1910, some twenty years later, that the council had another look at the law relating to dogs and finally defined a vicious dog as one which had been known to have bitten someone, so again, the free bite situation remained in place until the early 1970's, when dog owners were made totally responsible for any and all of their dogs actions and behavior.